Blood clouded the sea where he'd been hit

Bolan intended to sink the rowboat. Holding the two-handed sword like a spear he bent his legs and pushed off hard against the ocean floor. He erupted upward and arrowed for the bottom of the rowboat.

As Bolan closed in, he rammed the sword upward with all of his strength. The blade punched through the thin wood. Bolan inverted himself, putting both feet against the bottom for leverage, and wrenched the blade sideways. The aged planking cracked and split.

Yaqoob was leaning over the side and stabbing at Bolan with his own blade. The Executioner roared with effort and ripped the ancient Damascus steel free. The effort drove Bolan down into the depths as the spade harpooned for him. Bolan heard the crack as the keel snapped under human weight.

Daylight drew a ragged incandescent line across the perforated bottom of the rowboat as its spine broke.

MACK BOLAN
The Executioner

The Executioner®
Don Pendleton's

BLOOD TIDE

A GOLD EAGLE BOOK FROM
WORLDWIDE®

TORONTO • NEW YORK • LONDON
AMSTERDAM • PARIS • SYDNEY • HAMBURG
STOCKHOLM • ATHENS • TOKYO • MILAN
MADRID • WARSAW • BUDAPEST • AUCKLAND

First edition January 2006
ISBN 0-373-64326-8

Special thanks and acknowledgment to
Chuck Rogers for his contribution to this work.

BLOOD TIDE

The logical end of a war of creeds is the final destruction of one.

—T.E. Lawrence, 1888–1935

No man has the right to harm innocent people, even in the name of his god. I will continue the fight against murderous fanatics until I meet my maker.

—Mack Bolan

THE
MACK BOLAN
LEGEND

Nothing less than a war could have fashioned the destiny of the man called Mack Bolan. Bolan earned the Executioner title in the jungle hell of Vietnam.

But this soldier also wore another name—Sergeant Mercy. He was so tagged because of the compassion he showed to wounded comrades-in-arms and Vietnamese civilians.

Mack Bolan's second tour of duty ended prematurely when he was given emergency leave to return home and bury his family, victims of the Mob. Then he declared a one-man war against the Mafia.

He confronted the Families head-on from coast to coast, and soon a hope of victory began to appear. But Bolan had broken society's every rule. That same society started gunning for this elusive warrior—to no avail.

So Bolan was offered amnesty to work within the system against terrorism. This time, as an employee of Uncle Sam, Bolan became Colonel John Phoenix. With a command center at Stony Man Farm in Virginia, he and his new allies—Able Team and Phoenix Force—waged relentless war on a new adversary: the KGB.

But when his one true love, April Rose, died at the hands of the Soviet terror machine, Bolan severed all ties with Establishment authority.

Now, after a lengthy lone-wolf struggle and much soul-searching, the Executioner has agreed to enter an "arm's-length" alliance with his government once more, reserving the right to pursue personal missions in his Everlasting War.

1

Malay Archipelago

The killers were coming. Their outrigger canoes slid through the water beneath the starless, storm-warning-black South Pacific sky, knifing through whitecaps toward the yacht.

Mack Bolan touched his throat mike. "Contact."

"Striker!" Barbara Price's voice was urgent in Bolan's earpiece. The mission controller back in Virginia was clearly unhappy. "Twenty-two minutes until satellite window! We do not have visual! Repeat! We do not have you!"

"Doesn't matter," Bolan said.

The enemy showed up clearly in tones of green and gray in the Executioner's night-vision goggles. They were half naked, wearing turbans and sarongs and festooned with weapons.

"They have us."

"Striker, be advised strategic withdrawal recommended."

The premonsoon winds moaned through the rigging of Bolan's yacht. The craft lay anchored thirty yards from the beach. The tiny atoll was little more than a crescent of palm trees jutting a few feet above sea level. The canoes aimed for the mouth of the lagoon to cut off the yacht from the open ocean. The paddlers did not need night-vision equipment to acquire their target. The yacht's dim deck lights marked it as a pool of radiance in the velvet dark of the shallow harbor.

Bolan checked the loads in his weapon system as the jaws of the trap closed. He was a sitting duck.

And that was just the way the Executioner wanted it.

"Noted, Control. Standby," he whispered.

The killers would be in boarding range in less than a minute.

Across the galley Bolan's wife checked her weapon.

Marcie "The Mouse" Mei was barely five feet tall, and the mass of highly modified, blackened steel and plastic she was toting appeared impossibly large in her tiny hands. She manipulated the weapon's controls with practiced ease. If an Olympic gymnast and a pixie had spawned a warchild in the Philippines, Marcie Mei would be it. Only her snub nose and generous mouth showed beneath her night-vision goggles.

The CIA field agent's big smile flashed at Bolan in the dark of the hold. "Platoon strength," she said as she flicked off the safeties on her weapon system. "Closing fast."

"Roger that." Bolan spoke low. "Scott?"

Escotto Clellande nodded from the other side of the cabin. In comparison, the M-4 carbine looked like a toy in the hulking ex-Philippine special operation commando's hands. "Yeah, I make it about forty hostiles. Heavily armed." Scott grunted to himself with relief. "No support weapons visible."

Bolan was silently relieved, as well. The yacht was not a normal pleasure craft by any stretch of the imagination, but RPG-7 rocket-propelled grenade launchers were the ocean-borne artillery of choice in the South Pacific. A few broadsides of antiarmor rockets with shaped-charge warheads would burn the old girl down to the waterline.

Scott grimaced as the killers closed in. "Whole lotta cutlery, though."

Bolan nodded. Pirates the world over had an anachronistic love of edged weapons.

Piracy in the South Pacific had recently taken a very ugly turn. Boats had been found adrift from the Sulu to the Andaman Sea. Everything from private yachts to cargo vessels had been taken. The ships were stripped of their cargo and any valuables, and the passengers, whether professional seamen or sport fisherman out for a trophy, were ritually butchered to the last man, woman and child. The stripped hulks were left to drift like floating slaughter yards.

Mack Bolan was sailing the South Pacific in a million-dollar yacht off the Philippines. To all appearances he was a rich westerner with a native wife, asking in every port of call for private coves and beautiful, secluded spots off the beaten path.

The atoll where they lay anchored had no name. It was picture-postcard beautiful, well off the beaten path, very secluded, and Bolan, Mei and the yacht made for a very tempting target.

Someone had just taken the bait.

Clellande was posing as their hired crewman and cook. He was an able sailor, and Bolan would have wanted him along for his culinary skills alone, not withstanding his skills as a Special Forces operator.

The pair was on loan from the CIA station in Manila. Clellande peered at the incoming enemy. "They're slowing down."

"Jesus…" Mei's ever-present smile went down in wattage. "They're slinging their rifles."

"And out comes the cutlery." Bolan watched as a platoon of pirates drew razor-sharp kris daggers, parangs, and bolo knives. Elaborate curved, razor-sharp steel of every description flashed and glittered in the Executioner's night vision.

The men in the canoes were bent on slaughter.

Bolan clicked the seven-inch, saw-toothed blade of his bayonet onto the muzzle of his carbine. "Control, high-level of probability that targets are prime."

"Affirmative, Striker. Choppers are in the air. ETA twenty minutes."

Bolan signaled his team. "I think these are some of the boys we're looking for. Be ready."

Mei and Clelland fixed bayonets.

Bolan's strategy was simple. He had lifted it from British

WWII naval tactics. In the battle for the Atlantic, German submarines had initially ruled the waves. The U-boats sank allied shipping with impunity, but U-boats were small and could carry only two dozen torpedoes, and those were reserved for enemy warships and large transports. To engage smaller merchant vessels, the German submarines would surface and use their deck guns. The British had invented the Q-boat in response. They had adapted merchant ships, mounting them with powerful six-inch cannons hidden amidships. When German submarines surfaced, the British sailors had flung open the Q-boat's trapdoors and blown the exposed U-boats to hell in a floating ambush.

Disguise equaled surprise, and surprise was the most precious weapon in any operator's arsenal. The yacht didn't have a pair of six-inch British naval guns hidden beneath the mast, but she did have some very nasty surprises, courtesy of Hermann "Gadgets" Schwarz.

Bolan reached down and punched a few keys on the portable computer perched on the galley counter. "Arming countermeasures." Tiny green LED lights on the black box next to the laptop turned red. Wires snaked from the box throughout the yacht.

The pirates closed to within ten yards.

Bolan lifted his nose and sniffed the air. Mei cocked her head. "You smell that?" she asked.

Bolan did. It was the sweet stench of hashish, and it didn't bode anything good. He pressed a key on the laptop and hit Enter. "Here we go."

The hull shook as the two dozen hidden smoke dischargers fired simultaneously in a 360-degree arc around the yacht. They were the same kind of smoke dischargers that tanks and armored vehicles used to screen themselves from enemy fire. Only those on the yacht weren't loaded with canisters of smoke-emitting hydrogen carbon powder.

They were loaded with military strength CS tear gas.

Bolan and the agents clicked their respirators into place beneath their night-vision goggles as they were instantly shrouded in blossoming clouds of CS.

The pirates shouted in a ragged chorus of surprise and anger. Wooden canoes thudded against the hull of the yacht. A war cry sounded a few feet away from Bolan's porthole. *"Allah Akhbar!"*

The killers hurled their voices to the heavens in response to the call.

Bolan hit another key and closed his eyes.

The second ring of dischargers fired.

Twenty-four Magnum ultra-flash stun grenades detonated like a ring of exploding suns around the ship. Each grenade lit off in a two million candlepower flash into the tear-gas streaming eyes of the pirates. At the same instant each grenade blasted out an eardrum-shattering 185 decibels of sound.

"Back to back, stay close," Bolan ordered Bolan. "I want one or two alive, but don't risk yourself to do it."

The Executioner raced up the tiny stairwell and threw open the hatch. Mei followed as Clellande exploded up from the forward hatch.

A dozen pirates blinked, wept and groped their way across the deck of the yacht. Others struggled to clamber aboard in their temporarily deafened and half-blind condition. Thousands of sparks drifted through the thick fog of tear gas, blinking and whirling like drunken fireflies in the stun grenade's disorienting secondary pyrotechnic effect.

A bare-chested, tattooed pirate stumbled toward Bolan with a bolo knife in each hand. The Executioner squeezed the trigger of his carbine and sent a burst into the killer's chest. The pirate staggered back a step and let out a blood-curdling scream of rage. He lunged forward blindly, his blades crisscrossing before him in a frantic attempt to fillet his unseen opponent.

Bolan punched a second burst through the killer's turban and dropped him half headless to the deck. Mei's and Clellande's weapons snarled on full-auto on Bolan's flanks. The range was point-blank, and they wielded their weapons like buzz saws. The pirates stumbled and tottered but did not go down.

More pirates climbed aboard. They lurched through the gas and the dark, guided to their opponents only by the strobing muzzle-flash of Bolan's and his team's weapons. Bolan put ten rounds into one of the killers, and only the eleventh shot that transversed the assassin's spinal cord finally put him down.

"These guys are hopped up out of their minds!" Bolan shouted into his respirator's microphone. "Go for a head shot!"

A screaming pirate to Bolan's left dropped his knife and un-slung his AK-47. Mei's M-4 spit fire and hammered the pirate's head into ruin.

A streamer of fire streaked into the air.

"Flare!" Bolan roared. The team snarled and squinted as a unit. Their light amplifying night vision went whiteout as the incandescent illumination round turned night into day. Bolan ripped away his night-vision goggles, and the respirator came with it. He swung his carbine aft. A second flare trailed up into the night from a canoe full of killers. Bolan aimed the M-203 grenade launcher beneath his carbine and squeezed the trigger. The personal defense round sent a thirty-six pellet swarm of buckshot like a wall of lead sweeping through the canoe.

The damage was done. Bolan and his team had lost the cover of darkness. The Executioner felt the sting in his eyes and the burn of the gas streak down his throat. He had been exposed to CS and worse before and fought on, but now the playing field had been leveled.

It would come down to a question of will.

Bolan inflicted his will. The carbine went hot in his hands as he swept it from target to target. He staggered as a bullet struck the ceramic trauma plate of his armor. Bolan spun and put a 3-round burst through the shooter's eye socket. The Executioner's own eyes streamed, and he struggled to breathe as the gas entered his lungs.

Bolan's carbine slammed open on an empty chamber.

A pirate who couldn't have been more than sixteen screamed and charged waving an escrima stick. Bolan squinted against the chemical burn engulfing his eyes and decided the young man was POW material. He aimed his empty carbine and thumbed the pressure switch on the forestock. The X26 Taser mounted on his weapon chuffed twice, and the two barbed probes streaked into the young pirate's chest trailing their conductive wires.

Bolan pressed the switch a second time and held it down. The stun gun crackled as Bolan pumped the five watt shaped pulse into his target at eighteen pulses per second. The force should have dropped the young fighter into the fetal position on the deck.

It did not.

The pirate let out a scream and ripped the bloody, sparking probes from his chest. He gasped and fell shuddering to his knees as he inhaled CS.

Bolan realized he would have to take his prisoner old school style. He rammed the aluminum buttplate of his carbine between the young man's eyes and dropped him limp to the deck.

Marcie Mei gasped raggedly behind Bolan. "Striker!"

Bolan ducked as a pirate flew past him. The killer's heavy parang passed inches from Bolan's temple and sliced splinters from the boom of the mainsail. The blade rang off Bolan's bayonet as he parried the second blow. The Executioner rammed his shoulder into the pirate's chest, pinning the killer's sword arm and shoulder-blocking him against the mast. Bolan shoved his bayonet beneath the pirate's chin, ramming the razor-sharp steel up. The pirate slid to a sitting position against the mast.

Bolan let his spent carbine fall and slapped leather for the pistols strapped to his thighs.

A pirate came at Bolan wielding a machete overhead like a samurai sword. The Desert Eagle rolled like thunder in Bolan's hand. The pirate folded as the .50-caliber bullet smashed him down the hatchway.

Clellande's grenade launcher belched yellow flame as he blasted a 40 mm buckshot round into a canoe off the bow. He moved along the grab rail, his carbine spraying the canoes astern.

Two pirates levered themselves up from the water, pulling themselves up into the push pit with daggers in their teeth. Bolan extended the Beretta 93-R machine pistol in his left hand in a fencer's lunge. The Beretta snarled as he touched off two 3-round bursts. The first pirate fell back from the stern with his turban unspooling in ribbons of cloth and brain behind him. The second hung tangled in the rail with his throat blasted open.

Bolan spun, the big .50 and the 9 mm rolling in his hands like a gunslinger. The Desert Eagle hammered a howling pirate into the jib, and the machine pistol painted the white canvas with the arterial spray of his target's life.

The pirates were not acting like pirates. They weren't cutting their losses and running. They were coming on like feudal Japanese samurai bent on death before dishonor. In the light of the flare, Bolan could make out the fins of sharks churning the dark waters of the lagoon as they feasted upon the dozens of fallen.

Mei knelt before the hatch, half-gagging from the gas as she rammed a fresh magazine into her carbine with streaming, swollen eyes. She held her trigger on full-auto as she swept the pirates off the port side of the deck. Clellande's weapon snarled in continuous fire as he put thirty rounds into a canoe full of steel-wielding cutthroats.

A pirate erupted out of the water at the bow and heaved himself up into the forward pulpit. Metal flashed and red fiber fluttered from the end as he threw a piece of glittering steel. Bolan and Clelland swung around, their weapons hammering the pirate in ruptured ruins to the black water below.

Bolan dropped to one knee. He struggled to bark out an order through the gas sizzling in his chest. "Hold your fire!"

Mei and Clellande knelt with their weapons ready.

"Scott! Anything off the bow?"

The man hacked and coughed. "Nothing moving! All targets down!"

"Marcie! Port?"

"No…hostiles all down," she replied, struggling for air.

Bolan scanned to starboard and astern. Nothing moved. He rose to take in the bigger picture as the second flare drifted low toward the water. The wind was dispersing the gas. The yacht was littered with bodies from stem to stern. Head shots at point-blank range were not pretty business. Neither was buckshot raking canoes out of 40 mm tubes. The canoes drifted dead in the water. None of the occupants moved.

Bolan reloaded his pistols. "Marcie, secure the prisoner and get him below before he chokes to death. Scott, let's clean up the deck and call for extraction. We keep two bodies for forensics, the rest go over the side."

"Affirmative, Striker, I…" the big man stumbled slightly.

Bolan moved toward the bow. "Scott?"

"Nothing, just a scratch." Clellande plucked a tuft of red fiber at the collar of his armored vest. "What the hell?"

Clellande went rigid as blood geysered between his fingers. "Jesus!"

Bolan lunged. "Leave it in!"

Clellande was already going into shock, and his first instinct was to get the intruding metal out of his neck. The shard fell to the deck with a clatter as Clellande fell facefirst onto the roof of the cabin.

"I need immediate medevac!" Bolan roared into his radio. "The big man is down!"

"Affirmative, Striker!" Price came back. "Choppers inbound."

Boland rolled Clellande over. Blood was pouring out of him like a river that had jumped its banks. The soldier applied pressure to the wound. He grimaced as his fingers sank through the gruesome, multiple channels the blade had dug into him. "Marcie! Field dressing!"

"Scott!" Mei raced to help.

Bolan grimly applied pressure while she ripped open a field dressing. Bolan pressed the dressing into the wound, and it instantly bled through. He pressed down as Mei ripped open another. The dressing bled through again. "Give me another!"

"Scott!" Mei screamed as she ripped open another dressing. "Scott!"

Bolan sat back on his heels. Escotto Clellande was gone.

The Executioner stared at the deadly gleaming weapon on the deck. It was a strangely shaped piece of razor-sharp steel. It resembled a hawthorn leaf save that it was six inches long, slitted and had a tail of red fiber to stabilize it in flight.

It was about the ugliest implement the Executioner had ever seen.

He pressed his thumb into his throat mike. "Control, be advised the big man is KIA. Tell command we have a prisoner." He shook his head bitterly. "We are ready for extraction."

2

Manila Station, Philippines

Aaron Kurtzman's face stared unhappily at Bolan from the computer monitor connected to the satellite link. He forced a smile. "You did real good, Striker. In the two months we figure these guys have been operating, no one who's laid eyes on them has lived to tell about it. You took out a platoon of them and brought in a boatload of useful evidence."

Bolan frowned. A good man had gone down. "Yeah."

"You took a prisoner," Kurtzman said. "That's the biggest break we've had since the Farm got involved in this."

Bolan considered the fight on the yacht and his young opponent. "I need more wattage."

"What?"

"I juiced that kid for two and a half seconds before he ripped out the probes, Bear." Bolan glanced at the weapon system on the table. "And that was after at least a full fifteen seconds of exposure to military strength CS."

Kurtzman blinked. "Really?"

"I had to brain him like an ox to bring him down." Bolan shrugged at the X26 slaved to the side of his carbine. "I need more wattage."

"I find that hard to believe, Striker. The X26 is the latest in EMD technology. With the old M26, each of its eighteen pulses per second had to break through the resistance of the subject's clothing and skin. Every jolt had to push its way in." Kurtzman warmed up as the talk turned technical. "Now, the X26? It's a brilliant piece of engineering. Rather than every pulse having to batter its way into the subject, it uses part of its charge to maintain the electrical opening. Holding the door open, so to speak. That lets nearly every single one of its pulses hit at full strength. It's been tested on SWAT officers, Special Forces operators and trained martial artists. They all go down. You sure you had a good connection?"

"The kid was sixteen, half-naked, took both probes in the chest and he was still salty," Bolan replied.

"Well, blood tests on the prisoner tested positive for some very powerful hashish, but even if he was high on PCP, the—"

"He was high on God, Bear."

Kurtzman's brow furrowed thoughtfully.

"Take two professional wrestlers," Bolan suggested. "Lock them in a cell, and toss in the key. One's high on drugs. One's high on God. You tell me. Who's walking out?"

Kurtzman answered immediately. The team from Stony Man Farm had dealt with fanatics before. "I'm betting on the guy with God on his side."

"Right." Bolan looked at Kurtzman pointedly. "And punky and his pals were high on both."

Kurtzman conceded with a sigh. "I'll tell the Cowboy you want more wattage."

"Thank you." Bolan considered his young opponent. "What information do we have on the prisoner?"

"We caught some luck there. Most of the bodies were unidentifiable, but your POW's fingerprints were on file with the Philippine National Police. The young man's name is Ali Mohammed Apilado, formerly Arturo Florio Apilado."

Bolan raised an eyebrow. "He converted?"

"That's right. Arturo was born on the southern island of Mindanao, but his parents were Christians. They were migrant field workers who moved to the city to get factory work in the textile mills. From the ages of twelve to fifteen, Arturo was involved in petty crime on the street. He was arrested for theft and assault and spent a year in jail. While he was inside, he converted to Islam and changed his name. When he was released, he disappeared without a trace. No one had seen him until he turned up on your yacht last night collecting for the Red Cross."

"Interesting."

Kurtzman snorted. "How so?"

An idea began forming in Bolan's mind. Religious fanatics born and raised were bad enough. Converted fanatics were worse. The born again of all religions hurled themselves into their new purpose with utter devotion, whatever that purpose might be.

Including slaughtering innocents with suicidal abandon.

Bolan nodded as his thoughts continued. The flip side of that coin was that the converted, unlike those raised in their religions, were often just as susceptible to deprogramming.

The Bear watched the wheels turn behind Bolan's eyes. "What are you thinking?"

"Where's Arturo now?"

"Philippine Military Intelligence has him about two blocks from your position. They play rough, Striker. I don't envy him. I suspect the beatings started this morning and haven't stopped."

"The kid's tough."

Kurtzman's eyes narrowed. "Somehow I see the good cop-bad cop routine shaping up nicely."

"Yeah, but I'm still a blue-eyed devil, and I need more than a successful interrogation."

"What are you saying, Striker?"

"I'm saying someone needs to have a 'Come to Jesus' with that boy."

Kurtzman snorted. "You mean a 'Come to Mohammed,' but I can have the CIA fly in a psychological warfare team from Langley and—"

Bolan cut in. "Send me Pol."

Orani

THE SUN WAS SETTING behind Bolan and Marcie Mei. The restaurant was made up of four bamboo poles with a thatched roof. The kitchen consisted of three converted fuel drums that were sending barbecue smoke to the sky. The dining area was the beach. The couple sat outside at a table with the tide lapping at their bare feet and the legs of their table and chairs. They drank beer and ate spareribs smothered in ginger-plum sauce as the lights of Manila began winking on like stars across Manila Bay.

Bolan took a long pull on his San Miguel. Marcie gnawed on the bones of her meal as if she hadn't eaten in a week. Her irrepressible smile flashed around the rib. "High metabolism."

Bolan smiled. Marcie's tiny frame was clad in a sarong and a bikini top. Plum sauce smeared her chin. She looked good enough to eat, bones and all.

Mei read Bolan's look and her smile threatened to reach her ears.

Bolan took another swig, acknowledging that the chemistry was occurring, but kept his mind on business. "What have you found out on your end?"

For once, Mei actually stopped smiling. "Nothing good. You noticed that when those guys thought they had us with our pants down they laid their guns aside and went with the cleavers?"

"Yeah, I noticed that."

Mei wiped her hands and stared at them reflectively. "I'm Catholic, myself, but I've had to impersonate a Muslim many times in the field. I've read the Koran. I know it pretty well."

"And?"

"The Prophet Mohammed makes many exhortations to his followers. One goes, 'Oh, True Believers, wage war against such of the infidels as are near you.'"

Bolan nodded. "I've heard it."

"I'm sure, but that one was heard a lot in the preceding centuries here in the Philippines. Usually right alongside this one. 'When ye encounter the unbelievers, strike off their heads until ye have made a great slaughter among them.'"

Bolan sighed. It sounded a lot like what was happening in the Asian shipping lanes, and he'd been thinking along the same lines, himself. "You're talking about the *juramentado*."

Mei nodded.

Bolan had done some research of his own. By some accounts 'running *juramentado*' had begun on the Philippine Island of Jolo during Spanish occupation in the 1800s. It was a religious rite among the Philippine Muslims, bound with the act of waging jihad, or Holy War, against the Christian invaders. Young Moro men would seek permission from the Sultan to run *juramentado* and swear oaths upon the Koran. They would then whip themselves into religious frenzy and attack Christians, singly or in groups, with bladed weapons. They fought with absolute disregard for death, killing until they, themselves, were killed. They believed with total conviction that their bravery and sacrifice would win them great renown and reward in the afterlife, with the added benefit that every Christian they killed followed them to Paradise as their personal slave.

The Moros had used the act of running *juramentado* against the Spanish colonizers, the American occupiers and the Japanese invaders throughout the region.

"You think these guys fit the bill?" Bolan asked.

"If they weren't running *juramentado*, they were sure as hell running a damn close copy. The white turbans are a historical match, and they'd all shaved their bodies and cut their hair short. That was supposed to make them appear more pleasing to God." Mei held up a file. "What's most interesting was the physical prep work."

"What do you mean?"

"It was hard to notice while we were fighting and breathing our own CS, but each of the pirates was wearing a tight waist-supporting band, like a weightlifter's belt, and had woven hemp cords tied around their elbows and knees. The CIA forensics team believes the waistband would obviously help someone who'd been wounded in the torso to keep fighting. The arm and leg bindings they're not so sure about, call it acupressure or something. Every one of them had also tightly bound their genitals with cords. That raised some eyebrows, but you and I saw the effect the other night. If we didn't blow out their hearts or blow off their heads, those guys kept coming. You add hash and fanatical conviction…" Mei trailed off grimly.

"Any other religious corroboration?"

"They were all wearing religious charms that supposedly ward off the blows of the enemy."

Bolan leaned back in his chair and let the water trickle around his feet. "So they're textbook *juramentado*."

"Well, technically speaking, you run *juramentado*, it's an activity, not a person. In the Moro dialect, what they actually call themselves is *mag-sabils*."

Bolan almost didn't want to know. "Which means?"

"Those Who Endure the Pangs of Death."

"Swell." Bolan finished his beer. "I can buy a revivalist *juramentado* movement here in the Sulu Archipelago. It's where the pastime was founded, but we've had similar attacks from New Guinea to the west coast of Thailand."

"That is disturbing," Mei agreed.

"What about your contacts in Philippine Intelligence?"

"They haven't found much. Whatever this movement is, it's highly secretive. It's hard to get operatives into the Muslim movements. Trust me, I've done it, and it isn't easy. Most of the power and wealth in the Philippines is concentrated in the hands of the Catholic majority in the big cities of the north. The Muslims tend to be rural, and most live in the southern islands.

Philippine Military Intelligence was built on the U.S. model, but the Philippine military was still based on patronage and loyalty to individual generals, and most of its assets were in the north. The military was clannish, and interservice cooperation was dismal, at best. For the most part, intelligence gathering consisted almost entirely of bribing informants or sending special operations commandos to shoot up suspicious villages and torture suspects. Neither tactic was ideal against fanatic terror cells.

Bolan stared out across the bay. "I need to get inside."

Mei rested her chin in her hands. "That, Blue-eyes, is something I'd like to see."

Bolan had to admit to himself it would be a challenge. "So we have nothing else on this end?"

"Like I said, Philippine Intelligence thinks there might be a movement in the southern islands, but there are always movements in the southern islands. That's were al Qaeda, the separatists, and every other violent group in the Philippines does their recruiting."

"Someone has to know something."

Mei gazed out over the water reluctantly.

Bolan read her look. "You have an idea."

"I know a guy who makes it his business to know things. He owes me a favor." She frowned. "But this may be stretching the mark to the breaking point."

"Maybe we should go have a talk with this guy."

"This guy's a real wild card." Mei's frown deepened. "I don't know if you want to get in bed with him."

Bolan shrugged. "I usually don't get in bed with anyone on the first date."

Mei burst out laughing.

"What's so funny?"

Mei waggled her eyebrows. "You'll know when you meet him."

"I don't get it." Bolan finished his beer. "And I'm not sure I want to."

3

Macao

Bolan stepped off the hydrofoil that had taken them from Hong Kong to the estuary of the Pearl River and onto the waterfront. At first glance, Macao looked like every other economically emerging city in Asia. Construction was everywhere. High-rise apartments and office buildings relentlessly clawed their way into the skyline. The streets were jammed with traffic, and hellish pollution surrounded them in the three dimensions of the air, the water and the streets. Casinos jammed the waterfront, and tourists crowded the casinos to overflowing.

Rickshaw men pounced on disembarkees from the hydrofoil, each working for a casino and affiliated hotel. Marcie Mei ignored them as she curled her thumb and forefinger against her teeth and let out a whistle that could have hailed a cab all the way from Manhattan.

A small man with massive calves and the shoulders of an ox looked up from his lunch. He took up the yoke of his rickshaw and trotted over to the pier. He and Mei spoke in rapid-fire Cantonese for a moment, and the woman gestured at Bolan. "Du, this is Cooper. Cooper, this is Du. There's hardly anything I don't owe Du, including my life."

Du grinned up at Bolan through gold teeth and stuck out a callused hand that seemed too big for his body. His English had strange inflections. He spoke his English more like a Brazilian than Chinese. "How you doin', hot rod?"

Bolan shook Du's hand. The rickshaw man squeezed, testing Bolan's strength. The calluses spread across his knuckles as well as his palms. Bolan suspected he hadn't developed them from pulling carts. The Executioner smiled and squeezed back. "Nice to meet you, Du."

Du grinned. He and Bolan silently agreed not crush each other's hands and relaxed their grips. Du grabbed what little baggage there was and threw it in back as Bolan and Mei climbed aboard. He took up the yoke and swiftly pulled his passengers away from the waterfront and into the sprawl. He chattered back over his shoulder, pointing out the sights.

He jerked his head off toward a tower of glass. "The Hilton?"

Mei sank back against Bolan. "Head for *Rua da Felicidade*."

Bolan perked an eyebrow. "The Street of Happiness?"

Mei nodded.

"Awww…man!" Du shook his head as he trotted past cars, bikes and scooters, and swerved around an ox. "Tell me you're not going to Ming's."

"Directly," Mei confirmed. "We're expected."

Du hunched his shoulders fatalistically and turned away from the glass and light of the downtown sprawl.

Macao was unique among Chinese cities in that it had once been a Portuguese possession. Once they pulled onto the *Rua da Felicidade*, they might as well have been in prewar China. Mediterranean architecture abutted ancient style Chinese houses and shops. The *Rua da Felicidade* had once been Macao's red light district. Now the street was lined with shops and street vendors and food stalls. The bright colors of silk were everywhere as were the smells of spices and roasting meat. For all of China's gustatory glory as one of the world's great cuisines, the art of barbecue was almost unknown there. Except in Macao. The Portuguese had brought their grills with them, and to this very day smoke filled the air. They passed a bamboo cage filled with a half dozen small, tapir-like animals. A metal trough lined with live coals and multiple spits glowed red hot and ready next to them. Bolan suspected few of the beasts would survive the lunch-time rush.

Bolan crooked two fingers and thrust out a note as the rickshaw passed a stall. Marcie's eyebrows shot in surprised approval as Bolan took two sheets of au jok khon wrapped in paper. The barbecued strips were a sweet, salty, cholesterol blowing form of pork-jerky sheathed in crispy fat.

Du pulled past the shops and took them deeper into the maze.

Bolan thought about their contact. He had consulted Kurtzman via satellite and was surprised Kurtzman had come up goose eggs. Neither the Farm, US, nor British Intelligence had anything on the man. He was an enigma.

Ming Jinrong was a part of the Chinese underworld.

Mei had been very closemouthed about the man. He was a valuable resource, and she was taking pains to protect him.

Bolan decided to try again. "What can you tell me about Jinrong?"

"I've had some dealings with him. He was Red League in Shanghai, but his…proclivities kept getting him in trouble, and he had to flee. He's been in Macao for twenty years," she said.

Bolan considered the tidbit of information. He had fought the Chinese triads before. The Red League was a secret society that had begun as a patriotic anti-Manchu organization of martial artists and merchants dedicated to the overthrow of the Qing Dynasty centuries ago. Like most of the other secret societies in China, as the ages passed, they had become runners of opium, heroin and prostitutes. They had taken their place as the heads of Chinese gambling, extortion, assassination and political manipulation.

The Communist revolution had only driven them further underground and made their business dealings even more Byzantine.

"So what does he do now?"

"He's kind of on the outs, but one of his strengths is that he's unconventional. Since he got pushed out of normal Chinese crime, he's specialized in peddling information. He's also interested in high tech. At this point, I believe the old men of the Red League council consider him a useful embarrassment."

"What does that mean?"

Mei locked eyes with Bolan. "It means he's not what you're expecting to meet, and when you meet him you be respectful."

"I'm always respectful." Bolan shrugged. "Until it's time not to be."

"Yeah, you just let me do the talking, and if you have to say something, mention the Eight Trigrams Double Broadsword."

Bolan nodded. "Got it."

Du pulled them down one side street and then another, each more narrow than the last, until he brought them to a halt before the wooden gate of a Portuguese villa that looked at least three hundred years old. The tile and stucco were faded and cracked, but the stonework was still incredible. It was a picture of lost colonial glory. Men with rifles peered down from the ornamental minarets at the wall corners.

Du set down his yoke and rapped the brass, lion-head knocker on the gate.

A pair of men with AK-47s opened the gate and let them in. Bolan, Mei and Du walked into the courtyard. A Spanish-style fountain with a potted flowering lemon tree in its middle dominated the tiled courtyard. Peacocks strutted freely, pecking among the rose beds.

Bolan locked eyes with their hosts.

The man was huge. He sat artfully draped across a cerulean chair, enthroned beneath a pink silk awning. Ming Jinrong looked like a six-foot-six, 270-pound Chinese version of Oscar Wilde. Right down to the wine-colored crushed velvet suit and the lily he held across his breast. A jaw like a steam shovel and a massive brow belied his soft eyes, cheeks and lips. His hair fell away from his face in languorous black curls.

Ming Jinrong danced the razor's edge between effeminate and Frankensteinian.

"Marcie." A half smile lifted one corner of his mouth as he spoke in an Oxford-accented baritone. "Such a pleasure to see you once again, and you have brought me an American." He looked Bolan up and down through thick lashes and met the Executioner's gaze without blinking. "And such blue eyes…"

He raised an eyebrow at the third member of their party. "Oh, and I see you've brought little Du."

Du's knuckles creaked into fists.

"Tell me." Ming cocked his leonine head at Mei. "Did you ever become proficient with the Southern Butterfly knives I gave you?"

"I'm sorry, Ming. The weapons you gave me hang in a place of honor in my home." Mei grinned impishly. "But I'm an island girl, and the kris is my life."

"Ah…the Serpent Waving Blade." Jinrong gazed off into the distance for a moment. "Well, then, how may I assist you? You know I can deny you nothing."

"I ask only for your expertise." Mei held the leaf-shaped throwing weapon that had ended Scott Clellande's life. The muzzles of automatic rifles along the walls raised slightly as the woman stepped forward with the blade.

Ming raised his eyes heavenward as if in infinite weariness at his guards. "Oh, please."

The weapons lowered as Mei set the blade on the low table before the gangster. "What do you make of it?"

Jinrong took up the red-tasseled weapon between immaculately manicured fingers and pursed his lips at it. "Why, it's a *piau*." His eyes widened slightly as he examined the slitted blade. "*Piau* is a loose term for a family of throwing weapons." He set the weapon back down on the table. "But this *piau* is not Chinese."

"Can you identify it?" Mei asked.

"Where did you find it?" Ming countered.

Bolan stepped forward. "In the throat of a friend."

"Ah." Jinrong sighed and sniffed at his lily. "Well, I can tell you what I know, which is that this weapon is Javanese and very likely the weapon of a *prisai sakti* practitioner."

"Javan?" Bolan and Mei exchanged glances. "Not Philippine? From a Muslim style of Arnis or Kali? Perhaps an esoteric one?"

"Oh, no, no, no. I have a similar weapon in my collection. As I mentioned, this form of *piau* is a specialty of the *prisai sakti* style of *pentjak-silat*. *Prisai sakti* means Holy Shield, and far from being a Muslim style, *prisai sakti* is affiliated with the Christian Javanese."

Bolan decided to be blunt. "You've heard of the rash of piracy in the South Seas."

Ming leaned back in his chair. "Yes, and such a distasteful way of doing business. It is bad for everybody." He waved a dismissing hand. It was clear he wished to change the subject. "Gau, bring our guests tea."

Bolan looked into Ming Jinrong's eyes. The man was an aficionado. Some men obsessively devoted themselves to baseball, blondes or bullfighting. The gangster's encyclopedic knowledge showed that his all-consuming passion was martial arts, and Bolan suspected it bordered on the fetishistic. "I've heard you are a master of the Eight Trigram Double Broadsword set."

"A master?" Ming raised a condescending eyebrow at Bolan and then looked at Mei disappointedly for clearly having fed the American information.

Bolan smiled. He was a master of no martial art, but he knew men who were. "I have a friend who is proficient in Monkey Kung Fu."

Ming tossed his hair distractedly. "What form?"

"Lost Monkey."

Ming reluctantly showed interest as Bolan continued.

"He also has some skill in the Seven Stars Mantis broadsword technique. He once told me that double broadswords are almost impossible to learn. They restrict each other's movements and endanger the practitioner. Only a master can wield them together effectively."

Mei stared at Bolan in shock.

Bolan kept his eyes on the man before him and knew he'd hit pay dirt. Ming Jinrong's eyes had lit up. Gau arrived with the tea, and Ming waved it away as he spoke rapidly, this time in Mandarin. The servant scampered away as Ming rose and removed his velvet jacket. He stood slightly stooped, as if he were embarrassed by his height and size, but he straightened to his full height as Gau returned with a silken pillow upon which he bore a pair of Chinese broadswords.

Gau took a brass-inlayed wooden sheath in each hand and presented the hilts to his master. Ming drew his weapons. The wide, curved blades made a loud rasping sound as they came free. Sharpening steels had been set within the sheaths so that the blades would be honed every time they were drawn or put away.

"This—" the man smiled at Bolan as he stepped into the courtyard with a dragon inlayed blade in either hand "—would interest your friend."

Ming stamped his foot and began striking the empty air. He held the blades parallel, so that each strike was a double attack as he cut to one side, twisted and cut again. The blades hissed through the air as his double cuts grew wider and he began slicing vertically and on the diagonal. His feet walked an octagon pattern of deep stances and quick leaps. Sweat began to sheen his face as he forced the heavy weapons to his will. With a shout the parallel blades began pinwheeling in the mobster's hands.

Bolan's eyes narrowed with appreciation. He was watching a master.

The blades blurred around Ming's body like counterrotating propellers and smeared into bright flashes. How he did it without clanging the blades or cutting himself was a mystery to Bolan. He whipped the blades so fast they made a noise like tearing cloth as they sliced the air. The grace, speed and control was astounding. The light gleaming in Ming's unblinking eyes revealed that his consummate skill was wedded with homicidal impulse.

Ming stamped his foot and the quicksilver blades clanged together in a scissoring attack that could only be intended to behead an opponent.

He lowered his swords and bowed to Bolan.

The guards burst into applause. Bolan and Mei joined them. Bolan knew it was a privilege to observe such a performance, particularly for a westerner. Even Du clapped his hands in open appreciation.

Jinrong sheathed his swords. Gau bore them away as the master sagged back into his chair. He was pale and trembling, and sweat dripped from his temples. He waved a shaky hand at another servant who produced a pipe. The man packed the pipe with a black blob and lit the pipe for his master. The black chunk in the bowl glowed red as Ming drew on the pipe. The huge gangster stopped trembling with the first puff of blue-white smoke, and the fragrant, sweet scent of opium drifted across the courtyard.

"Once…upon a time—" Ming sighed as his breathing returned to normal "—I was something to see. But opium, young men and gambling have left me—" he heaved another sigh "—distracted."

Mei's eyes were shining. "Your performance was magnificent."

"Thank you, my dear. I have always marveled at your skill at Kali, and little Du's Tiger-Crane is feared throughout the waterfront." He suddenly turned his eyes on Bolan. "But you, Mr. Cooper? Of what are you a master?"

"I am a master of no acknowledged style." Bolan shrugged.

Jinrong pursed his lips and puffed on his pipe in disappointment.

"But," Bolan said, smiling in mock shyness and looking down, "I am proficient at the Seven Triple Bursting technique."

Ming sat up straight. His brow furrowed at the thought of a technique he did no know. "I demand a demonstration."

Mei simply stared.

Bolan shrugged again. "I'll need seven plates."

Ming spoke some words, and servants scampered. He and his small army of guards looked on keenly as seven of the household servants returned each bearing a plate.

Bolan nodded. "Have them stand in a line to my left, fifty paces back."

Ming gave orders and the servants lined up along the wall to Bolan's left and eyed him nervously.

"Tell them to throw the plates in the air across the courtyard, as high as they can, when I say go."

The master leaned forward with keen interest as he translated the instructions. The tension of the servants grew palpable as they obeyed.

Bolan's hands dropped loosely to his sides.

Mack Bolan was a master of no martial art, but he was an incredibly lethal man with his bare hands. And, long ago, the Green Berets had made Bolan a master sniper. His War Everlasting had made him the most lethal living exponent of combat sharpshooting on the planet.

"Go!"

The china spun into the air like awkward porcelain dishes.

The servants didn't have time to cower as the Beretta 93-R cleared leather. A machine pistol was a specialist's weapon. Most respected firearms' authorities eschewed them altogether. They were too heavy for a pistol, but much too light for a submachine gun. Their rate of fire made them almost uncontrollable on full-auto. A few gun experts grudgingly opined that they made a good weapon for the point man of an entry team, but that man would require prohibitive amounts of training to make it worthwhile.

Bolan had trained with the 93-R for hundreds of hours and fought with the weapon in his hand for more years than he cared to think about. The smooth rosewood grips had been custom fitted to his hand and the action tuned to oil-on-glass slick perfection. Bolan knew the weapon's recoil and rapid cycling like old friends.

The Beretta 93-R had become an extension of his will.

Seven plates spun into the air. The white dot front sight of the Beretta whipped toward the farthest and lowest flying plate. Both of Bolan's eyes were open, bringing the front sight blade and the plate into convergence. His finger caressed the trigger, and the machine pistol cycled in his hand.

Bolan's speed had left the guards no time to react. They jumped as the pistol spit its first burst and the plate came apart. The spell broke, and they swung their automatic rifles up as Bolan's second 3-round burst snarled from his gun.

The Executioner ignored the riflemen. He concentrated on the plates as they hit their apogee and began falling back to earth. The front sight of his pistol whipped from target to target without conscious thought. Each time the white dot eclipsed a plate, Bolan squeezed the trigger and the Italian steel snarled off a 3-round burst cycling at just over eighteen rounds per second.

Plate after plate shattered. Bolan grimaced and dropped his aim as he touched off his last burst. The seventh plate shattered less than three feet from the ground. The lead servant in line shrieked as his robes were harmlessly sprayed with bits of ceramic shrapnel.

The Beretta 93-R racked open on a smoking empty chamber.

The seven plates had been shattered in as many heartbeats.

The sudden silence in the courtyard was deafening.

The guards dropped their rifles on their slings and began applauding wildly. Mei and Du joined them. There was renewed respect in Du's eyes. Ming tossed his lily at Bolan's feet in tribute. "Ah!" He rolled his eyes at Mei, and his smile was ecstatic. "You brought me not just an American, but—" he savored the words like fine wine as he spoke them "—a gunfighter."

Bolan slid a loaded magazine into his pistol and pressed the slide release home on a fresh round before he holstered it. He had done fancier shooting, often on the field of battle and in the face of oncoming fire. Bolan allowed himself a small smile. Seven plates in one and a half seconds...

Ming sat up in his chair. "Gau, have some of the men light some firecrackers in the street to allay the neighbor's suspicions."

The gangster turned back to Bolan. "I believe I know what it is you wish of me, and I believe it would be my pleasure to render you assistance. Give me a week while I send forth my agents. In the mean time," the gangster said, opening a huge but graceful hand in invitation, "be my guests. I insist."

Bolan frowned. A week of downtime, and who knew how many more innocent targets would get hit. Ming caught the look and shrugged.

"During that time, it would be my honor to teach you something of the sword." He smiled enigmatically. "I believe you may have some need of one where you will be going."

4

Macao

"Cut! Cut! Cut!" Ming's blade hurtled down at Bolan like a gleaming meteor. Sweat dripped from Bolan's brow as he fought. Ming's crushed velvet suit of the day was lime green, but he had shoved off his suspenders and fought in his sleeveless T-shirt beneath the southern Chinese sun. Bolan fought stripped to the waist as Ming attacked him, the giant mobster shouting at him all the while like an angry headmaster.

Bolan was bleeding from numerous superficial cuts that could easily have lopped off limbs had Ming wanted. Purple bruises blossomed beneath the skin of Bolan's cheek and his arms and shoulders where Ming had struck him with the flat of the blade or hit him with the pommel. Bolan ignored his blood dripping on the hot tiles and the sweat stinging his eyes and fought on.

"Cut!" Ming roared.

Chinese martial-arts masters did not encourage their students. They beat on them, literally and figuratively, until they mastered the technique or quit.

Bolan held a two-handed sword. It was barely three feet long, and the massive, curved blade seemed much too short and far too wide. The cord-wrapped handle was one-third as long as the blade and mounted with a thick, rigid, black iron ring at the bottom. Although it was a two-handed sword, Ming forbade

Bolan to touch it with his left hand. Once Bolan had picked it up he had found it amazingly well balanced and lightning fast.

"You are forcing it!" Ming shouted. "Use your wrist! Let the blade do the work! Do not chop at me! I am not a goat! This is not a butcher's stall in the market! Cut!"

Ming's own broadsword whirled around his wrist, flashing like lightning. "Like this! And this! And this!"

The slender saber whipped up, down and sideways in a dazzling array of cuts. Their swords rang with blow after blow as Bolan barely blocked the incoming barrage.

"Cut! Cut! Cut!" Ming said. "I see your left hand yearning to grip the blade for a two-handed blow! I see you have had training in the Japanese sword, and you desire to pull the hilt toward you for the slice! Cut! This is not a kendo dojo! Chinese swords express themselves outwardly! Let your wrist succumb to the curve! Let your weapon's weight do your work for you!"

Bolan knew intuitively that Ming was right. The few sword fights Bolan had been in and the little formal training he had received in swordsmanship were with the Japanese katana and its smaller, straight cousin, the *ninja-to*. Those instincts were interfering with the morning's lesson.

Bolan had to empty his cup before more knowledge could be poured in.

The Executioner let his wrist succumb to the curve of the blade. He stopped defending, and his blade licked out in series of blindingly fast attacks.

"Better!" Ming grinned delightedly as he parried the attacks. "Better!"

The giant gangster counterattacked. They fought back and forth, blades ringing beneath the watchful eyes of Ming's guards. Ming no longer punished Bolan for his mistakes but let him explore the blade, now that he was using it properly. He grunted corrections, and every time Bolan made a mistake Ming stopped and made him do the move ten times correctly, and then resumed the battle.

Forty-five minutes later the noon sun hammered down on the courtyard.

"Enough!" Ming stepped back. "You will learn nothing more at this point but the mistakes of fatigue."

Bolan didn't argue. His arm felt like lead. He had been fatigued two hours ago. At this point he was staggering with exhaustion.

"Now that we have cured you of your samurai impulses…" Ming took Bolan's sword and walked to a rack loaded with Chinese kung fu weaponry of every description. He picked up a length of bloodred silk ribbon and tied it to the ring in Bolan's hilt. "Observe."

Ming slowly swished the blade through the air, the red ribbon twirling behind it like an angry serpent. "The dadao is called the war sword. One reason is that you could issue it to a raw recruit and with little training he could take it in both hands and smite an enemy with some effectiveness. However, in the hands of an adept, the dadao becomes a thing of great subtlety."

Bolan watched as Ming wove a web of steel with the blade. The ribbon twirled along in its wake like the prop of an Olympic rhythmic gymnast. "The ribbon can be used to distract the enemy…or worse." Ming suddenly snapped his wrist and the end of the ribbon licked out and whipped against the vase of flowers on the table. The pottery cracked and Bolan realized the end of the ribbon was weighted. Ming let go of the sword as he swung it and caught the silk ribbon by its weighted ends. The gangster dropped low into a spinning crouch. The sword deployed at the end of the ribbon, adding three feet to Ming's reach. It scythed around at ankle level and sank into the wood of a courtyard beam.

Ming yanked the ribbon, and sword's hilt leaped back into his hand. "The dadao has endless possibilities."

Ming nodded at a samurai sword in the rack, and Bolan drew it. Ming motioned for Bolan to attack.

"Now the iron ring pommel," Ming lectured, "cannot only be used to strike an opponent, but to trap his weapon and disarm him."

Bolan slashed, and Ming twirled his weapon like a baton. He slapped the pommel ring around the tip of Bolan's sword and yanked it halfway down the blade. It took all of Bolan's strength not to have the sword ripped from his grip as Ming twisted and yanked.

Ming grinned as they played tug of war for a moment with the trapped blades, testing each other's strength. "But should your opponent prove too strong for you to take his weapon away…" Ming roared like a lion and torqued his wrists. The blade of Bolan's trapped katana snapped in two. "You may destroy it, and then him."

Ming sighed as he held up the weapon and ran his eyes along the edge. "The dadao is a two-handed sword, but you have discovered that a strong man may easily wield it like a saber in one. Thus, in the morning you shall practice one handed, and then again in the afternoon we shall practice with two hands. There your training on the Japanese katana may be of some assistance to you."

He handed the blade back to Bolan.

"I thank you, *Sifu*." Bolan bowed slightly and used the Chinese honorific for teacher.

"It is my pleasure." Ming bowed too. He clapped his hands, and two beautiful women appeared in the silk robes and coiffures of medieval Chinese courtesans. "Butterfly, Jade, see to our guest's injuries." Ming leered. "See to his every need."

Butterfly and Jade bowed to Bolan. Beneath their thick lashes, the women's eyes roved over Bolan's naked and bloody torso like horse traders presented with a strange and powerful new breed they did not recognize.

"Gau," Ming called. Gau instantly appeared at Ming's right hand. "Summon Du, and tell him to bring his butterfly knives." Ming drew his broadsword once more. "I feel…invigorated."

Bolan didn't envy Du. He paused a moment as Jade and Butterfly gently took him by the elbow to lead him back to his chambers. *"Sifu?"*

"The lesson is over. You may call me Ming. All my friends do."

Bolan bowed slightly. "May I inquire, my friend, if you have heard from any of your agents since yesterday?"

"Indeed. Three of my men have made inquiries into the matter and reported back already." Ming clapped his hands. "Ho!"

A hulking, shaven-headed servant Bolan had not seen before came through the curtains behind Ming's throne. He bore a large carved box and held it out for Bolan, who lifted the lid.

Three severed heads lay nested in the box. They gazed up at him, their faces frozen in the contortion of their final fear and agony.

"I will need to send more men." Ming smiled his enigmatic smile once more and dropped his eyes to the dadao in Bolan's hands. "In the meantime, I suggest you practice."

CIA Safehouse, Macao

BOLAN DRANK SOME TEA. Butterfly and Jade had taken him to his chambers and applied liniment to his bruises and ointments to his cuts. He smelled like a Chinese herbalist shop, but his bruises had subsided and the cuts had been reduced to thin pink lines.

Once they had been assured of his survival, they had been insistent on seeing to Bolan's other needs, as well. He smiled at the memory and wondered if he'd have any strength left for the evening's sword lesson. He'd been limp when Du had taken him by rickshaw to the safehouse. Du had been sullen, silent and covered with bruises himself. His knife technique had not been enough to save him from a beating at Ming's hands.

Bolan checked the time and hit a key on the laptop. Kurtzman's face appeared on the monitor via satellite link. He cocked his head at Bolan's salve-smeared body.

"Do I want to ask?"

Bolan thought about Butterfly and Jade. "You might."

Kurtzman read Bolan's expression. "Man…you have all the fun."

Bolan shrugged and drank more tea.

"Well, tell me about Ming, then. I hear he's quite a character."

"That's an understatement."

Kurtzman looked curious. "And?"

Bolan smiled proudly. "He says my swordsmanship is salvageable."

Kurtzman blinked. "Well, that's good news."

"I think he's taken a shine to me."

Kurtzman paused. "That's a good thing?"

"If we want his cooperation, yes. I get the impression he's been kind of lonely since the triads pushed him out of Shanghai. He's been wasting away in exile like fallen royalty. I got his blood moving again. He really seems to be enjoying having a student."

"That's all well and good, but where's the mission payoff?"

"In China, the criminal underworld and the martial arts are deeply intertwined. Both have their code of honor. By taking me on as his student, his code obliges him to help me against my enemies. It's his plausible excuse to himself and his superiors for getting involved in business he shouldn't."

"So what have you learned?"

"So far, not much. Ming apparently got a few nibbles, and his agents promptly got their heads cut off. The interesting thing was that they were spread out. One was in the Philippines, one in Malaysia and one in Java."

"A real pan-Southeast Asian movement." Kurtzman chewed his lower lip. "It's not good, but if it's a charismatic movement like you suspect—"

"Then I'll have to find that charismatic head and cut it off," Bolan finished.

Kurtzman scowled. "That'll be a neat trick, especially doing it without turning him into a martyr."

"Yeah." Bolan considered the fanatical movements he'd fought before. "I'll just have to do it in a way that doesn't leave any doubts."

"First, you've got to find him."

"Speaking of which, where's Rosario?"

"He's in Central America. He says he and Calvin can extract and be in Manila in twenty-four hours."

"Good enough. Tell them I'll meet them in the Polillo Islands safehouse. That should do for our purposes."

"What kind of purpose?"

"How's our young friend doing in custody?"

"According to Manila station, the Philippine military police have stopped just short of rubber hoses and jumper cables, and that was only at the direct request of the station chief."

"Good, I think in twenty-four hours he'll be about ready to see a friendly face."

Kurtzman grimaced. "You're playing kind of rough with this kid, aren't you, Striker?"

"That kid boarded a private yacht in the middle of the night, blade in hand, with the intention of beheading every man, woman and child he found, Bear."

"Well…granted," Kurtzman replied. "But he was under the influence of drugs, and—"

"Running *juramentado* is an all-volunteer activity. You sign up. Our boy was excited about the plan and thankful to be a part of it, and that was before the hash, the trance and the ball-binding." Bolan's voice went ice cold. "Young, dumb and brainwashed, I'll grant you. We'll let him live. But he's going to make good on what he owes humanity, one way or the other."

"Yeah." Kurtzman shifted uncomfortably in his wheelchair. "I hear you. So what are you going to do?"

"I'm going to fly back to the Philippines and take a meeting with Pol and the kid. Assuming all goes well, I'll leave Pol to it and come back here to Macao. The last leads we generated came by setting out bait. I figure I might as well try it again while Pol goes to work."

"The yacht trick again?"

"Yeah, but I'm thinking bigger."

"Bigger?"

"Ming's had a few interesting suggestions."

Kurtzman raised a bemused eyebrow. "I bet he has."

Bolan ignored the innuendo. "Meantime, I've got a job for you, Bear."

"Oh?" Both of Kurtzman's eyebrows rose with interest. Aaron Kurtzman was a genuine, certified genius, and when Mack Bolan said "I have a job for you, Bear," it meant the big guy had a whopper of a challenge for him.

"Yeah, this is a Southeast Asian mission."

"Yes…" Kurtzman waited for the rub. "And?"

"And I need a Muslim cover."

Kurtzman stared blankly into the Webcam.

Bolan nodded in empathy. "Work on it."

5

Polillo Islands, Philippines

"Has he snapped, yet?" Bolan walked up the steps to the beach house. The yellow Piper Super-Cub seaplane lay at anchor in the lagoon. Rosario "Politician" Blancanales' bull-like figure stood on the veranda holding two cups of coffee in one hand. Bolan could smell it as he mounted the steps.

Stony Man Farm's psychological warfare expert shook his head. Bolan tossed a manila folder onto the table as both he and Blancanales sank into rattan chairs.

"Not yet," Blancanales said over his mug, "but he's just about ready."

Bolan nodded. "Snapping" was the point in cult deprogramming when the cultist realized he had been deceived by his cult and snapped out of his delusion. "So what's the hold up?"

"Well, your boy wasn't exactly wearing saffron robes and handing out flowers at the airport. He's more than just a true believer. We're dealing with a genuine holy warrior here, with martyrdom on his mind."

"So what's your strategy?"

"Same as always. Force Ali to think. Someone once said thinking is the hardest activity man is capable of, and that's why so few men do it. People in cults have surrendered their minds. In many respects, their minds are actually turned off." Blancanales stared intently at the seaplane as it bobbed on the water.

"The first time you lay eyes on a person, you can tell if their mind is working or not. As you question them, you can tell exactly how they've been programmed. I agree with your initial assessment. It began in prison. Ali was fifteen when he was incarcerated. As you can imagine, a fifteen-year-old boy is in for some very rough times in prison. He hasn't come out and said it, but I suspect the cultists inside saved him from being punked, which immediately engendered gratitude, and more importantly, trust. The minute a cult gains your trust—" Blancanales snapped his fingers "—they have you. You're in."

"And to snap him out of it?" Bolan asked.

"Like I said, this isn't some rich man's daughter signing away her trust fund at an ashram. Ali's a hard case. He came from poverty-stricken parents and grew up on the streets. He went in for robbery and assault, and when the cult sucked him in it gave him instant family, instant support, instant purpose. That's a tough one to beat."

Bolan waited. "And?"

"And it's a matter of language. It's talking and knowing what to talk about. I've started moving his mind around, slowly pushing it with questions. Ali hasn't just turned his mind off, he's given it to someone else. He's been taught that thinking and questioning are wrong. They're the equivalent of doubting. Thinking is a sin. He's been told not to think, but to implicitly trust."

"Our boy is operating on faith."

"Exactly. As I question him, I watch every move his mind makes. I know where it's going to go, and when I hit on a point or question that sparks a response, I push it. I stay with it and don't let him get around it with the lies he's been told or circular dogma. I drive it home."

"And then you snap him."

"Sooner or later." Blancanales leaned back and sipped his coffee.

"So how's it been going?"

"Pretty rough on everyone. His first instinct was violence, so we had to restrain him. Even shackled, he made a pretty decent attempt at taking my head off with a standing mule kick. When he realized I wouldn't let him hurt me, he went sullen and refused to talk at all. That's par for the course. At that point, I had Calvin treat his injuries and administer him two low doses of sodium Pentothal to loosen his inhibitions. Then Calvin pulled his Black Muslim routine. Once Ali started talking to Calvin as his doctor and a fellow Muslim, Ali's strategy turned to feigned compliance while looking to escape. That, however, was a strategic mistake on his part." Blancanales grinned. "Because that got him talking to me."

Bolan nodded in acknowledgment. "And that is everyone's downfall."

"Darn tootin'!" agreed Pol.

"So where is Ali now?"

Blancanales lifted his chin eastward. "Calvin took him for his morning walk on the beach."

"Is that wise?"

"A growing boy needs his exercise. Besides, this is an island." Blancanales shrugged. "Ali can't swim, and he's shackled. Short of pulling a Man from Atlantis, he's not going anywhere."

Bolan smiled wearily through his jet lag. Blancanales was a people person. When it came to getting inside an enemy's head, he was a genuine "hearts and minds" lubricant. If he thought the boy deserved a walk, Bolan would take his word for it.

"So, you want to meet him?"

"Sure." Bolan scooped up his folder and followed Blancanales down the back stairs into the jungle. They walked a hundred yards inland through the trees and came to the other side of the island. Blancanales gave him a basic sitrep. "Ali speaks English, Spanish and Tagalog. To him, I'm Dr. Blancanales and a Mindanao native. He knows Calvin is an American but thinks he's a Muslim doctor. He has no idea who you are, and I doubt he'd recognize you. He sure as hell isn't expecting you, so you can play it any way you want. You going straight in, or are you working with a cover?"

"Cover."

"Really? This should be interesting."

Bolan nodded. He'd given Kurtzman a challenge, and the man had come up with something so crazy it might actually work. "Thanks for the psych profile. Any personal observations?"

"Yeah. As a matter of fact, this Ali kid? I like him."

Bolan frowned.

Blancanales's dark eyes stared right back at Bolan. "Listen, I know he's an intelligence asset, but the kid's got guts. Deep down, there's a decent human being in there."

Bolan nodded. His life was going to depend on it. "All right."

Blancanales gestured through the trees. "There's the lad now."

Ali Mohammed Apilado sat slump-shouldered by the water's edge. He dejectedly watched the sun rise over the Philippine Sea. He wore blaze orange prisoner-of-war garb, and Bolan could see the glint of the shackles and handcuffs that bound him. Twenty yards back, Calvin James leaned against a palm tree. A prayer rug lay near his feet. The lanky black man turned and smiled at Bolan.

"Hey, big guy."

"Morning, Calvin. How's the patient today?"

"He's a bit pouty." The ex-Navy SEAL shrugged. "I'm giving him some space. I opened the cellar door this morning and then followed him at a respectful distance. He's just finished with his morning prayers."

"This is the calm before the storm," Blancanales said. "Ali's been getting angrier and angrier. Right now he's directing it at me. Let's go say hi."

Three of the most dangerous men on Earth walked across the sand toward the prisoner. Ali's prayer rug lay rolled to one side. Blancanales strolled up and smiled in a fatherly fashion. *"Buenos dias, amigo."*

Calvin James nodded. *"Asalaam aleikum."*

Bolan glanced at the rising sun and smiled down at the young man and wished him good morning in Tagalog.

Ali's bruises were fading, but his face was still lumped and misshapen from his treatment at the hands of Philippine Intelligence. He ignored Blancanales and Bolan and grunted glumly at James. *"Aleiku salaam."*

"Ali?" Blancanales extended a hand toward Bolan. He had modulated his English with a perfect Philippine accent. "I would like you to meet a friend of mine."

Ali Mohammed Apilado regarded Bolan with grave suspicion. Bolan bowed slightly. *"Asalaam aleikum."*

Ali stiffened in anger but did not respond.

Bolan played the hand that Kurtzman had drawn him. "My name is Makeen al-Boulus. Do you recognize me?"

Ali stared into Bolan's blue eyes intently but without recognition. Blancanales and James both shot Bolan surprised looks. Bolan held the young man's gaze and smiled benevolently. "Strange, it was one week ago this morning that you ran *juramentado* and tried to cut off my head."

Ali's jaw dropped.

Bolan knew he'd hit pay dirt. Blancanales folded his arms across his chest, nodding. James grinned his approval. Bolan reached into the manila folder and showed Ali a picture of Marcie Mei. "This is my wife. She is pregnant with my child, yet you and your brothers tried to take her head, as well."

Ali paled.

Bolan turned a picture of Escotto Clellande like a tarot card of fate. "This was my first mate. A pious man." The Executioner took the *piau* from the folder and let the razor-sharp shard of steel fall to stick point first in the sand. Its red fiber tail fluttered in the morning breeze. "He pulled this from his throat as he drowned in his own blood."

Ali Apilado looked as if he might vomit.

"You are young and devout so much may be forgiven, but can you truly be so ignorant that you would attack the faithful?"

Rage, fear and betrayal rose unstoppably from the young man's soul. He rolled to his hands and knees and heaved up his guts into the surf.

Bolan spit into the sand. "May God forgive you."

The Executioner turned and walked away. Blancanales followed, while James knelt and put a consoling hand on Ali's shoulder.

"Jesus…" Blancanales shook his head as they walked back through the jungle. "Did anyone ever tell you you're hard core?"

Bolan shrugged as he went past the beachhouse. "Is he snapped?"

"Yeah."

"Good. I need him."

Blancanales let out a long breath. "Striker, we need to have a talk about recidivism and the need for follow-up rehabilitation after the snap."

"I'm going fishing with Ming and Marcie." Bolan kept walking toward his plane. "You have a week."

Coloane Island, Macao

"BEHOLD!" MING CLAPPED his hands, and his men yanked back the bolts holding the steel container vessel together. The top of the container had been cut off, and the four sides fell away with a tremendous clang to the foredeck of the steamer.

Bolan simply stared.

"Do you like it?" Ming clasped his huge hands together and looked at Bolan expectantly.

"I…" Bolan opened his mouth and closed it.

"I listened with great interest to your story of how you used your yacht as a pirate trap," Ming gushed, "and the lesson of the British Q-boats in the World War II."

"I can see that."

Ming raised a hesitant eyebrow. "You do know how to load and fire a 106 mm recoilless rifle?"

"I do," Bolan said.

He now had six of them.

Bolan stared at the tiny armored vehicle that squatted on deck. What Bolan was looking at was a former United States Marine Corps Ontos tank destroyer. Ontos was a Greek word that literally meant "thing." It was an apt description. The tank was barely taller than Bolan, himself. At twelve-and-a-half-feet long and eight-and-a-half-feet wide, it was not a tank so much as a tankette. The most remarkable thing about the Ontos was the steel arm sprouting from each side of the tiny, open turret, each of which held three, externally mounted 106 mm recoilless rifles on stalks.

It looked ridiculous, but undeniably hostile.

Bolan eyed the Ontos critically. It had to be at least fifty years old. The thin steel hull was streaked and pitted with rust. A black welding line ran the circumference of the top hull. Both of its tracks were gone, and it sat chalked in place on its road wheels. However, the guns appeared to be in decent condition. "Does it run?"

"No." Ming gestured at a tiny man in a stained coverall. "My mechanic, Fung, says the engine is hopelessly corroded."

Bolan let out a long breath. "The guns will have to be manually traversed."

"So says Fung," Ming concurred.

"Where did you, uh…" Bolan shook his head. "Get it?"

"A Vietnamese associate of mine sold it to me a year ago. The Vietnamese army captured it from you Americans long ago. With the engine gone, the Vietnamese had intended on using it as a static field gun. However, moving it to any place of use proved prohibitive, so it languished for decades in a warehouse in Da Nang. I had thought to strip it of its cannons and sell them but…" Ming gazed upon the six barreled monstrosity and sighed. "But I became fond of it."

Bolan reserved comment. Ming Jinrong was a very complicated man.

"The Viet Cong greatly feared it, you know. When all six

barrels were loaded with 'beehive' ammunition and fired together, it was said to be able to clear a quarter mile of jungle. The Marines called it the rolling shotgun.

"The problem was that each of the six recoilless rifles were externally mounted on a stalk, which meant that once it was fired someone had to go outside the tank and reload it by hand. However, for a first salvo it was capable of incredible firepower." Ming paused once again to admire the Ontos.

"Your Q-boat!" Ming spread his arms, encompassing the ancient, rusty steamer and the equally decrepit armored vehicle squatting on the bow. "I have named her *Flawless Victory*." He gazed at Bolan expectantly again. "Do you like it?"

Bolan nodded. "I love it."

"I am so glad." Ming sighed.

"We have 106 mm shells?" Bolan asked hopefully.

"Oh, we have an assortment." The gangster glowed. "I have a crew ready and shall give you twenty of my best men. You shall have to train your gun crew at sea." Ming gazed proudly at what he had wrought. "We sail with the tide."

6

South China Sea

Bolan fought Marcie Mei on the stern deck of the *Flawless Victory*. The tiny woman fought with a two-and-a-half-foot kris in one hand and a twelve-inch blade in the other. Ming Jinrong stood by the bridge, straddle-stanced and arms akimbo like a judging Buddha. He held a rattan stick like a rod of correction in his right hand. Every mistake Bolan made was pointed out with the baton and punctuated with a blow for emphasis. Ming had invited Bolan to resist correction if he felt so motivated.

Bolan took the blows and learned.

Ming had decided that facing a kung fu master would not help Bolan where he was going. Now that he had a grudgingly admitted "feeble grasp of the basics," Bolan needed more practical opponents. Mei and Du had been called off the bench. Ming had ordered the woman to "pink" Bolan with her blades when he left himself open, but not to cut him too badly. As a result, Bolan was lumped and bleeding again.

However, Bolan's swordsmanship with the dadao was rapidly improving.

They had been at sea for three days, and Ming's soldiers and crew without current duties attended the sparring sessions with the avidness of ancient Romans attending the gladiatorial games.

Wagers were flying from stem to stern.

Bolan was larger, stronger, faster. But Mei?

She was tricky.

Bolan knew he was quite good, but a feeble grasp of dadao basics wouldn't be enough to save him. Mei's father had been an accomplished fighter on the island of Mindoro, and he had wanted a boy. A kris had been shoved in his diminutive daughter's hand at age five.

The Mouse had pinked Bolan twice and was moving in for the kill.

"Ting!" Ming threw his baton down between them to halt the action. The triad lord leaned down as the *Flawless Victory*'s first mate spoke in his ear.

Mei lowered her blades and raised a disappointed eyebrow at Bolan. "Your bacon just got saved, buddy."

Bolan didn't bother denying it. He sheathed his sword as Ming beckoned. "What's up?" he asked.

Ming's eyes were alight with excitement. "We can expect company tonight, Mr. Cooper."

"What kind of company?"

"Well, according to registry, this boat is officially loaded with palm oil headed for Australia. However, in certain circles I let it slip that I am transferring some of my fortune and that this boat is actually carrying a million dollars' worth of gold ingots and one hundred kilos of opium."

Bolan nodded. "Is it?"

Ming smiled. "What good is a trap that does not smell of fresh bait?"

"Are we expecting the company I want?"

"Alas, not. Your true quarry continues to elude me." Ming shrugged. "However, I have found that if you cannot find your enemy, then find his enemy. These people you seek are poaching. They are stepping on established toes and making things hot for everyone. They are making people angry. Perhaps those people know something."

Bolan agreed. It was sound logic. "So we're going to get hit by a different pirate group?"

"Indeed."

The Executioner considered the nature of piracy in the South Seas. "Speedboats before dawn?"

"A veritable armada." Ming sighed happily.

"Who?"

Ming draped himself across his massive chair. "Why, none other than the Pirate King of the South China Sea."

Bolan had done a lot of recent research on Southeast Asian piracy. "Rustam Megawatti?" he asked.

"Indeed." Ming looked impressed.

Bolan shook his head. They had attracted some serious attention. "The Megawatt, himself?"

"So it would seem." Ming laid a massive hand ruefully upon his breast. "And I fear he is no friend of mine."

"Tell me what you know about him."

"He is owned by the Red League, who in turn have paid the old men in Beijing handsomely for his…what was the word the English pirates of old used?" Ming pursed his lips as he savored the term. "Letters of mark and reprisal. Megawatti has official sanction from the Chinese authorities to commit acts of piracy in the China Sea as he long as he kicks profit back up the line."

Bolan regarded his sword master frankly. Ming was already on the outs with the Red League. "You're treading dangerous ground," Bolan said in warning.

"I thrive upon danger." Ming looked at Bolan, his expression all seriousness. "Indeed, I have languished from the lack of it."

Bolan shrugged. Ming Jinrong was an interesting man, he thought and then turned to business. "When?"

"Somewhat past midnight I believe we shall be tested." Ming ran an appreciative eye over Bolan's battered physique. "I suggest you take a nap."

It was a good suggestion.

Bolan went below. He and Du shared a small steel cube with two cots and a single light bulb hanging from the ceiling. The crew's quarters of the ancient steamer were dilapidated, but Ming's servants had scrubbed them clean. Bolan's weapons and gear took up a quarter of the cell. He had folded his cot and spread his bedding on the floor. The Executioner staunched his bleeding, stripped and sacked out on top of his blankets.

BOLAN STRAPPED HIS pistols to his thighs and his sword over his right shoulder. He scooped up his Farm-modified carbine and he made his way to the bridge. The room was clustered with men carrying automatic rifles. Ming and his men were all dressed for combat in khaki coveralls and red head scarves. His men all carried M-16 rifles and a bladed weapon of one sort or another. Ming, himself, stood among his men with his broadswords strapped in an X behind his back, and a pair of Chinese Type 80 machine pistols hung from his hips like a gunfighter.

"Ah!" He looked up as Bolan came in and handed him a red scarf. "For identification."

The Executioner tied the red silk bandanna around his head. He suspected he and Ming's forces looked more like pirates than the approaching pirates did. "Where's my gun crew?"

Fung and his four men marched in on cue. They looked from Ming to Bolan expectantly. They were well drilled. They had fired the four inert training rounds in Ming's stock and knew how to load, reload and traverse the turret.

Live firing at night was going to be exciting to say the least.

Du and Mei trotted in armed to the teeth. The woman was wearing a black raid suit, armor and carrying her carbine. Du had a shotgun across his shoulders, and both fighters were wearing red scarves.

"Du, Fung." Bolan jerked his head toward the stern as he put on his headset. "You're with me."

The Executioner and his artillery team marched out onto the deck. Bolan climbed the rope ladder, lowered himself into the open container vessel and dropped on top of the Ontos. All six rifles were loaded, three with high-explosive and three with beehive rounds. Bolan squeezed his frame into the tiny commander-gunner's position in the turret and clicked on his radio. "I'm in position."

"Affirmative, Cooper." Ming was clearly excited. "My sources tell me we can expect a large attacking force. They know I am heavily armed wherever I go, and my spies tell me the Red League considers this an ideal opportunity to finally wash their hands of me."

"How large?" Bolan asked.

"Perhaps six to ten boatloads of Megawatti's men. Heavily armed with automatic weapons and rocket propelled grenades."

Bolan glanced around his gun emplacement. The frontal armor of the Ontos was one inch of armored steel and of no protective value at all against an antitank weapon. "How soon?"

"My sources say our enemies departed the islands an hour ago."

"So they should be right on top of us."

"Almost certainly, they—" Bolan could hear shouting in the background. "They are upon us!"

Bolan raised his voice to parade ground decibels. "Du!"

The bolts holding the container vessels shrieked as they were pulled. Illumination flares burst into incandescence overhead. The sides wobbled and fell open like a corrugated steel flower and hit the deck clanging like thunder. The ship's lights blazed on, and Du, Fung and the artillery team scampered into place. Bolan could see a dozen speedboats approaching across the bow. Automatic rifles strobed at the *Flawless Victory* as Megawatti's forces came on.

"Left! Twenty degrees!" Bolan's voice boomed.

The Vietnamese had cut through the turret so that it could be rotated 360 degrees. Without the engine, the turret had to be turned manually. Fung and his team grabbed the sides of the turret and heaved. Fung had greased the crudely welded track, but the turret still screeched as the men heaved themselves against the ancient metal behemoth.

"Stop!" Du shouted, and the turret stopped turning.

The pirates were coming straight on. Bolan tilted his guns. "Aiming!" He squeezed his trigger, and the spotting rifle on top of his top-right recoilless weapon fired. The tracer round streaked through the night and impacted the prow of the lead boat. Bolan pressed the electrical trigger of the main weapon. "Firing!"

Du, Fung and the team covered their ears and cringed against the armored sides of the Ontos.

The principle behind the recoilless rifle was simple and based on one of Newton's basic laws of physics. Every action had an equal and opposite reaction. Recoilless rifle shells were perforated at the bottom. When the rifle fired, approximately four-fifths of the propellant gas blasted backward through vents in the breech while the remaining gas sent the cannon shell flying forward. The two forces canceled each other out, making a weapon that had no recoil and could used on very light mounts. But it also meant the weapon spewed fire out of both ends like a two-headed dragon.

The back blast rolled across the stern of *Flawless Victory* and shattered the windows of the bridge. Three hundred yards out to sea, the lead speedboat disappeared in a ball of orange fire.

Fung and his men pumped their fists and cheered.

Bolan shouted at the top of his lungs and pointed. His traversing team had been deafened by the first shot, but Fung watched Bolan's hands like a hawk. The turret began turning. The speedboats began to split off evasively as Bolan fired his spotting rifle and then triggered the top-left weapon.

The recoilless rifle lit up the stern deck like Armageddon. Bolan's shot went wide and hurled up a geyser in the dark water. Bolan knifed his hand through the air as Fung and his men heaved against the turret. Bolan couldn't track the speedboats fast enough. He tilted his guns as his muzzles swung past the target and fired. Back blast blackened the deck as the 106 mm rifle fired.

One hundred darts bloomed from the muzzle. The invisible

swarm of steel expanded outward at 1700 feet per second. The speedboat lurched as it flew into the hail of darts, and splinters erupted along its length. The dozen pirates aboard shuddered like wheat in the wind as the killing cloud rippled through the open cockpit.

The pirate armada closed to rocket range. RPG-7 rocket-propelled grenades hissed from their launch tubes. One rocket shrieked by the Ontos and detonated over the bridge, blasting shrapnel against the superstructure. The second hit the bow, killing two of Ming's riflemen. Ming's men opened up with their M-16s. Red and green tracers crisscrossed in the night.

Bolan fired his fourth round, but the speedboats were too close and moving too fast. His beehive round ripped a hundred white-water geysers in the wake of a pirate boat. Megawatti's men were determined to capture the prize. Rustam Megawatti wanted the gold and the opium. The Red League wanted Ming Jinrong dead.

Bolan fired his fifth and six barrels, barely clipping the nose of one boat and missing the other entirely. "Reload!" he shouted while signaling to Fung.

Fung and Du pulled fresh shells out of the back hatch of the Ontos while the other men flung open the six smoking breeches and yanked out the spent cases. The speedboats encircled *Flawless Victory* like a pack of orcas around a gray whale. They fired their RPGs high into the deck rather than into her sides so that she wouldn't sink or have her cargo be damaged.

Bolan's crew slammed the breeches shut on the recoilless weapons. Du shouted to be heard, "Top four beehive! Bottom HE!"

The speedboats were already beneath the Ontos's maximum declination. Hooked rope ladders and grapnels clanked over the rail, and pirates streamed up *Flawless Victory*'s sides.

Bolan whipped his hand in a half circle. "One-eighty!"

Fung and his men heaved on the turret and brought the Ontos's smoking 106 mm muzzles to bear on *Flawless Victory*, herself. Ming's voice thundered across the loudspeaker in Mandarin, and then again in English. "Prepare to repel boarders!"

"Ming," Bolan shouted into his radio, "get your men flat on the deck!"

The loudspeaker boomed. Bolan had to give Ming credit. His men were well trained. As a unit, they dropped flat to the deck as if they had been shot.

Pirates came over the rails spraying automatic weapons port and starboard.

Bolan aimed his top right gun along the starboard rail. "Firing!"

Fung and his team crouched as Bolan fired. Sparks shrieked off the side of the bridge as the stream of darts swept the starboard rail from stem to stern.

"Port!" Bolan roared.

Rifle fire hammered the front of the Ontos like hail, and two of Bolan's gun crew went down. His top-left barrel came online, and the weapon swept the port rail like a fire hose. Ming's men leaped up, slaughtering the survivors and shooting down into the sitting speedboats.

"Cooper!" Ming stood in the shattered window of the bridge, pointing frantically. Bolan looked back and saw a dozen men climbing over the bow. They couldn't shift the turret in time. Du, Fung and the two remaining gun crewman clawed for their pistols.

"Down!" Bolan shouted. "Everyone down!"

Ming's voice thundered like god on high from the loudspeakers. His men dropped once more to the deck.

The pirates came straight for the Ontos, guns blazing.

Bolan pumped his electrical trigger, firing rifles three, four and five. The left-hand beehive round swept the starboard rail again, and the HE round in the barrel beneath it streaked out into the night. The right-hand gun sent a swarm of darts directly into the bridge.

Three plumes of superheated gas and fire erupted across the

bow as the 106 mm weapons back-vented. The pirates charging the Ontos were engulfed in the multiple back blasts. Their blackened and smoldering bodies folded in upon themselves as they fell out of the smoke.

The pistols of Bolan's gun crew cracked as they finished off any charred pirate still twitching. Bolan leaped out of the turret and moved astern. The attack had ended as quickly as it had begun. Four of the speedboats were streaking away into the night in full retreat. The deck was littered with dead pirates. Ming and his men crouched with their rifles pointed at a cluster of fuel drums. Bolan approached Mei and Ming. "What's going on?"

"We have a situation," Mei responded.

The fuel drums had been filled with concrete as a makeshift fortification for Ming's men. Bolan could see that someone was crouching behind them. "I can see his knee. I can take him from here," he said.

"He says he has a bomb," Mei replied calmly.

"Really? Who is he?"

"He is the prize." Ming continued to peer down the sights of his M-16. "He is Isfan Megawatti."

Bolan was surprised. "The Megawatt's son?"

"The little Megawatt," Ming said. "He says one of the speedboats is loaded with two, one hundred-pound charges of C-4 plastique with which they had intended to scuttle my ship after they had relieved her of her cargo."

"On a deadman's switch?" Bolan asked, already sure of the answer.

"So he claims," Ming replied.

"Does he speak English?"

"Indeed."

"Okay." Bolan rose. "Isfan Megawatti! My name is Cooper! I'm an American with Interpol! I am prepared to negotiate with you!"

"Don't shoot!" A young Indonesian man of about twenty

stood up slowly. He was wearing a blue tracksuit with body armor over it. In his hands he held an AK-74 and a black box. "I'll blow us all to hell!"

Bolan walked slowly to the port rail. A speedboat was hooked to the side of *Flawless Victory* by a rope ladder. Two bulging canvas rifle bags sat across the seats. Bolan walked back and spoke quietly to Ming and Mei. "He doesn't have enough to blow up the ship, but he has enough to sink her."

"Unacceptable," Ming declared.

"Negotiate?" Mei suggested.

"With the man who came to rob and assassinate me?" Ming lifted his chin imperiously. "Cooper, can you not do something?"

"Yeah." Bolan sighed wearily. "I'll do something."

"Isfan!" The Executioner began walking forward. "Disarm the charges. I promise you I will not allow you to be harmed."

"I will recall my boats. The opium and the gold will be loaded onto them." Isfan Megawatti smiled to reveal gold teeth. "Ming may keep his life, for now."

Bolan raised his carbine as he kept walking forward. "Disarm the charges!"

"One more step!" Isfan brandished the box. "Just one more!"

Bolan stopped and lowered his carbine slightly. He was within twenty feet. The problem was his target was wearing Kevlar, and armored vests made excellent insulators. Bolan aimed at Isfan's legs. "I don't know if Ming will go for that deal."

"I shan't," Ming declared.

"You'd goddamn better go for the goddamn deal!" Isfan was shaking. He had come to collect the opium, the gold and Ming's head, and had planned to return to his father a hero. Now, he was one-half of a Mexican standoff.

"Listen, we can work this—" Bolan snarled at one of Ming's men. "Stand down!"

Isfan turned to look, and Bolan pressed the button on his weapon system's laser sight. A ruby dot appeared on Isfan's pant leg.

The young pirate's head snapped around. "What—"

Bolan squeezed the trigger on the X26. The twin probes flew through the air trailing their wires. They plunged into Megawatti's right thigh. Bolan held down his trigger. The weapon had been modified to Bolan's specifications. The Executioner pumped a full twenty-six watts into Isfan Megawatti on continuous pulse.

The Indonesian's automatic carbine sprayed on full-auto as his finger clamped spasmodically on the trigger. Bolan sprang as the man's body locked and began to fall. Bolan tossed away his carbine as he dived, cutting the charge as he hit the pirate like a fullback. He slammed both of his hands around Megawatti's fingers and the detonator box. His shoulder smashed into the pirate's chest, and the two of them flew in a tangle of limbs up and over the fuel drums. The young man gasped, ribs cracking, as Bolan landed on top of him. He twitched and spit as Bolan held his hand between his in a death grip.

Feet thudded on the deck, and Bolan was suddenly surrounded in a ring of M-16 rifles. Ming peered down over his front sight. "You have it?"

Bolan grimaced as he held Megawatti's hand and the box in a white-knuckled vise. "We're fine as long as he doesn't raise his thumb."

Ming slung his rifle and drew one of his broadswords. "Shall I cut off his hand?"

"Marcie, peel his fingers back from the box, one at a time, starting with the little one," Bolan said.

Mei knelt and began peeling fingers back from the black plastic box. Megawatti struggled. Bolan pressed his thumb down against the edge of the red button as Marcie pulled the young man's thumb away. He took the box and slid the arming switch back to safe. Ming's men sighed collectively as Bolan rose and handed the box to Ming.

The Chinese gangster shook his head in wonder as he took the detonator. "I know kung fu masters who cannot move with your speed, Mr. Cooper. Breathtaking, simply breathtaking."

"Listen, I know he came to kill you, but I need him. He's an intelligence asset," Bolan said.

"Oh, indeed, I suspect he has information I wish to know, as well." Ming dropped to his heels beside Megawatti. "You wish to live. My friend and student here has urgent questions." Ming loomed over the twitching pirate prince. "We are now going to renegotiate your release."

7

Polillo Island

Rosario Blancanales's six-foot Okinawan bo staff blurred toward Ali's head. The youth formed an X with his escrima sticks to block the strike.

Calvin James stood outside a ten-foot circle drawn in the sand, a copy of the Koran in his hand, quizzing Ali like a schoolmaster as the young man and Blancanales did battle within the tiny arena.

Ali's rattan batons hummed through the air and clacked against the six-foot white-oak staff in rapid staccato, seeking an opening in the older man's defenses.

Ali froze as the tapered end of Blancanales's staff suddenly slid past his batons in a brutal thrust that stopped a hairsbreadth from his exposed throat. Ali lowered his rods in recognition of the killing blow.

James had been testing the young man's knowledge of the laws of his faith. It was quite clear that Ali was fully aware he had broken every law of his adopted faith. He was clearly remorseful and grateful to the Stony Man fighters for their guidance.

James nodded and closed the Koran as Bolan walked out from the cluster of trees. "Ali, do you remember this man?"

Ali dropped to his knees and bowed at Bolan's feet. "He is the man I have offended."

"And what will you do to atone for it?" James asked.

Ali rose and looked into Bolan's eyes. "All that is required, including the giving of my life."

James knew how eager Ali was to make amends. "You have partaken of lies, Ali. You have broken the laws of Islam. Yet you were spared. You were spared for the purpose of saving the lives of the innocent. There is no higher tenet of Islam, other than that of freeing fellow Muslims from slavery. Those are your goals. To protect the innocent and free your fellow believers from the slavery of a faith that has been perverted. Do you accept this task?"

Ali bowed his head. "I do."

Bolan's blue eyes burned down on the young man. "Wait."

Ali looked up and blinked in surprise.

Bolan locked his gaze with Ali's and held it. "I am going to give you a choice. You can come with me, and see this thing through to the end. Or, if you wish, I will take you back to Mindanao. You will be given a new identity, money and the opportunity to start a new life."

"I will go with you—"

"My goal to destroy those you served, Ali," Bolan said. "I'll use treachery and every other device within my means to do so. It's possible I will die in the attempt, and you could too if you accompany me. You are young, and you've already escaped death once. Are you really so eager to risk it a second time?"

"I choose it. Of my own free will, and because Allah and honor demand it." Ali stared at Bolan defiantly.

James stepped into the circle and handed the Koran to Ali. He held out his hand to Blancanales. "Go with this man, Ali. Go with God."

Ali took the Koran without breaking eye contact with Bolan. "I am your man, Makeen. I will find you."

Bolan nodded once. The die was cast.

BOLAN AROSE. He had allowed himself the sleep his body needed. He rolled out of his bedding and followed the smell of coffee to the kitchen. James sat at the table reading *The Econ-*

omist. He glanced at Bolan and inclined his head toward the pot on the counter. "Morning."

"Morning." Bolan poured himself a cup of Javanese coffee. "Where is everybody?"

"Pol took Ali in the seaplane at dawn. You caught him off the Sulu Archipelago, so Pol's going to release him back into the wild on Tawi Tawi Island. His cover story is that he and his team attacked the wrong boat and that the yacht was owned by heavily armed drug dealers. There was a fight and he got knocked overboard. He washed up on the beach. He was hurt, but after a couple of days he managed to signal a fishing boat and make his way back."

Bolan sipped his coffee. The story was plausible, but for rejoining a secret society, he knew it was as thin as hell.

James read his mind. "They'll probably kill him out of hand."

That was undoubtedly true. But Ali was young, brave and lower echelon. His chances were slim, but he had a chance. "He volunteered," Bolan said in reply.

"Jesus, Mack—"

"I know," Bolan said. "You like the kid."

"Yeah, well…" James shook his head ruefully.

"I like him, too, Cal, and he did volunteer. I gave him a choice."

"Yeah, I know. I guess Pol and I kind of adopted him. I know what he was, but I know what he is now. For good or ill, he's part of the team. I'm worried about him."

Bolan was worried, as well. "What kind of intel did you and Pol get out of him?"

"Not much. Ali was pretty much a rank and filer in the organization. We know he was indoctrinated in prison. When he got out, he was contacted by an agent of the sect and driven up into the hills blindfolded. It was a two-day trip, rural Philippine roads…" James trailed off with a shrug.

"So it could have been anywhere in the lower half of Mindanao."

"He says there was a kind of encampment and a farm where he was given religious training and worked for about three months. Then he was driven to the coast, blindfolded again and taken out to sea."

"Celebes or Sulu?"

"The boy doesn't know. They were at sea for about three days. He was taken to a small island where he and a dozen other young men received further bladed-weapon training by someone they simply called "Master" and rudimentary care and feeding of the AK-47 from a Chinese man who spoke Arabic and administered most of his instruction through pantomime and beatings. He was there for about a month when a minor cleric came and gave them instruction on how to prepare themselves physically and spiritually to run *juramentado*. They were taught how to put themselves into trance. They spent about two weeks on it."

"Then what happened?"

"Then they were told they were ready. They were told they had a target, and they received a visit from the Mahdi, himself."

"Mahdi?" Bolan set down his cup. "You're sure that's the word he used."

"That's the word Ali used, and that's the word he said all of them used."

Bolan's stomach sank with the implication. Mahdi meant "Expected One" or "Guided One of the Prophet." The long-awaited messiah of the Muslim faith. A Mahdi was the Muslim equivalent of a Second Coming of Christ. During the 1880s, the last self-proclaimed Mahdi had, with an army composed mostly of men armed with swords and spears, destroyed a well-armed Egyptian force and then drove the British out of the Sudan.

Bolan's worst fears of a strategic religious terror movement were being realized. "This isn't good," he said.

"No. No, it's not."

"What'd he say the Madhi was like?"

"The boy was kind of vague on that. The minor mojo man

on the island had them hopped up and tranced when the Mahdi and his entourage showed up. All Ali remembers is that he wore white, he looked like an angel and spoke like God. They made a night of it." James shook his head. "From Ali's description, it sounded like a real old-fashioned holy rolling and shaking revival meeting, but with a lot of machetes and hemp smoking involved."

"What happened after that?"

"Ali says the next day the Mahdi was gone, that it was like a dream. They spent the day purifying themselves according to the *juramentado* code, fasting, praying and burnishing their weapons. That night, they loaded canoes into a small cargo vessel and began their approach on you. They deployed the canoes about ten miles out and from the other side of the island where you were moored. They had exact intel on where you were. That's all we got."

Bolan knew it wasn't enough. "What about Ali's protectors in prison? Has Philippine intelligence gotten anything on them?"

"Yeah, I got a call from the Bear. We know exactly one thing."

Bolan closed his eyes. "They're gone," he said.

"Yeah, like ghosts. The prison officials identified three men, and it's as if they just walked out. What's more, their prison identities were false. Neither we nor the Philippine police have any idea who these guys really were."

"They had inside help."

"No doubt, but getting all the guards and prison employees interrogated is going to take time we don't have, even if we can get it done." Calvin James rolled his shoulders. "Mack, did Pol talk to you about recidivism?"

"Yeah, that's why I called you two in, to make sure that didn't happen."

"Ali's words were this Mahdi SOB looked like an angel and spoke like God. It'll be a classic fallen disciple and charismatic leader confrontation. We can't guarantee what's going to happen if they meet again. He could snap back."

"I thought you said you trusted him."

"I said I liked him, but I don't like this situation."

"There's nothing we can do about it now. The ball is in play. Where's my yacht?" Bolan asked.

"It's in Zamboanga, just north of the Sulu Archipelago. All battle damage has been repaired, and the retrofitting is complete. Three complete warloads arrived in Manila this morning. Everything's ready." James poured himself another cup of coffee. "What did you and Ming get out of the Megawatti kid?"

"Not much. Isfan's father and the Red League are none too happy about a rival pirate faction. Ming dropped a dime on Rustam, and the Pirate King of the South China Sea was willing to deal to get his son back. This group has done more than just poach his territory, they've hit his pirates directly, taking several of his ships and wiping out his men. Three times this month, alone, in the Malacca Strait."

"The Malacca Strait." James sighed into his coffee. "That stretch of water has been pirate central since the Middle Ages."

"That's right. That's why Megawatti is going to spill it in certain circles that he's after a man on a yacht who will be sailing the strait within the week."

"A week? You're going to sail a thousand miles in a week?"

"No, we're going to stuff the yacht into a C-147 out of Darwin and fly it to Singapore. Should be there in forty-eight hours."

James eyed Bolan critically. "As the medic on this team, I recommend you take forty-eight hours of downtime while Ali gets himself caught and Pol comes back with the seaplane."

Bolan yawned and stretched. "All right. A little R and R before I go to meet the Mahdi."

James raised his eyebrows in slight surprise. Getting Bolan to rest in the middle of a mission was like pulling teeth. "That was too easy," he said.

Bolan nodded at James. The ex-Navy SEAL was the most dangerous knife fighter Bolan had ever met. "How's your double kris technique?" he asked.

James lit up the kitchen with his smile. "Carve you like the Christmas goose, Whitey."

"I'll give you a chance to prove it," he said as he walked out of the kitchen.

8

Malacca Strait

Mack Bolan was prepared for whatever might happen next.

Bolan's cover was the thinnest it had ever been. He looked at the rising sun and thought it was a good day to die.

Barbara Price spoke through the stereo speaker in the cabin as Bolan gazed eastward. "Striker, you have company."

"How long?" he asked.

"Satellite imaging shows two small vessels coming around the point toward your position. ETA ten minutes. Armed men on deck." Price's voice rose slightly with concern. "You have time to rethink this. Bugging out is still an option. Last time, you had Marcie and Scott with you and your opponents were in canoes. This time, you're facing the enemy in platoon strength, and you're all by your lonesome."

"I know." Last time he had also had stun grenades, CS gas and darkness on his side. This time the yacht had been stripped of her armament. Bolan's only defenses were a sword and one of the biggest lies he had ever told.

"Striker, weigh anchor and head for open ocean. A pair of F-111 fighters are twenty minutes from your position. A stern chase is a long chase. Hit your diesels. If the pirates follow, I can order both vessels sunk with laser-guided bombs. Philippine naval cutters will sweep for survivors and we can do intelligence surveys from there."

"Negative, Control. This is an infiltration mission. Keep the fighters as Plan B if I am attacked and sunk. Otherwise, stand down. You have satellite imaging?"

"We have you for the next forty-five minutes."

"Affirmative, Control." Bolan strode into the cabin. "Breaking contact."

"Striker—"

Bolan disconnected his satellite link and packed the unit into its aluminum case. He walked to the stern and heaved it into the sea. The yacht was going to be taken by the enemy. There was no choice about that, but the last thing his cover needed was CIA hardware on board. He sat down on one of the folding galley seats and drew the dadao from its wood and leather scabbard. He slipped the sharpening steel from its pocket and ran it along the already shaving-sharp Damascus steel.

Four minutes.

The Executioner ceased his honing as he became aware of the sound of diesel engines. Twice the enemy had been caught by his Q-boat strategy. He wondered if they would come in the same way to—

Bolan threw himself down as automatic weapons opened up in a concerted roar. The windows of the cabin shattered and the wooden cabinets of the galleys ruptured into flying splinters as machine guns and automatic rifles raked the boat from stem to stern. The fusillade continued for nearly a minute as rifles and light support weapons were emptied and reloaded as fast as they could be fired.

Bolan had one thing in his favor. No RPG rockets had slammed into the yacht and set her on fire. The enemy wanted the ship intact for the final slaughter onboard.

The reconnaissance by fire was new.

The firestorm stopped as quickly as it had started. Bolan lay prone and listened to the sound of the engines as the pirate vessels chugged forward. He heard the clack and clatter of dozens of firearms being laid down on the deck. At the same time, dozens of bladed weapons rasped from their sheaths as the pirates came in for the kill. He could hear the simultaneous intake of four dozen men readying themselves for the war cry of jihad.

Bolan beat them to it.

The Executioner burst out of the hatch, stripped to the waist with the dadao raised overhead in both hands. *"Allah Akhbar!"*

A pair of shrimp boats bracketed the yacht ten yards to port and starboard. Dozens of Southeast Asian men in white turbans bearing bladed weapons stood on decks, ready to board the yacht.

They stared at Bolan in shock.

A fat little man burned brass colored by the sun lowered his sword. He wore a white turban and a short robe that barely covered his girth. His hashish-reddened eyes peered at Bolan with surprising lucidity. His thick brows bunched mightily as he spoke in a heavy accent.

"Muslim?"

Bolan didn't answer. The decks of both shrimp boats were strewed with set-aside automatic weapons. Any of the four dozen men could pick up a rifle and blow Bolan to pieces. He noted several RPG-7 launchers among the rifles. The Executioner stood like a statue of iron, the dadao cocked to kill the first man who set foot upon the yacht.

Bolan hid his surprise as a woman stepped out from the throng on the starboard shrimper. She was almost six feet tall and wore a white robe but no turban. Her blue-black hair fell to her waist. A bronze chain draped over her shoulders only enhanced her startlingly pronounced breasts as it crisscrossed between them.

Bolan made her for a Eurasian of Indonesian-Dutch descent. In each hand, she held pair of giant barbecue tongs that could only be described as combat pincers. Each weapon was a two-foot fold of iron with toothed tips so that when squeezed close would grab and tear flesh like the jaws of a shark. Bolan instantly grasped that such a device could easily grip and rip a bladed weapon from an opponent's hand while the second pair seized a man's trachea and ripped it from the moorings of neck bones.

The woman stared unblinkingly at Bolan with haunting black eyes. She snarled a few words that sounded Indonesian to Bolan, and a dozen men sheathed their blades and scooped up their assault rifles. The woman's lips curled up on one side and down on the other with disfavor as she spoke in English. "Who are you?"

Bolan had spent the past week in intensive cram sessions with CIA language tapes, modifying his English with an eastern European accent. "My name is Makeen Boulus."

"Makeen." The woman ran her gaze up and down Bolan's physique with interest. "The strong."

"So my father, Samir al-Boulus named me." Bolan lifted his chin impassively at the woman. "And who are you?"

She smiled without an ounce of warmth. "My name is Sujatmi Fass."

"Fass is a Dutch name." Bolan curled his own lip in derision. "A Christian name."

"So my father named me." Her face darkened with the word father, and her eyes flashed at Bolan in challenge. "Beg me for mercy, and explain to me why you should not endure the tortures of hell before we kill you."

"You are pirate scum," Bolan said, taunting the woman. "Do what you will, only tell your men to lay down their rifles and come to me with blades, so that I may meet Allah in Paradise with four dozen slaves at my side."

Fass glared at Bolan. She and the fat man spoke to each other in rapid Indonesian. Further conversations burst forth in Tagalog and Arabic among the pirate crews. The pincers clacked shut in the woman's hands. "We are not pirates," she said.

"I came here to grieve," Bolan said. "Deny that you have come to steal that which is mine!"

Fass blinked. "We have come to enjoin war against the infidels."

Bolan scoffed. "I see no such about."

Fass and the fat man had another hurried conversation. Fass gazed for a long moment at Bolan. "You will come with us," she said.

"And if I do not wish to?"

Fass shrugged and opened her pincers. "Then these men shall strip you and hold you down while I tear your manhood from your body."

"Very well." The dadao fell point first and lodged into the deck where it stood quivering. Bolan folded his arms across his chest. "I will come with you."

Stony Man Farm, Virginia

"THEY GOT HIM." Barbara Price bit her lip as she watched the satellite image on the giant plasma screen in the Computer Room. Pirates had swarmed the yacht quickly. They were hoisting the sails and weighing anchor.

"They're separating." Aaron Kurtzman leaned back in his wheelchair and watched as the two shrimpers and Bolan's yacht went off in three different directions. Concealed deep in the bowels of the yacht was a second satellite link and a full warload of weapons. The panel had been sealed, caulked and painted over. The pirates would literally have to start chopping into the lower hull to discover it.

There was also a homing beacon on the yacht, similarly embedded in the superstructure. Tracking the yacht's whereabouts would be no problem. The problem, Kurtzman was betting, was Bolan was no longer on the yacht. "What's our window with the satellite?"

"Thirty minutes left," Price replied.

"How about the fighters?"

Carmen Delahunt clicked keys at her station. "They each have another hour of loiter time before they have to fly to Australia and refuel."

"We have in-flight refueling?"

"We have a tanker flying out of Darwin," Price stated, "but it's going to be thin getting it there in time. I'm willing to risk it, and so are the pilots." She arched an eyebrow at Kurtzman.

She obviously thought that airborne surveillance was a good idea, Kurtzman thought as he drummed his fingers on the desktop. Bolan had said he didn't want a tail. He would initiate contact when the opportunity presented itself.

"Recall the fighters, but keep a pair hot in Diego Garcia. Keep in-flight refueling hot on the tarmac."

"So that's it?"

Kurtzman shrugged. "We have a lock on the beacon in the yacht?"

"Beacon activated, signal is strong," Price confirmed. "Battery is good for one hundred and sixty-eight hours."

"Pol and Calvin are ready?"

"Both are in Manila. They have full warloads, with one for Striker. They have a seaplane and can be airborne on 'go.'"

"What is Mr. Jinrong's status?"

"*Flawless Victory* is just slightly north of Singapore undertaking repair and taking on a few new crewmen. Ming says he can be underway in forty-eight hours and is prepared to go wherever he is needed."

"Marcie?"

"She's in place in Mindanao, her cover is established. She is ready to move when summoned."

"And our young friend?"

"Ali's been released back into the wild. He's disappeared and hasn't checked in, but according to Pol we should wait a week before we start worrying about it."

Kurtzman ceased drumming his fingers on the desk. "That's it, then. We've done all we can do." He watched the screen as the computer-generated image showed the three boats slowly moving farther apart. "It's all up to the big guy now."

9

A single shaft of light shone down in the shrimper's black belly through a hole in the deck. Bolan sat in half-lotus position on the sticky floor and watched it. If he raised his palm to it, the ray burned with the midday, tropical heat like light through a magnifying glass. The sweltering, dark chamber reeked with the fermenting remnants of a thousand generations of crustaceans that had been dredged up from the seas. The stench was overpowering and all pervasive. Bolan felt like he was absorbing it.

They had been at sea for three days. Bolan considered his options and found them extremely limited. He had been stripped of everything, including his clothes. The pirates had, however, allowed him to keep a prayer rug and a copy of the Koran. Each morning, he was given a bowl of steamed rice and a banana. In the evening, he had a bowl of the morning's leftover rice fried with bits of curried mystery meat on top. He was given a fresh slop bucket once a day and a bucket of water to drink.

The Executioner had been in a hell of a lot worse lockups in his life, but he knew it would be a long time before he willingly ate shrimp again, and he didn't fancy his chances of making his way out of the hold past forty pirates using two plastic buckets, a book and four feet of carpet.

Bolan watched the thin shaft of light as it went vertical. It was time for the noon prayer.

He decided he was just going to have to wait and see how things developed.

The Executioner unrolled his prayer mat and began the four silent cycles of prayer. He found he didn't have long to wait.

Light flooded in as the loading hatched squealed open. Fass, the fat man and half a dozen men with automatic rifles ringed the hatch in glaring silhouette. Bolan's shorts, sandals and T-shirt were tossed down to him. He finished the four cycles of silent prayer before dressing and clambering up the wooden ladder. He squinted into the world. After three days in the hold, the colors of Southeast Asia were almost unbearable. The sky and sea seemed too blue, and the island two dozen yards to starboard was an incredible shade of green. The sun was searing white and the strip of beach reflected it with ugly intensity.

Bolan had long since lost his sense of direction. As he surveyed his surroundings, all he was sure of was that the shrimper lay somewhere between New Guinea and Thailand. That left thousands of miles of ocean and ten of thousands of islands to choose from. The yacht and the other shrimper were gone. He was fully aware that no one knew where he was.

Bolan took a deep breath. He had emerged from the rotting oven of the hold. That was the first step, and the Executioner accepted the simple blessing of the ocean breeze filling his lungs.

Fass cocked her head at the filthy, naked man who had emerged from the hold. He was not beaten down or fearful. Nor was he angry and defiant.

The man was smiling as he tilted his face into the wind.

"You present a problem to us, Makeen," she announced. Neither she nor anyone else of the crew was wearing white robes or turbans. They wore khaki shorts and T-shirts, like any other of a thousand fishing crews in these waters. The fat man wore a battered Greek fisherman's cap, and Bolan made him out as the man in command. Only Fass and the prevalence of automatic weapons gave lie to the crew's appearance of hardworking fishermen.

"I am sorry to inconvenience you," Bolan said.

"If it is true that you are a believer, then it would be wrong for us to kill you, despite the fact that you are a westerner."

Bolan nodded at the wisdom of the statement.

"However, we cannot allow you to live after having seen us."

The Executioner accepted that with a shrug as well. "You have a solution?"

"I had voted to kill you and be done with it," the woman admitted, "but Hoja has become fond of you."

The fat man nodded at Bolan and smiled through a mouthful of buck teeth yellowed from chewing betel nut.

"Hoja approves of you." Fass regarded Bolan dryly. "You showed no fear when we took you."

Bolan inclined his head at Hoja. Fatty grinned back delightedly. Bolan returned his gaze to the woman. "And so?"

Fass extended a graceful hand at four men bound men by the prow. Hoja issued an order, and two of the rifleman drew knives and cut the prisoners' bonds. The four men rose. The first two appeared to be brothers. Both were short and built like kickboxers and looked to be Thai. The third man was the size of a refrigerator, huge and muscular but running to fat. Hints of Spanish features marked him as a Northern Island Filipino. The fourth man was blade thin with the hawk eyebrows and drooping mustache of a Turkic Chinese.

"The Mahdi has been informed of the situation. We received these four men yesterday. They have failed us, and yet, they expressed the desire to atone," Fass said.

Mahdi. Bolan took note of the term and was encouraged to know he was on the right trail even if he wasn't sure where it might lead next. It was a Muslim term. Literally translated it meant "The Expected One."

"And?" he asked the woman.

Fass gestured toward the beach. "And that is the Island of Trial."

Bolan understood the situation all too clearly.

"Akram, Al'alim, Guadaloupe and Yaqoob, have failed us.

Akram and Al'alim were drunk and gambling when the Mahdi required them. Guadaloupe—" Fass's nose wrinkled in disgust at the man "—his crimes are too vile to mention. Yaqoob is an opium addict and was absent and could not explain himself. Yet, in the past, each of these men have proved themselves in battle. So it is in battle they must prove themselves worthy to remain among us."

"Four against one." Bolan's joints popped as he rolled his neck and shoulders. It had been three days since he had stood straight. "And should I win?"

The woman's lips curved in amusement. "Then you shall join us in jihad and do the work of four men."

"I have already been on jihad." Bolan let his voice fill with scorn. "Why should I do so again at the behest of a naked-faced whore?"

Fass went white.

"Ah, I remember now." Bolan smiled. "You mentioned removing my manhood."

"With pleasure," Fass agreed. An ugly light kindled in her eyes as her gaze ran down Bolan's body. The Executioner became very aware of the fact that Fass was mentally disturbed.

Bolan turned an imperious gaze upon his opponents. "Then put my sword in my hand," he said.

Fass jerked her chin. Hoja came forward with the dadao in his hand. The blade was sheathed, and the leather retaining cord was knotted over the hilt. Bolan knew he would never live to draw it on board the boat. Hoja grinned and nodded as he handed Bolan the Chinese blade. He patted Bolan on the shoulder encouragingly. The soldier grinned and nodded back.

If he had one man in his cheering section, it was best to have it be the captain.

Hoja handed him a small, olive drab, drawstring cotton ditty bag. Inside was a plastic canteen of water and a bundle of sugar-cured, dried beef strips wrapped in newspaper. Bolan looped the bag over his neck and rested his sword across his shoulders. His opponents were each issued a similar ration bag, and Bolan watched with interest as the men were given weapons.

Akram and Al'alim were both handed sheathed kris daggers. The biggest man, Guadaloupe, took up a machete in one hand and a kris in the other. Bolan's eyes narrowed as Yaqoob accepted a polearm. The wooden shaft was five feet long. One end was tipped with a sharpened spade shaped like an inverted ax. The other end was fixed with a crescent moon of steel. Both ends glinted with razor sharpness. Bolan recognized the weapon from martial-arts demonstrations he'd seen. Ming Jin-rong had had a similar polearm in his courtyard weapon rack. It was called a "Monk's Spade" and was one of the ancient weapons of Shaolin kung fu.

Akram and Al'alim took their long-bladed daggers and spoke to each other in low voices. Guadaloupe was grinning at Bolan like a lifer in San Quentin sizing up a white-collar newbie in prison. Yaqoob ignored Bolan as he carefully inspected the edges of his weapon.

Bolan made a mental note. Yaqoob was trouble.

"When?" Bolan asked.

"Can you swim?" Fess asked in response.

"I can."

"Then I suggest you do so."

Bolan slung his sword. A cheer rose from the pirates as he took four strides and dived into the water. The ocean was sweat warm as it closed over him, but he had been in the cramped hold for three days and it felt good to stretch out. The salty water skimmed the stench from him and buoyed him as he swam. Bolan swam the thirty yards in moments, and his feet hit sand. He rose out of the surf and did not look back until he had hit the beach.

Bolan turned.

The four men had clambered into a wooden rowboat gray with age and had begun paddling in his direction. Bolan wondered if that implied some or all of them couldn't swim. He kicked off his sandals, threw down his provisions and ran back into the surf. Men began shouting as he dived beneath the water. The water was crystal clear, and Bolan stroked cleanly toward the dark silhouette of the rowboat. He rose once for air. The men on the shrimper were all pointing and shouting at him, but no one aimed their rifles in his direction.

Bolan drew the dadao from behind his back. Akram and Al'alim shouted in consternation as Bolan sank beneath the waves. The Executioner swam along the bottom. He judged the depth to be about twelve feet, more than enough for a man to drown but shallow enough for his purpose.

Bolan stopped as the rowboat eclipsed the sun overhead. The men in the rowboat were furiously slapping the water with their paddles hoping to club him when he tried to board. But Bolan didn't intend to take the rowboat. He planned to sink it. Bolan bent his legs and pushed off hard against the bottom. He erupted upward and holding the two-handed sword like a spear, he shot toward the bottom of the rowboat.

As Bolan closed in, he rammed the sword upward with all of his strength.

The blade punched easily through the thin wood. Bolan inverted himself, putting both feet against the boat for leverage, and wrenched the dadao sideways. The aged planking cracked and split. Bolan ripped the blade free and stroked for the ocean floor. He put his feet against the sand and shot for the surface a second time. The sword blade crashed through the wood and jammed halfway through the keel. Bolan inverted himself with his feet against the bottom of the boat and torqued the two-handed sword. Bubbles blew out his mouth as he grimaced with effort. Oxygen debt began darkening the edges of his vision as he shoved with his feet and heaved against the hilt of his sword.

Cold steel suddenly burned just above Bolan's left elbow. Blood blossomed into the sea where he'd been hit. Yaqoob was leaning over the side and jigging for Bolan with his Monk's Spade.

The Executioner roared with effort and ripped his blade free of the rowboat's bottom. The effort drove Bolan down into the depths as the spade harpooned for him. Bolan heard the crack as the mortally wounded keel snapped under human weight.

Daylight drew a ragged incandescent line across the perforated bottom of the rowboat as its spine broke.

Bolan swam for distance until his lungs screamed and he surfaced. He gasped for air and took stock.

The rowboat had split in two. Akram flailed and screamed in the water. Yaqoob held Al'alim in a headlock and tried to manage his Monk's Spade as well as the screaming man who seemed bound and determined to drown the both of them. Guadaloupe held on to a broken section of the boat and glared at Bolan.

Akram suddenly dropped beneath the water. Bolan descended as well to see if the Thai was coming for him.

There was no need.

Akram's kris sank to the sand. The Thai vomited up huge bubbles as he swallowed seawater and inadvertently emptied his lungs. The pirate's struggles slowed as he sank to the bottom. Sand puffed beneath him as he sat down next to his knife. He looked at the weapon and then looked around. His mouth opened and a single small bubble escaped. Akram relaxed into the embrace of the ocean and stopped moving.

Bolan surfaced.

Yaqoob was slowly but surely dragging Al'alim toward shore. Guadaloupe was dogpaddling toward Bolan with his dagger in his teeth. Bolan considered trying to finish it there. He was a trained combat swimmer, and even with the awkward dadao he was sure he could take Guadaloupe either above or below the water. Yaqoob was another matter. The Monk's Spade gave him reach. The man had stopped swimming and was watching Bolan like a hawk even as he controlled Al'alim. Bolan revised his assessment.

Yaqoob was big trouble.

Bolan noticed he was treading water in a growing cloud of his own blood. He was also exhausted. Three days in the shrimp cellar hadn't done him any favors. Bolan sheathed his sword and stroked for shore. He staggered up through the surf and looked backward.

Guadaloupe was awkwardly treading water and waiting for Yaqoob. Back on the shrimper, men were shouting in half a dozen languages. Bolan stood in the sand with his chest heaving. He didn't speak any of the languages, but the activity was very clear.

The odds had changed to 3:1.

The wagers were flying back and forth among the pirates.

Bolan scooped up his sandals and the little sack of provisions. He waved to Hoja, and the pirate captain waved back. The Executioner turned bleeding and exhausted for the jungle.

10

A good rock was hard to find.

It was a problem with tiny tropical islands barely above sea level. They were almost all sand and palm trees.

The Executioner eyed his handiwork. Without a suitable missile it would be useless, but the craftsmanship wasn't bad. He had cut his sword's sling lengthwise to produce two lengths of cord. It had taken only moments to cut a palm-sized pocket of leather from the footbed of one of his sandals and tie the cords to either end.

Bolan had manufactured a sling.

He preferred his slings around three feet long, the distance from his heart to his left hand. At two and half feet, his make-shift weapon was a little short by Goliath slaying standards, but Bolan supposed it would do for Guadaloupe.

If only he could find a rock.

Bolan's left arm ached like hell. He had cut his T-shirt into bandages to bind the wound Yaqoob had given him in the water. It had bled through five layers before it had begun to crust over. The Executioner ate half of his dried, sugared beef and drank half of his canteen. Both were salty from his swim. He scanned the sand for stones as he began retreating through the trees.

"Hey! White Boy!" Guadaloupe's voiced boomed through the jungle in a baritone that would have done Goliath proud. "Come on out! We'll make it quick! You make us come get you…we have fun, you know?"

Bolan remembered Guadaloupe's crimes being "too vile to mention" and Fass as her perfectly formed upper lip curled with revulsion. Whatever the big man's idea of fun was, Bolan was pretty sure he didn't want any part of it. All three men had obviously been raised in the culture of the blade. Armed with a Chinese two-handed sword, Bolan was not confident in taking any of his hunters, much less all three at the same time.

The Executioner faded back, knowing full well he was running out of island.

A hard rock would be good to find.

Bolan winced and crouched as something jabbed painfully into the arch of his foot. The Executioner squatted on his heels and stared at the treasure he had trodden upon. Three smooth stones the size of hen's eggs rested half covered in the sand in a loose triangle.

Bolan smiled.

A week of praying five times a day had done him some good.

Two of the rocks were smooth oblongs and nearly perfect projectiles. One was nearly triangular and would provide interesting flight characteristics. Bolan scooped up his stones and unsheathed his sword. He tucked the naked blade under his arm as he loaded one of the round stones into his sling. The Executioner began walking toward his enemies. They weren't hard to find.

Guadaloupe was being helpful in that regard.

"White Boy!" the giant bellowed. For such a huge man, he moved with simple grace.

Bolan lifted his elbow as he sighted his adversaries. He let his sword fall. The blade half sheathed itself in the sand, the hilt standing ready. Bolan let his loaded sling hang loose by his right leg as he stepped out of the trees.

"You know what I'm going to do to you?" called out the big man. "I'm going to gouge out your eyes."

The three men were sticking together. They walked in a loose arrow formation through the palms. Guadaloupe strode carelessly at the apex, tapping his machete rhythmically against his calf with each step. He held his kris in his left hand with his thumb on the blade. To his flank, Al'alim walked with his chest thrust out and his kris in one hand and a baton he'd cut of bamboo in the other. Bolan eyed Yaqoob. The Chinese man walked with his Monk's Spade held in a middle guard position, like a rifleman walking point with his bayonet fixed.

The Executioner stepped into line of sight with Guadaloupe, and the big man froze for a moment and presented a stationary target. They were twenty yards apart, a distance at which Bolan could bust cantaloupes with a sling with monotonous precision. The sling hissed diagonally across Bolan's body and blurred back around behind his head. He took a lunging step forward like a baseball pitcher, and the leather cracked liked a whip in a brutal side-arm cast as he released.

Guadaloupe's head snapped back as blood exploded from his brow. Bolan was already reloading as the man fell facedown on the ground like the biblical Goliath.

Al'alim screamed in rage and charged forward, his stick and dagger weaving before him. Bolan's sling whirled around him and snapped like a rifle shot. True to form the triangular stone arced in flight. Bolan had been going for the head shot. Al'Alim staggered as his collarbone broke.

The Executioner reloaded, stepped into line with Yaqoob and cast. The sling snapped and the shovel blade of the Monk's Spade rang like a bell as Yaqoob brought it in front of his face and blocked. Al'Alim's face contorted in insensate rage. His baton fell from the nerveless fingers of his hanging arm, but he continued to scream, spittle flying from the corners of his mouth as he brandished his kris in his good hand.

Bolan drew his sword from the sand.

The Executioner spun like an Olympic hammer thrower as Al'alim closed in. Bolan released the hilt of his sword as Ming had taught him. He seized the end of the silk ribbon unreeling through his hands and dropped to one knee. He turned 360 degrees like the center of his own hurricane of steel. The two-handed sword scythed six inches above the sand at the end of the silk ribbons like a bladed ball and chain.

The Thai shrieked as the dadao sliced both of his legs as it passed. Bolan rose, and the hilt of his flying blade slapped into his outstretched left hand as he completed his turn.

Al'alim hurtled through space trailing blood from his flailing legs. He tumbled and landed on his back, howling.

Bolan took his sword in both hands and planted it like a spike through the Thai's chest. Al'alim's arms and legs jerked once as he was pinned to the sand and lay still. Ribs splintered as Bolan put his foot against the dead man's chest and ripped his blade free.

The Executioner then regarded Yaqoob.

The man had not rushed in. He had slowly circled toward Bolan's left. His almond eyes measured the Executioner over the gleaming twelve-inch curve of his spade.

Bolan cocked his head. "You're not one of the Mahdi's men," he said in challenge.

Yaqoob stopped and eyed Bolan without blinking.

The Executioner let the point of his sword lower to a less threatening guard. "You're PRC Special Reconnaissance."

"People's Special Armed Police, Anti-Terror Infiltration Unit." Yaqoob spoke with an English accent. "You're an American."

Bolan nodded.

"You had me fooled." One of the agent's hawklike brows rose slightly. "Tell me. How did you know?"

"The fight in the water. You handled a five-pound Spade and a drowning man at the same time with the efficiency of a trained combat swimmer." Bolan shrugged. "An interesting talent for a Ugyur boy from the plains of Xinjiang."

It wasn't a huge guess. Yaqoob's features revealed him for a far-West Chinese, and Xianjang province had one of the largest Muslim populations in China. He had undoubtedly been raised Muslim. Bolan figured Yaqoob was just the sort of man PRC Special Forces would recruit into their antiterrorist, Muslim infiltration units.

The spy was still impressed. "You are good."

Bolan let his sword drop to his side. "We should work together. Two agents can work better than one, and our governments' goals are the same. These pirates represent more than just a threat to shipping. They have a larger plan. We should pool our information. Together we stand a better chance of success."

"An intriguing proposition." Yaqoob shrugged. "But Hoja and Sujatmi are expecting our heads, or yours, and you have already claimed three."

"You can say Guadaloupe and Al'alim turned on you. We fought together. We present their heads. Hoja likes me." Bolan opened his hand. "We can make it work."

"It is possible it could work." Yaqoob's smile spread his drooping mustache. "But I have orders to kill anyone who discovers me. I think presenting your head to the Mahdi will solidify my cover. He likes killers. I think your death will be best. But aspects of your idea have merit. I will make you a deal. Give me whatever information you have, and I will use it to help accomplish the mission."

Bolan frowned. "Not much of a deal."

"But it is. Tell me what you know and I will kill you cleanly. Refuse, and I will be forced to cut off your hands and feet and extract the information through interrogation." Yaqoob smiled without an ounce of warmth. "And while I do not have access to my acupuncture needles, I assure you bamboo slivers, while cruder, are quite efficacious."

The Executioner looked into the Chinese agent's eyes and knew the man was speaking from personal experience. Bolan raised his sword into the high guard Ming had taught him.

Yaqoob sighed. "You have made an error. I have trained with the Shaolin Monk's Spade for ten years, and while your technique was impressive, I can tell by your stances you have had less than two or three years at most with the dadao."

Bolan nearly smiled at the compliment. "I've had a week."

Yaqoob blinked.

"But my *sifu* was Ming Jinrong, master of the Lost Track style."

Yaqoob's eyes narrowed to slits. The fallen Red League smuggler of Macao was clearly well-known to Chinese intelligence. The agent raised his weapon high over head and dropped into a low stance. "Then show me what the sodomite has taught you."

Bolan turned and ran.

Yaqoob shouted in outraged Mandarin. Bolan scooped his sling from the sand without breaking stride. He knew he couldn't go hand-to-hand against ten years of Shaolin Monk's Spade tutelage. Bolan needed distance.

And a rock.

The Executioner opened his stride. Three days in the hold hadn't done him any favors, but for decades every day that he had not been on a mission he had run a 10 k, and run it for top speed. For a man who operated alone, outmarching and outrunning the enemy was a key skill. Bolan forgot his wound and his exhaustion and ran all out. He needed distance and a few free moments to stack the deck in his favor.

Bolan checked and saw Yaqoob following him through the trees at an easy jog. He judged that a mistake. The Chinese agent should have made every effort to run down his opponent and kill him blade to blade. Then, again, Yaqoob had blocked a sling stone in midflight. His confidence was based on ability.

Bolan burst out of the trees and found himself on the other end of the island. The golden strip of beach sloped down toward the achingly blue water. It was postcard perfect and unblemished by anything even remotely resembling a rock. Bolan jogged down the beach scanning for a projectile. A handful of pebbles would suffice as a distraction, but all Bolan saw was a black patch a hundred yards ahead.

Someone had made a fire.

The small black hole was filled with dead embers, and the

bones of a decent-sized fish with the blackened stick it had been spitted on still thrust through it. Bolan dropped to his heels and considered his find. Four empty, green Bintang pilsner beer bottles lay in the sand, their labels faded with age and peeling in the sun. Bolan picked up a bottle and considered the ballistics of the equation.

Modifications would have to be made.

He drew his sword and wedged the hilt firmly between his feet as he squatted over the blade. Bolan took the bottle by the neck and carefully cracked it across the edge. He grimaced as the bottle broke and collapsed into shards. He took up a second bottle and tried again, but the bottle broke apart leaving him nothing but the neck between his fingers.

"Hey!" Yaqoob called jovially from down the beach.

Bolan took aim and snapped the third bottle against his sword blade. He tossed away the neck and picked up the fallen piece. He held a jagged glass cup about two and half inches tall and two inches in diameter.

Yaqoob strode down the beach with his Spade resting jauntily across his shoulders. He was sixty yards and closing. "What are you doing?"

Bolan ignored the approach of his assassin and filled the broken bottle with sand. With such an ungainly projectile, he figured the release was going to be problematic. He would have to get to point-blank. The filling was another problem. He was bound to get spin and the force would fling the sand out.

"What do you have there?" Yaqoob called out. He took his Spade in both hands at fifty yards.

Bolan hunched to hide what he was doing. He took his canteen out of his bag and began pouring his water slowly into the broken bottle. The hot sand drank up the liquid quickly, but he stopped before the sand turned to slop. Bolan gulped the remaining water and tossed away the canteen.

"Did you find a rock?" Yaqoob was thirty yards away.

Bolan tamped down the damp sand with his thumb.

Yaqoob closed to twenty yards. "What is it you think you are doing?"

Bolan took his sword from between his feet and stabbed it point-first into the sand. He placed the broken bottle in the pouch of his sling and wrapped his left hand around it. The Executioner rose and began walking toward his assailant.

At fifteen yards, Yaqoob brought up his Spade at midguard like a bayonet fighter. Bolan drew the cords of his sling tight at ten yards. Yaqoob's hooded eyes regarded Bolan frostily over the edge of his blade.

"You should have taken the deal."

Bolan raised his sling for the cast at five.

Yaqoob spit. "You only have one sh—"

Bolan slung at three yards. He did not engage in a windup. The pouched sling blurred behind him and back up in a ripping, uppercut of a cast at Yaqoob's head. Green glass flashed in the sun. The unbalanced projectile took spin and flew slightly off course as Bolan had thought it might. Yaqoob finished Bolan's job as he'd hoped. Instead of dodging, the agent instinctively whipped his weapon up to block Bolan's shot. He caught it on edge, and half of the projectile splattered against the blade of his Spade. The other half exploded into a cloud of wet sand and shattered glass that expanded into the left side of Yaqoob's face at 100 miles per hour.

Bolan leaped back as Yaqoob screamed and whipped his Spade in a defensive figure-eight pattern. The Executioner ran back and picked up his sword. Yaqoob had ceased his swinging. Bolan surveyed the damage as he came forward. Yaqoob's left eye was gone. The left side of his face was a hideous, wet mosaic of broken glass and blood set in sand. His right eye squinted and blinked as it teared over.

Bolan began circling to Yaqoob's left.

The Executioner had to jump as the crescent blade scythed around to hamstring him. He landed and jumped a few feet away.

Yaqoob was far from done.

"You are going to be a long time dying..." the agent snarled. "You will—"

Bolan attacked without warning. The sword-and-Spade clash rang across the beach. The Executioner aimed his blows toward Yaqoob's blind side, but the Chinese agent parried them with ease. "I am going to gouge out both your eyes," Yaqoob announced as they crossed blades. "And fill the sockets with—"

Bolan snapped the hilt of his sword as Ming had taught him. Under Ming's watchful eye, he had practiced snapping out the red silk ribbon five hundred times each morning of training. Bolan could reliably crack a dozen eggs with a dozen snaps.

The weighted tips of the ribbons snapped directly into Yaqoob's remaining eye.

Yaqoob let out a high thin scream. The agent was a man who could fight by feel, and even blind he was still dangerous. Bolan slammed his sword against Yaqoob's Spade and then ripped his blade down the wooden shaft.

Wood shaved away, and the fingers of Yaqoob's right hand were sliced to the bone.

The agent struggled to control his weapon one-handed.

Bolan stepped in and pushed the iron ring pommel of his sword under Yaqoob's jaw. Yaqoob went up on his toes with the force of the blow. Bolan swung the sword back down with all his might, and the dadao cleaved Yaqoob's collarbone and grated to a halt.

Bolan let go of his sword and yanked the Monk's Spade from Yaqoob's hand as the man fell back in a heap. His mouth worked, and the pulverized orbs in his eye sockets gaped up blindly.

"You have any information for me?" Bolan asked.

"Or...what?" Yaqoob gasped.

"Or nothing," Bolan answered, "but I'll put you down easy if you want."

Blood spilled over Yaqoob's lips. "We have...a second agent."

Bolan dropped to one knee. "Who is he?"

"The...lepers."

"Lepers?" Bolan frowned. "Your fellow agent?"

Yaqoob's head fell to one side as his body relaxed into the sand.

Bolan frowned. A second Chinese infiltrator and lepers. Or a leper agent. That was interesting. Bolan pulled his sword from the dead man's corpse and retrieved his sling. He walked back across the island, stopping by the bodies of Al'alim and Guadaloupe and to gather their weapons. Bolan retraced his steps to the opposite shore. The shrimper still lay at anchor.

Fass, Hoja and six of the pirates stood on the beach with rifles in their hands.

Bolan threw his captured steel in a pile at the woman's feet. He retained his sword.

Fass smiled at Bolan. The curve of her lips was predatory.

11

It was quite a party. Although they prohibited the imbibing of alcohol, this sect in the South Seas had no issue with smoking hemp. Water pipes gurgled while happily hopped up pirates inhaled huge quantities of spit-roasted goat. A second boat had come to meet them on the island, and they had brought portable stereos and prostitutes.

The faithful were being rewarded.

Stereos blasted Indonesian pop music and extended-disco versions of Pakistani music and the men danced with abandon. The prostitutes were wide-eyed with fear as they danced with the pirates, flinching as men fired their automatic rifles into the air in celebration.

"Makeen!" Someone shoved a pipe into Bolan's hand. The Executioner made a show of accepting the offering but did not need to feign smoking it as the stone man simply clapped Bolan on the shoulder happily and tottered off toward a woman.

Bolan watched the celebrations. His single-handed defeat of four men in trial by combat had been taken as a sign of great good luck. The Executioner sat back and gnawed on perfectly barbecued haunch of goat. The meat had been rubbed with cumin and basted with clarified butter until it was practically falling off the bone.

"Makeen." A hand draped across Bolan's shoulder. "You do not smoke deep, nor do you dance. Why?"

Bolan glanced up at Fass. She wore a blue button-down

man's shirt that was four sizes too large. The billowing cotton clung to her curves in the breeze coming off the sea. He swallowed his food. "You know why."

She raised an eyebrow in challenge. "Oh?"

Bolan tossed away the naked bone and gave her his most roguish smile. "I was waiting for you."

Her thick lashes drooped at him as the corners of her lips turned upward. "That is a good reason."

Fass took his hand. She quickly led him away from the light of the fires. They walked silently through the palms to a small grotto. A pair of blankets was laid out near a palm. Fass hesitated and stepped back from Bolan as if she had suddenly become aware of what she was doing. She leaned against the trunk as Bolan came to her.

"Makeen, I do not—"

Bolan kissed her. The tensed muscles in her arms and shoulders melted as her lips opened beneath his. He took the collar of her shirt and pulled her up to him. She gasped as he yanked his hands apart. Cotton tore, and the buttons of her shirt popped in a line. He leaned back slightly, examining her naked body by the starlight as his hands ran over her flesh. He felt the lean flatness of her stomach and the rails of her ribs. Her breasts filled his hands, their startling size, torpedo shape and almost hostile firmness and defiance of gravity revealing them to be a product of science rather than nature. His hands went back to her hips and pulled them against his. Her hands yanked and pulled at the button and fly of his shorts.

Her voice moaned low in his ear as he kissed her throat and lowered her to the blankets.

THE WOMAN'S ARM DRIFTED across Bolan's chest in sleep. Bolan's hand closed around the hilt of his sword as his eyes slitted open. He suddenly sensed they were not alone.

"You will not need that," a strange voice said.

Bolan looked up. Hoja and four of his pirates flanked a six-foot-tall, rail-thin Asian man. He wore a small red turban, and a wispy mustache and beard attempted to fill out a face like a hatchet. Every exposed muscle and tendon in his body stood out in high relief. Bolan thought he looked like a bodybuilder who had spent six months in a death camp. A Tokarev pistol was holstered on his right hip. A double-pointed, curved Indonesian sword hung from his left. A hand ax was thrust through the front of his belt. Bolan had not seen the man at the previous evening's festivities, and highly doubted he ever engaged in such things.

The man radiated command authority.

"I am Jusuf." He gazed down at Bolan in open suspicion. "You will come with me."

Bolan rolled out of the blankets and pulled on his shorts. One of Hoja's men picked up Bolan's sword. The captain knelt by Fass's side, and the two of them began speaking in low voices.

She was being obviously debriefed.

Bolan thought about the night they'd spent together, their pillow talk and the many questions she had asked after their lovemaking. He had given her most of his cover story. He had been sure that his night with Fass had been the opening round of interrogation. If they were going to play good cop–bad cop, she had been a very good cop.

If his story didn't stand up, Bolan suspected Jusuf would be a very bad cop.

Bolan followed Jusuf while two pirates with fixed bayonets followed him. Jusuf did not speak. They walked to shore and began walking along the beach. They were doing a lap around the island, and Bolan knew that someone else was getting the briefing.

The Executioner enjoyed the sunrise, knowing that it might be his last. They had circled most of the island when they came to a small camp. A small, blue tent stood near the tree line. Outside of it, a Persian carpet had been laid in the sand. A teapot hung from a tripod over a small fire. Bolan's sword and sling lay on the carpet.

The Executioner came face to face with the Expected One.

The Mahdi was a sparrow of a man. He sat cross-legged on the rug, his stick-thin legs visible beneath his short white robe. A gray shawl covered his narrow shoulders and the top of his shaven head against the morning chill. His skin was the color of saddle leather but was as unlined as a baby's. His short snow-white beard and mustache were startling against his face. He could have been forty years old or eighty. He could have passed for Asian, Indian, South American or perhaps a little old Swiss man who had spent long years in the equatorial sun. His black eyes were huge, somewhat sunken and stared up at Bolan from beneath his snowy brows with startling intensity.

Bolan had seen such eyes before.

The dark pools of his eyes were warm, all seeing, all encompassing, all understanding. Bolan was reminded somewhat of Rosario Blancanales. The man from Able Team had eyes that could look inside another human being with empathy. He could make you feel like he was the father you wished you'd had. Bolan reflected that Pol was a man who could take a damaged, invaded individual and push them to the right side of the line. He could speak to the weak and hurt, the scarred and jaded, and make them do the right thing.

The Executioner could see immediately that the Mahdi was a man who could look inside another human being and make them do wrong. He was a man who could take the damaged and disadvantaged, the weak and the marginalized, and give their suffering meaning by having them inflict horror on an enemy of his choosing.

Behind him stood a quartet of armed bodyguards. A black man built like a sumo wrestler knelt behind the Mahdi holding a massive, cross-hilted sword ready for the Expected One to draw. The straight, double-edged blade looked like it belonged in the hands of an armored medieval knight rather than a 110-pound holy man.

The Mahdi smiled to reveal a mouth of blazing white teeth. "Greetings, Makeen."

Bolan smiled back as the force of the man's personality hit him like a wave.

The Mahdi was a leader, pure and simple, and he had something that Pol could not call upon.

The Mahdi had God on his side.

The Executioner knelt in all humility before his enemy. "Greetings, Imam."

The Mahdi smiled and waved a hand dismissively for Bolan to rise. "Will you take tea with me?"

His voice had an accent Bolan did not recognize. One of the Mahdi's servants poured tiny cups of mint tea thickly sweetened with cane sugar. Bolan sat cross-legged on the carpet and took the tea.

"Makeen Boulus." The little man seemed to savor the sound of the name.

Bolan nodded.

"You are Bosnian?"

Bolan nodded again.

"I understand you are Bektasi."

Bolan gazed out into the dawn, his eyes fixing on the middle distance. The Bektasi were a dervish sect, brought to the Balkans by the Turkish Janissary armies in the fifteenth century. They proclaimed themselves part of Sunni Islam, but their doctrines contained aspects of ancient Turkish paganism, Buddhism and had strong elements of Shia Islam and even Christian influences.

The main difference between the Bektasi sect and Orthodox Sunnis was the Becktasi belief that all religions were valid. Some even preached that Christians and Jews were not really infidels. It made them popular among the conquered Balkan Christians, and the sect attracted many of the conquered Christians who chose to convert.

The Bektasis acted as chaplains to the Turkish armies and would fight beside Turkish troops, wielding enormous iron axes inscribed with Koranic verse.

Bolan started quoting from the scripture he had studied for his cover.

The Mahdi smiled beatifically. He ran his fingertips spider-like across the ancient gold inlay in the blade of Bolan's sword.

"The sword is an heirloom, Imam. A gift to my forebear," Bolan said as he bowed again. "Always have the eldest sons of my family practiced with the blade."

"Ah." The Expected One touched Bolan's sword again and then his sling. It was obvious the weapons gave him great pleasure. "With the Sling of David, and a sword fit for Goliath, you slew the Philistines among us."

"The sling I learned as a boy, herding my father's sheep. There are still wolves in the Balkans." Bolan bowed once more in humility. "As for the killing of your men, I was given little choice, Imam."

"Indeed, but now you have a choice, Makeen."

"To embark upon jihad." Bolan let out a bitter sigh. "It is a road I have walked before."

It was not far from the truth. The Executioner's War Everlasting had been a very personal Holy War of biblical proportions.

The Mahdi tilted his head understandingly. "The war in Bosnia," he said.

Bolan nodded.

"The war against the Christians and the ethnic cleansing."

Bolan stared out stone-faced across the waves. "My family lived in Kosovo. I was a soldier, a member of the Special Purpose Corps. When the trouble started, all Muslims in the corps were detained. During my detainment, my fellow soldiers, Orthodox Serbs, raped and killed my wife. I escaped, and I killed them. Then I took my family away to relatives, near the coast. Catholic Croats, armed by the Germans, bombed the village with fighters and then their soldiers put it to the torch. I lost my sister and my daughter there. My son was of age, so I took up my rifle and my sword, and he and I returned to Kosovo. We fought for the Kosovo Liberation

Army, until my son was killed by U.S.—" Bolan's face twisted as he spit the word "—peacekeepers."

The Mahdi put a consoling hand on Bolan's shoulder. His other hand stretched out to encompass the South Pacific. "What has brought you here, among us?"

"After my son was killed, I fell from grace. I continued to kill Serbs, but only because I could think of nothing else to do. One day we raided the house of a very wealthy man who lived in the mountains. It was a bitter fight. He had many men, but after the fight I found gold in his cellars, heaps of it, like the treasure of Ali Baba. During the war, he and his soldiers had specialized in attacking refugee caravans and camps in the mountains. They were easy prey, poorly defended, and carried their wealth on their backs. It was the gold stolen by the Serbs in their ethnic cleansing."

Bolan sighed again, as if speaking of such things somehow lifted some of the burden of carrying them. "I was the son of a shepherd, but the army taught me coastal warfare. I knew how to sail a boat. I was weary, and I decided I had had enough. I took as much of the gold as I could carry and crossed the border into Macedonia. I made my way to Greece and bought a boat. I sought the solace of the sea. I sailed for a long time, across many oceans. Drinking, whoring, fallen. When I came to the Philippines, I met a Muslim girl in Mindanao, a pious girl. The daughter of a farmer. I returned to Allah's embrace, and we were married. I went to the capital to make arrangements to sell my boat, and use the money to start a business, to buy more land for the farm."

Bolan's set his face in stone.

The Mahdi gently squeezed his shoulder in encouragement.

Bolan's cheeks flexed. He willed the sting of tears to his eyes with the memories of his own fallen loved ones. "I received word the village had been attacked. The government thought there were Muslim terrorists operating in the area. They attacked the village with the aid of American Special Forces advisers. The village was wiped out. The farm was burned." Bolan grimaced. "They left no one alive. Since then, once more, I have…drifted."

"Sujatmi said that you grieved for someone." The Mahdi's voice was clear but tears sparkled on his cheeks. "But I had no idea you had suffered so much."

The best lies were woven with truth. Bolan had stepped onto the Executioner's path with the loss of his family, and the ensuing war had cost him enough suffering and loss to crush a hundred lesser men.

"The world is empty. You feel alone." The Mahdi sighed understandingly. "As if you have no place."

"Indeed, Imam," Bolan agreed.

"Perhaps you have a place here."

Jusuf hissed in a disapproving breath.

The Mahdi ignored his lieutenant. "Among us."

Bolan gazed back out across the sea.

The Mahdi shrugged his thin shoulders with regret. "Alas, you have seen us. You have seen me. We cannot allow you to leave us alive. You must join us, or join Allah as a martyr."

The last Bolan had heard, martyrs gave their lives willingly to the cause. He took a long breath and let it out slowly. "I know what I must do," he said.

"Good, Makeen." The Mahdi smiled upon Bolan like a proud angel. "Good."

A boombox a mile down the beach howled out the Fajr, the dawn Call to Prayer. The Mahdi turned toward Mecca. "Let us pray together."

Bolan knelt beside the Mahdi.

He could feel Jusuf's eyes burning into his back.

12

BOLAN JUMPED into the surf. He stretched and surveyed his new home. A row of sun-bleached huts on stilts straggled along the water, with fishing canoes tied to the poles. Fishing nets hung between them. The real village was inside the trees. Within the tree line, Bolan could see camouflage netting strung like giant green spiderwebs beneath the jungle canopy. Numerous huts squatted in the shade in haphazard fashion, and chickens and goats roamed freely. Four speedboats had been pulled up beneath the netting and laid up in dry dock. Men with rifles lounged about smoking, while others worked at repairing things and working around the village under the trees.

If this wasn't *juramentado* central, Bolan knew he was getting close.

The problem was he had no idea where he was. He had spent the past week belowdecks, only allowed up briefly five times each day to pray with the crew. They had been sailing for a week and had picked up six more passengers, all of them Southeast Asians of one nationality or another who appeared to have converted to the cause.

"You will stay here for a time." Sujatmi Fass walked up with the beach with him. Bolan's week belowdecks hadn't been without reward. The tawny Indonesian had visited him nightly.

The Executioner looked around the bustling jungle camp. "What am I to do?"

"What is it that you can do?" Jusuf challenged, appearing suddenly.

Bolan shrugged. "Show me your armory."

Jusuf shook his head once. "No."

"Show him," Fass urged. "The Mahdi's word was to bring him here so that he could serve."

"Very well." Jusuf stalked through the trees past the bamboo and palm leaf huts to a squat, solid cabin made of logs. He took a key from a leather string around his neck and opened the padlock securing the door. A single bulb connected to the generator outside blinked on. "Here."

Bolan looked around at the armory. Rifles of every description were piled, racked or leaning against the wall in various states of disrepair.

"Yaqoob was our armorer." Jusuf shot Bolan an arch look. "You killed him."

Bolan picked up an Austrian AUG rifle and stared down the cracked optical sight and the powder fouling on the ejection port. Yaqoob had been shirking his duties. Bolan reracked the weapon and went to a pyramid of crates in the corner. The top crate was open, and Bolan pulled out an AK-47 type rifle with a folding stock. Much of its finish was missing, and swathes of hardened cosmoline caked the weapon. The action moved as if it was full of sand when Bolan worked the bolt. He held the weapon up to the light. He couldn't read the AK clone's markings, but he knew the weapon by the slight differences in its receiver and folding stock. "North Korean Type 68," he said.

Fass smirked at Jusuf.

Jusuf frowned.

Bolan ignored the interchange. The rest of the rifles in the open crate were wrapped in wax paper, and a simple feel told him the cosmoline grease had been exposed to the tropical climate and had hardened to rocklike consistency around the rifles they were supposed to protect, trapping them like flies in amber. Bolan sighed. It was going to be a long night. He hunted through the clutter and found a pile of field-cleaning kits in a canvas bag. He took out the oil bottles and shook each one to see if they had congealed. He dropped the usable cleaning gear in a pile and stepped back outside. A small crowd of men had gathered around the armory to see the white man who had appeared in their camp.

Ali Mohammed Apilado stood among them. He had fresh bruises on his face, arms and ribs. He stood like the rest, arms folded across his chest, staring at Bolan with a mixture of mild hostility and interest.

Jusuf jerked his head at the armory. "And so?"

"I'm going to need two liters of gasoline and as many rags as you can find."

Jusuf nodded. "Ah."

"I need machine oil, though palm oil will do if we don't have it. I'm going to need an assistant. One who speaks enough English so that he can understand my directions." Bolan looked around at the cluster of young men. "Anyone here speak good English?"

Ali raised his hand and stepped forward.

"No." Jusuf shook his head.

Ali froze in his tracks.

"Ali is on…" Jusuf searched for a word. "Probation, and even if he is accepted back, he must still be punished."

Bolan shrugged. "Punished for what?"

"Failure."

Ali's shoulders hunched at the word.

"I understand." Bolan nodded. "But tell me something, Jusuf."

Jusuf's eyes slitted. "Tell you what, Makeen?"

Bolan grinned. "Do you consider stripping, cleaning and reassembling seventy rifles a privilege, or a punishment?"

Ali's shoulders sank.

One corner of Jusuf's mouth quirked upward against his will. Fass seemed amused.

"Ali." Jusuf jerked his head. "Go to the boat shed. Draw gasoline and take a can of oil. Go to the huts of the women and tell them to give you all the rags they can find and then return here. You will work with Makeen, today, tonight, and tomorrow if necessary, until all of the weapons are burnished…" The thin man looked from Ali to Bolan with an unpleasant smile. "And I am satisfied."

BOLAN'S FINGERS BURNED from the gasoline and ached from assembling thousands of parts. Seventy-two Type 68 rifles were stacked in tripods in front of the armory. They would have sparkled if it hadn't been for their dull gray phosphate finish. Their bayonets were affixed, polished and sharpened. Ali's fingers were swollen and bleeding from the scrubbing and cleaning. Both men's eyes were bloodshot with exhaustion and gasoline fumes. They had finished with the consignment of North Korean weapons and begun cleaning and inventorying every other weapon. Those that were too rusted out or obviously damaged had been stripped and cannibalized for parts.

Ali had wanted to talk, but Bolan had kept their conversation to bolt assemblies, breechblocks and firing pins for the past twelve hours. Only during the last minutes before dawn when Bolan was certain they were alone, and he knew Ali was exhausted to the point Bolan could easily catch him in a lie did he drop his cover.

"So how did it go?"

Ali blinked in surprise and wiped his eyes with the back of his wrist. "Dr. Blancanales released me on Tawi Tawi. I went to the mosque, and it was not long before I was contacted. I was blindfolded and taken out to sea. Two days later, another boat met ours in the lagoon of an island I did not know. Jusuf was on the other boat." Ali's shoulders twitched. It was clear he was afraid of the Indonesian.

"What happened?"

"Jusuf questioned me. I told the story of attacking your boat and how the occupants were heavily armed and how we were slaughtered." Ali met Bolan's gaze. "All of which was true. Then I told him of being knocked overboard, and that I do not know how to swim."

"Then what?"

"Jusuf told me to defend myself. We fought for a moment, but I was like a child before him." The young man rubbed the fading bruise on his jaw. "I did not even see the kick that knocked me overboard."

Bolan nodded tiredly. "He let you sink."

"To the bottom of the lagoon," Ali said. "He waited until he saw no more bubbles rise to the surface and then waited some more before diving after me and pulling me up by the hair. I do not remember much of this. I remember fighting for a moment and then awaking as I threw up half the lagoon."

Bolan considered a Dragunov sniper rifle. The battery to the optics had long since corroded, but all that meant was that the infrared sensing unit and the dim-light illuminator were nonfunctional. The optics themselves were clean, and the bore was clean. Bolan set the sniper rifle aside. "Jusuf believed your story?"

Ali shook his head ruefully as he ran a rag over an M-60 machine gun. "Jusuf said he believed that I did not know how to swim."

Bolan nodded. Jusuf was going to be trouble. "What have you heard since you've been here?"

"There is a rumor that we are going to attack someone. A big target, an enemy of the Mahdi. More warriors are being recruited, and as you see there are new shipments of guns."

A big target. Bolan suspected that Rustam Megawatti might be in for some trouble.

Ali finished reassembling a rifle. "I think perhaps—"

Bolan cut him off. "Check the action again."

Ali worked the M-60's bolt several times as Jusuf came striding through the trees. The thin man peered at the racked, stacked and shining weapons. One eyebrow rose a millimeter. He took in Ali's disheveled and grease-stained appearance and nodded once. "You have worked well, Ali. Go, sleep."

"Thank you, Jusuf." Ali leaned the machine gun against the wall of the armory and trotted off wearily into the dawn.

Jusuf ran his eyes over the well-serviced weapons again. "You have done good work."

Bolan pointed at the pistol holstered at Jusuf's hip. The thin man stared at Bolan for a moment before drawing the Browning Hi-Power and handing it over. His hand drifted to the cleaver thrust through his belt. Bolan swiftly field stripped the pistol, cleaned it, oiled it and reassembled it. Jusuf took the gun, inspected it with a grunt and reholstered it.

"You seem to know many weapons," Jusuf said.

"You know of the fighting in Kosovo?"

"I have heard of it," the thin man admitted.

Bolan picked up an old submachine gun and began removing its barrel. "The Serbs seized most of the arms factories in Yugoslavia and were given much equipment by the Russians. Germany gave surplus ex-East German equipment to the Croats. We Muslims?" Bolan frowned through the barrel and its pitted rifling. "We had to beg, borrow and steal whatever we could find. One of my jobs was to keep my unit's weapons shooting."

"You and Ali have worked well together."

"He is a hard worker." Bolan took out the bolt assembly. It was serviceable. "He wants to prove himself."

"You have spoken, then?"

Bolan nodded. "We have been cleaning and repairing guns for fourteen long hours."

"He has told you his story?" Jusuf asked.

Bolan replaced the pitted barrel with one he had cannibalized from another weapon. "He has," he said.

"And you believe him?"

Bolan looked up from his work and feigned amusement. "I believe that he does not know how to swim."

Jusuf's thin smile ghosted across his face. "Sleep, Makeen. You and Ali may finish the work after you have rested. Then we shall talk again."

Bolan racked the submachine gun back into battery and put it aside. He stretched and walked down to the water's edge where the fishing huts rose up out of the tide on their stilts. He clambered up a bamboo ladder and threw himself down on a reed matt next to Fess and listened to the tide. She rolled over and wrinkled her nose at him. "You stink of gasoline and guns."

"There was much that needed doing."

She sat up and poured water from a gourd into an old GI canvas basin. She took his hands one at a time and began washing them. Bolan lay back as she cleaned the grease and powder fouling from beneath his fingernails. She frowned in bemused disgust. "You are filthy. I should throw you over the rail and let the sea do this."

Bolan smiled as she straddled his hips, lathered his face and began shaving him. He took in the view as she leaned over him and ran the razor over his jaw. The woman noticed where his eyes lingered. The razor paused. "You like them," she said.

Bolan reached for her breasts even as the blade pressed against his throat. "Very much," he said.

The look of amused disgust returned to her face. "Most men do." The razor continued smoothly on its path.

Bolan's hands moved to her face. Her Eurasian features gave her a slight hardness in the lines of her jaw and cheekbones. Even in repose, her face seemed to radiate a submerged, angry challenge.

She was beautiful, he thought.

Bolan believed he knew the answer but asked anyway. "Why did you feel the need—"

"My pimp thought they would make me more profitable," she said. She rinsed the razor and went to work on Bolan's chin. "I was born in Bandung. My father was an expatriate Dutch, as you guessed. I loved him very much, but he had two unfortunate habits, one was opium and the other was gambling. It was not a favorable combination. He sold me when his debts became insurmountable. I was taken to Jakarta. My features made me exotic and popular there, but I soon grew too tall for those who prefer little girls. My pimp decided I would make more money as a dancer and in…film." She looked down at her enhancements coldly. "So this was done to me."

It was an old story and far too common. Many fathers in Southeast Asia sold unwanted daughters even without the excuse of drug or gambling debts. Bolan cupped her chin in his hand. "How did you escape?"

"One morning I was hanging out the brothel's wash when I heard a voice. A man was speaking in the square. He called out to all. The weak and the strong, the rich and poor, to all come to him. His voice drew me. He said to come to Allah. To rise up and make war against all infidels that were near you. He looked into my eyes when he said it, and something within me moved."

She stared into the middle distance. Her eyes were seeing her past instead of Bolan. "I was twelve when my father sold me, and since that time my spirit had been broken and I had become addicted to drugs. Yet when the Mahdi spoke, something within me moved. I arose. I returned to the brothel. I came upon my pimp and killed him. I fled to the Madhi and showed him the blood on my hands. I confessed all that I was, all that I had done and begged him for sanctuary. He gave me sanctuary and sent forth his followers to slay the gang my pimp belonged to. I have followed him ever since."

Her eyes blinked into ice-cold focus on Bolan. "There is no perversion you can imagine that I have not done or had done to me. My hands are red with the blood of infidels." Her barely submerged anger blazed to the surface. Her features hardened into a mask of defiance, daring him to despise her. "What do you think of me now?"

Bolan spoke the truth. "I think you're beautiful."

The angry mask broke as she made a choking noise. "You do not—"

Bolan put a finger against her lips and spoke the truth once more. "I've killed more men than you can imagine. Good men, innocents and loved ones have died because of my actions." Bolan gazed up into her eyes. He was not a judge. He was not a jury. He was an Executioner. It was the path he had chosen. He would not turn away from his War Everlasting until it claimed his life, but neither could he deny the sea of blood that was the collateral damage he had left in his wake. Nor could he deny the likelihood that Sujatmi Fass would drown in that same sea before this task was done. It was a burden as heavy as a mountain. He would carry it to his grave and would be forced to bear it before him when he met his maker on the Judgment Day. "Suja, you—"

Bolan tasted the salt of her tears as she pressed her lips against his to silence him. Both of them bore terrible scars. Their pasts were full of debts unpaid, their futures dark with bloodstained blades and the roar of gunfire. Only that moment had meaning.

They made love with a new and terrible urgency.

13

"Fire."

Pedoy let out a scream. *"Allah Akhbar!"*

The Type 68 rifle burst into life. Spent brass shell casings sprayed the right side of the firing line as the North Korean weapon burned its 30-round magazine in three seconds. The bolt racked open on an empty chamber. Pedoy stood shaking and blinking. He smiled at Bolan hopefully. Then he flinched and slammed his gaze down at his toes as Jusuf glared at him.

Bolan peered downrange.

The distance was twenty-five yards. The rusted-out jerrican serving as the target sat unscarred by bullet holes. Bolan returned his gaze to Pedoy and then to his rifle. Pedoy's bayonet was fixed. His folding stock was not. He had not bothered to use his sights, but the ladder was set fully forward at eight hundred yards. Pedoy had held the rifle like a giant handgun. His firing technique had consisted of screaming, closing his eyes and holding the trigger down on full-auto.

Bolan took Pedoy's rifle with a sigh. "Ali, translate for me."

The Philippines had been a blade culture since time out of mind. Pedoy looked crestfallen as Bolan removed the bayonet and handed it back to him. "This is your bayonet." Bolan pointed toward Jusuf while Ali translated his words into Tagalog. "You do not fix bayonets until your commanding officer tells you to."

Jusuf grunted at the wisdom of the statement as Pedoy sadly sheathed the blade.

"This is your shoulder stock. Your shoulder stock is your friend." Bolan pulled the folding metal stock down and locked it into place. "It goes against your shoulder."

"These are your sights." He took the ladder sight and set it for the one hundred yard minimum. "You look through the rear, but concentrate on the front."

Pedoy nodded as Ali dropped knowledge on him in his native tongue.

"This is your selector." Bolan took a loaded 30-round magazine from Pedoy's belt and clicked it into the rifle. "This is safe." He held up the rifle and nothing happened as he squeezed the trigger. He slid the selector down with a metallic clack. "Semiautomatic, one shot per each pull of the trigger."

Bolan brought the rifle to his shoulder and aimed at a coconut tree a hundred yards away. "You never pull your trigger. You squeeze it."

Ali spoke and the Executioner squeezed the trigger three times. Three coconuts burst apart in white sprays of meat and milk.

The men on the firing line sighed happily at the carnage.

Bolan considered killing them.

Jusuf was watching him like a hawk with one hand resting on the butt of the pistol holstered at his hip. Bolan was fairly certain he could put a burst into Jusuf's skull before the Indonesian could react. But killing the other twelve men would be tight. Their rifles were unloaded, but all of them had bladed weapons and the range was spitting distance. On top of that, he did not know where the Mahdi was or the nature of his master plan. Bolan flicked his selector lever to full-auto.

"Automatic fire." Bolan squeezed the trigger. The jerrican tumbled as a 5-round burst tore through it. Bolan fired short bursts, walking the besieged fuel container along the ground. A bullet kicked the can up in the air, and Bolan's final round swatted it into a violent spin that sent it whistling into the trees.

Bolan took another magazine and reloaded the rifle. He handed it to Pedoy and pointed at a cardboard box downrange. "Shoot it."

Pedoy eagerly put the rifle to his shoulder and peered down the sights.

"Keep your eyes open. Don't pull the trigger, squeeze it. Slowly."

Pedoy's trigger finger tightened. The rifle barked. The box skidded along the ground. A black hole had appeared in its lower right-hand corner.

The volunteer killers along the firing line clapped enthusiastically. Pedoy blushed like a schoolboy. Hitting a cardboard box at twenty-five yards with an assault rifle ranked right up with hitting a barn with a baseball bat, but it was the first hit of his life.

Bolan nodded approvingly. "Again."

Pedoy pulled the trigger. Holes began appearing in the box with monotonous precision. After twenty-two hits the devastated box collapsed upon itself.

"Everyone load a magazine. Fix your stocks. Pull your rear sight all the way back. Set your selectors on semiauto. Pick a target and start firing."

Bolan stepped back as the men on the firing line began to shoot. Boxes and buckets began to scud and jump as they were hit with .30-caliber slugs. Bolan knew he might very well have to kill all of these men, and he was making them better killers in the meantime.

"Soon they will be ready."

Bolan turned at Jusuf's cryptic remark. "I want them to be able to reliably hit a man-sized target at one hundred yards."

"As do I, Makeen." Jusuf nodded. "There is a time for the blade of the *juramentado* and a time for the gun. The time of the gun approaches." Jusuf spoke over his shoulder as he turned and walked back toward the village. "Keep them at it until noon prayers."

THE EXECUTIONER'S EYES flicked open. His hand closed around the grips of his pistol a second before Jusuf spoke at the bottom of the ladder to his hut. "Makeen."

Bolan relaxed his grip. He had presented Jusuf with a list of the weapons that were unserviceable and shown him the junk pile of discarded components. However, from four rusted-out and corroded Tokarev automatics of Russian, Chinese, North Korean and Yugoslavian manufacture, Bolan had cobbled together a cannibal pistol. The bore was not good and the springs a little sloppy, but Bolan figured he had a pistol that would reliably empty a magazine into someone before blowing up in his hand.

He pushed the pitted and worn pistol back into the niche he had created between the reed wall facing the sea and a floor beam. Fass made a sleepy noise and rolled over as Bolan rose. He knotted a sarong around his hips and put his sword across his shoulder as he stepped out onto the tiny balcony. Jusuf stood below with the surf lapping around his ankles. A few feet back from the water the Mahdi was surrounded by a phalanx of armed guards. All of them stood in the sand smiling up at Bolan.

Ducks in a row.

Bolan knew he had no choice but to wait for a better opportunity.

The Mahdi crooked his fingers at Bolan. "Come, Makeen. Come. Walk with me."

Bolan went down the steps, and one of the Mahdi's guards bowed slightly and held out his hands for Bolan's sword. He handed over his blade, and the Mahdi reached up and embraced him warmly. "I hear many good things about you."

Bolan returned the little man's embrace. "Jusuf has given me a good many things to do," he replied.

The Mahdi put a hand on Bolan's back and they began walking down the beach. "I understand the armory is in order, and men who could not…" The little man searched for the phrase in English and his smiled as he found it. "Hit the broad side of a barn…can now do so."

"Jusuf told me there was a time for the blade of the *juramentado*, and a time for the gun. I have done what I can with your men and your guns."

"And you have done well." The Mahdi sighed. "Did you know I have enemies?"

"The righteous are beset with them. Always has it been so," Bolan said.

"Indeed." They walked along for a few moments in silence as the sun rose. "You have proved yourself quite useful."

"Thank you."

"Yet, you have not proved yourself."

Bolan nodded. "I fear so."

"Your position among us is unique. You are not one of us. You did not come to me because you were called. You appear to be a righteous man caught in an unfortunate situation."

Bolan nodded. "What would you have me do, Imam?"

"I have an enemy." They stopped walking and the Mahdi gripped Bolan's arm. "Would you rid me of him?"

Bolan frowned. "I have trained and broken bread with your men. I know enough to know that I do not know the rituals, and I have not been initiated into the mysteries of the *juramentado*."

"I would not initiate you yet. I would not reveal our mysteries or our true purpose to you yet." The little man took Bolan's hands in his own. "But as Jusuf told you, there is a time for the blade of the *juramentado*, and a time for the gun."

Bolan's set his jaw. "I will tell you this, Holy One, even if it means my death. In Kosovo we fought the Crusaders, Roman and Orthodox. I was raised Bektasi. My father was a Dervish, and yet I fought beside both Shia and Sunni. I fought beside Muslims of many nations who had come to make jihad against those who sought to cleanse the land of those of the faith. I fought beside Asians, Arabs and Persians and saw them martyr themselves in the war against the Christians. I will not raise my hand against my fellow Muslim."

"I would not ask such a thing." The little man's eyes shone, and again Bolan felt the power of his personality like a battering ram. "Jusuf warned me that you could be a danger, and yet I would not allow you to be callously slain for the same reason."

"You have my thanks."

"Yet, you are a warrior, you have made jihad. We have a purpose, and you must join us, or I fear you must pay a terrible price."

Bolan stood silently.

"I see you are a man of conscience." The Mahdi's snowy brows rose slightly. "Yet what if I told you my enemy is an infidel?"

"That would make things significantly easier. What is he?" Bolan put a scowl on his face. "A Christian?"

The Mahdi smiled like a fisherman who feels a nibble. "My enemy worships four things. Graven idols, gold, opium and whores."

"Then he is damned."

"Indeed," the Mahdi said. "And constantly he seeks to send his spies among the brethren and destroy me, but unfortunately for him, I have many more spies among those who cleave unto him. They tell me he now conspires with western powers we fight to see me fall. I have had enough. I would see him fall."

"Who is your enemy?"

"Why, my enemy is Rustam Megawatti, the Pirate King of the China Sea." The tiny man's fingers gripped Bolan's hands with a strength that belied his size. The eyes of the Expected One blazed into those of the Executioner. "And now is the time of the gun."

14

Kouprey Island, Cambodia

The men were nervous, and they had every right to be. Most of them had never been in a firefight in their lives, and they were going up against hardened killers. The enemy were pirates who had spent their lives savaging the sea lanes and taking what they wanted by force. Bolan's platoon had received exactly one week of the equivalent of US Army Ranger training. Most of that had been marksmanship, weapons maintenance and the use of cover.

Very little of that would serve them well.

The Mahdi and Jusuf had taken Bolan's fledgling marksmen and decided to use them as shock troops. Behind them were nearly a hundred fighters, armed with whatever firearm they could find. They would come flooding in when Bolan's corps had broken the defenses.

Bolan thought a much better idea would be to have the one hundred hopped-up yahoos do the charging and screaming while his men used their newfound skills to cover the assault, or better yet, make a flanking attack during the diversion. Unfortunately, Bolan had not been consulted during the grand strategy session. He and his team had simply been issued their orders.

They were the tip of spear.

Sneaking up on Rustam Megawatti had not been difficult. The Mahdi had spies in Megawatti's household who knew his every movement. The Pirate King was making inroads into "legitimate" business enterprises. He was using his considerable connections and a great deal of under-the-table PRC financial backing to open up a string of casinos along the Cambodian coast. The tiny island the Cambodian government had leased to him was named after the national animal. The kouprey was a very rare, forest-dwelling cow that stood over six feet at the shoulder and weighed over a ton.

The Mahdi's army had unloaded outrigger canoes from the belly of a steamer and spent a day and a night under sail and oar to insert on the island's southern tip.

Megawatti's French colonial manor was lit up like a Christmas tree. The sound of music and laughter wafted over the twelve-foot walls of stone. A military truckload of prostitutes had been driven into the compound earlier. The Mahdi's spies said the manor had at least fifty armed men. The son, Isfan, was on the island, and he had brought a dozen of his bodyguards with him. Armed men walked the walls and guarded the gate. The French-style iron gate had been replaced by heavy beams reinforced with iron bands. Within the walls, a twenty-foot bamboo guard tower surveyed all approaches to the villa.

The assault was going to be ugly.

Bolan could smell the sweet smoke as the men prepared for *juramentado*. They smoked, tied their testicles and worked themselves into a religious frenzy back in the trees. The Executioner's men were stone-cold sober. Their balls were not bound. Indeed, they were hanging in the breeze on this one, and each and every one of them knew it. Bolan wished he had the Dragunov sniper rifle, but he knew it would not serve him in the current situation he was leading from the front.

Bolan spoke low. "Hey, Pedoy."

Pedoy's head jerked around.

Bolan's smile flashed out of the black greasepaint camouflaging his face "Now you can fix your bayonet," he said while miming the action.

Pedoy grinned and the men who had been on the firing line laughed low. Bolan nodded at Ali. "Tell the men to fix bayonets."

Ali gave the order down the line, and bayonets rasped from their sheaths and clicked into place. The order to hang sharpened steel on the end of his rifle never failed to focus a soldier's attention. Fear and uncertainty hardened into fierce determination. Bolan's chosen men all wore thin black cotton pyjamas and head wraps. Their faces were smeared with grease or ash.

Sujatmi Fass crept through the trees like a phantom in black and dropped to one knee beside Bolan. "They are prepared," she said.

Ali knelt beside them. "Bayonets are fixed. Shoulder stocks deployed. Sights set at one hundred yards." The young man grinned. "We shall die like real riflemen."

"Like chosen men."

"Yes." Ali nodded happily. "Chosen men."

"Good," Bolan said. "Let's prepare."

Ali took out a plastic butane lighter and handed it to Bolan. They crouched back deeper in the trees, and the Executioner nodded at a man even younger than Ali. "Abu, dynamite," he ordered.

Abu scampered forward carrying a canvas satchel. Bolan gave the contents of the satchel a final examination. His nose wrinkled as he caught the vague acrid-chemical stench coming from the bag.

The dynamite was sweating nitro in the tropical heat.

Bolan shook his head grimly at his demolition assistant. "Abu, wipe down the dynamite one more time. When we attack, you stay behind me, right on my heels. Ali, you and Section One stay back to cover the assault and then move forward once the gate is breached. Then— Damn it!"

A man came running through the trees like a white-robed ghost brandishing a knife in each hand. Bolan was tempted to shoot him as he broke into the killing ground between the trees and the manor. *"Allah Akhbar!"* the man shouted.

They had just lost the element of surprise.

"Allah Akhbar!" The one-hundred-man roar rose behind Bolan's corps in response. The pumped-up men were running *juramentado* early.

Bolan raised his rifle and put a burst through each of the two men guarding the gate. "Sections Two, Three, Four! Follow me! Go! Go! Go!"

The men streamed out of the jungle. Bolan and his crew were black shadows among the fanatics in white as they burst forth from hiding, desperately trying to cover the kill zone.

The floodlight snapped on, lighting the area like a football field.

Gunfire flashed along the wall as Megawatti's men responded to the sea of incoming targets.

The first men fell from a burst from an automatic rifle. Bolan's riflemen obeyed their training. The twelve men he had held back in the tree line with Ali used their sights and began engaging the guardsmen along the wall. Bolan's remaining thirty men charged forward firing short bursts as they came. Tracers crisscrossed the killing ground.

The heavy machine gun in the watchtower began ripping through the human wave like a scythe. Blood sprayed Bolan as a man beside him broke apart like a piñata. The big .50-caliber bullets blew through the oncoming men like tissue paper. Bolan ran on. Abu ran behind him with the satchel of sweating dynamite clutched in both hands. They'd lost thirty men in ten seconds, and the machine gun continued to reap men like wheat.

Bolan flung himself flat against the gate. "Abu!"

Abu produced a five-stick bundle of dynamite. Bolan struggled with the lighter. The flame finally held and the fuse lit. He pressed the bundle into place against the center of the gate. "Tape!"

Duct tape ripped in Abu's hands as he taped the hissing dynamite in place.

"Move!"

Bolan and Abu ran down the wall. The men running *jura-*

mentado swarmed screaming against the walls as the defenders shot down into them. Two of them ran up and began chopping at the gate with their parangs even as the dynamite burned.

Fass ran to Bolan's side. "Makeen! We must—"

"Down!" Bolan shoved Abu and the woman to the sand.

Thunder rolled along the wall. The gate and the two men pounding on it disappeared in a flash. The assaulting group roared in mindless victory and surged toward the smoking opening.

Bolan was already up. "Abu! Single stick!"

Abu fished out a stick of dynamite.

"Abu! Suja! Give a hand!"

The pair made stirrups out of their hands. Bolan tasted the iodine bitterness of nitroglycerine as he shoved the sweating stick of dynamite between his teeth and took a running step. Abu and Fass grunted as they took his weight and boosted him to the top of the wall. Bolan pulled himself up. A pair of guards stood on the catwalk a few feet away shooting into the mob streaming in through the gate.

Bolan's rifle ripped through the spine of one of the closest guards and ripped the head from the second. The .50-caliber gun was the real problem. The big Browning slaughtered all who came through the shattered gate.

The lighter in Bolan's hand was cracked from his climb but still lit after a few flicks. He pressed the fuse to the flame. Someone in the tower got wise, and the fifty caliber swung its smoking muzzle in Bolan's direction. He flung the dynamite. It turned end over end over in a sparking wheel, and the three men in the bamboo tower screamed as the stick of dynamite landed among them. The machine gunner dropped the spade grips of his fifty and leaped twenty feet to the courtyard to fall under the blades of the howling mob. One of the other two men tried to kick the stick off the platform. His sandal connected, and both he and the top of the tower were eclipsed by a thudding red ball of fire.

The Mahdi's men swarmed onto the grounds.

Guards were firing from the patio and the balconies of the mansion.

Bolan stood on the wall and faced the jungle. His voice boomed over the sound of battle. "Ali!"

Ali and his five surviving riflemen charged out of the trees.

Bolan's rifle corps clustered below him on the wall. Fifteen had survived the initial charge. He jumped from the wall. "Section Two! Flank right! Section Three, flank left! Four! You're with me! Abu, dynamite!"

Bolan slid the stick into his tunic while the remnants of Section Two and Section Three peeled off and began flanking the mansion. The rest of the men clustered around Bolan. "Spread out!" he shouted.

The riflemen spread into a skirmishing line and moved forward steadily. They walked fire into the windows and balconies as they came to suppress the enemy guns. Ali and his section came through the gate at a run and fell into the line.

The door of the mansion's triple garage was suddenly smashed off its hinges, and a black Hummer roared out with its lights blazing. Bolan's corps swung their weapons onto the vehicle and flicked their selector switches to full-auto. Hundreds of orange sparks flickered like berserk fireflies across the body panels and windshield. The Hummer was armored. The M-60 machine gun mounted on its roof began strobing into the attackers. The men with blades were simply run down beneath the wheels. The machine gunner had his sights set on Bolan's riflemen. The engine of the Hummer roared like Doomsday as it bore down on the line.

"Scatter!" Bolan roared. "Abu! Dyna—"

"Allah Akhbar!" Abu drew his kris and charged the Hummer. The machine gunner ignored him and shot down two more of Bolan's riflemen as they scattered. The driver saw Abu waving his blade in the headlights and gunned the engine.

Fass screamed, "Abu!"

The driver failed to notice the canvas satchel slung beneath Abu's arm. Abu ran straight at the Hummer's grill. *"Allah—"*

Abu's fifteen sticks of dynamite lit up the Hummer like an Air Force iron bomb on impact.

The force of the explosion knocked Bolan off his feet. Heat rolled over the compound in a wave. Bolan watched for a dazed moment as the back end of the Hummer rose twenty feet in the air trailing smoke and fire. The front of the Hummer was gone. The Executioner rolled as an axle came crashing down out of the stratosphere and thudded into the earth where he had just been. Half of his riflemen had been knocked down, and the others staggered dazedly. Bolan leaped to his feet, ignoring the rain of smoking metal all around him and pumped his rifle into the air.

"Abu!"

The dazed rifle corps rallied to the sight of their leader's rifle, bayonet fixed and held like a flag. The riflemen roared back. "Abu!"

The *juramentado* were hacking at the front door and smashing at the windows while the defenders fired outward. The demolition charge to breach the mansion was gone. However, the shattered garage lay open and lit from within like the chink in the enemy armor.

"Chosen men!" Bolan shouted. *"Allah Akhbar!"*

"Allah Akhbar!" Bolan's riflemen streamed after him in a wedge, firing their rifles from the hip-assault position. Bullets tore into the garage and sparked off the armored Mercedes limousine parked within. The fire-engine red Ferrari Testarossa fared much worse.

Bolan stopped beside the limo and tried the driver's-side door. It was unlocked. He opened the door, flipped down the sun visor and keys spilled into his hand. "Ali! Smash down the door! Assault the house! Room by room! I'll meet you in the middle!"

"Yes, Makeen!"

Ali and the riflemen began pouring fire up the step into the heavy oak door between the garage and the house.

"Suja!" Bolan folded the stock of his rifle and slid behind the wheel of the limo. "Get in!"

Fass crawled into the passenger seat as Bolan gunned the engine and slid the gear into reverse. The long Mercedes squealed out of the garage and fishtailed into a bootlegger's turn as Bolan yanked up on the parking brake and spun the wheel. He rammed the limousine back into gear, and the tires spat gravel as he accelerated toward the side of the house. The suspension bucked and shook as he took the Mercedes off the driveway and onto the grounds. Sections Two and Three had the back patio of the mansion in a cross fire, but they were meeting spirited resistance from the defenders. The few fighters who had made it around back were sprawled on the lawn and the patio steps where they had been cut down. Bolan's riflemen crouched behind trees and raised flowerbeds and engaged the defenders.

Dirt flew as Bolan brought the limo to a sliding halt in front of a flowerbed. He rolled down the window. The six remaining riflemen of Section Three stared at the black car that had miraculously appeared in front of them. "Get in!"

Bolan's riflemen grinned, leaping over the planter and piling into the back of the limo.

The Executioner slid the car into gear and accelerated straight for the mansion. The defenders suddenly realized the limousine no longer belonged to their boss and began shooting at it. The body of the Mercedes popped and ticked as if it were in a hailstorm. Sparks flashed off the windshield.

Fass gasped in alarm as Bolan put the pedal to the floor. "What are you—"

"Brace yourselves!" Bolan said in warning.

The engine screamed in protest as he rammed it into low gear. The limo lurched and bucked like a bronco as it hit the flight of steps up to the terrace.

"Allah Akhbar!" Bolan shouted for the benefit of his riflemen.

The six young men roared like lions in response. *"Allah Akhbar!"*

The limo thudded onto the terrace, and Bolan shoved it into second gear and accelerated. A guardsman recklessly stood before them, spraying the Mercedes with a pistol in each hand. He flapped like a ruptured bird as the limo hit him and he flew across the hood. Fass screamed as he hit the windshield and rolled off.

The armored limousine plunged through the double glass doors. Sofas, chairs, tables and guardsmen were broken and sent flying as the limo slammed into Megawatti's living room. Bolan hit the brakes, and the tires shrieked and slid on the marble floor.

"Hold on!"

The limo's rear wheels rose up as it slammed into the banister. The airbags deployed and pressed Bolan back into his seat. The rear wheels slammed down, and Bolan hit the button for the sunroof as the airbags deflated.

Two of Bolan's riflemen popped up through the sunroof and began spraying their rifles at the guards.

"Short bursts!" Bolan kicked open his door and crouched behind it as a man with an Uzi sprayed the armored glass window. The Executioner dropped low and fired off a burst under the door. Rifle bullets shattered the killer's ankles and knocked him off his feet.

Bolan's men spilled out of the limo. Section Two was down to four men, but they had cleaned out the last defenders on the terrace. They entered the mansion and linked up.

"Suja! Take Section Two! Get the front door open!"

Gunfire erupted from the top of the stairs.

"Section Three! Cover me!" Bolan jumped onto the hood and stepped to the roof of the limo as his men cut loose at the men on the landing above. He tossed away his rifle and leaped. His hands caught the marble rail and he swung his right foot up and jammed his sandaled foot between a pair of uprights. The gunmen on the landing stared in alarm at the black figure that suddenly hung before them on the railing like a giant black spider.

Bolan pulled the Philippine Army .45 out of his sash and shoved it through the rail. The Colt rolled in twin trip-hammer blows as Bolan double-tapped each of the three gunmen in the chest. "Chosen men! To me!"

Bolan's riflemen swarmed up the stairs. Below him, he heard the tearing scream of the crazed attackers as they entered the house. Bolan had no time for them. He hauled himself over the railing and dropped into a crouch as a door down the hallway burst open.

Rustam Megawatti emerged with two of his guards. The little Indonesian man wore a gold silk smoking jacket and not much else. Both he and his two men held gold-plated Sterling submachine guns in their hands. Women were screaming in the room behind them. Bolan took his .45 in both hands and the big Colt barked twice. Megawatti's bodyguards both fell with burst brows. Bolan flung his empty .45 at Megawatti and threw himself into a forward shoulder roll. The two-and-a-half pound pistol cracked into the Pirate King's chin and his gold-plated gun snarled off a burst into the mirrored ceiling.

Bolan slid his sword from over his shoulder as he rolled to his feet. The Indonesian spit teeth, staggered back a step and lowered his submachine gun for the kill. Bolan took a forward step and hurled the two-handed sword like a lumberjack at an ax-throwing competition. The sword revolved once and struck Megawatti's sunken chest. It pierced his sternum and pinned him to the doorjamb behind him like an insect.

The Pirate King of the South China Sea stared at the iron ring hilt jutting from his chest. His gold-plated gun fell from his fingers. His chin drooped to his chest as he sagged into the Chinese sword impaling him.

Bolan's riflemen hit the landing with Ali in the lead as Bolan took Megawatti's golden gun and stripped his bodyguards of their spare magazines.

"You have slain him!" Ali was jubilant.

Bolan nodded and stared back down the stairs. The men running *juramentado* were in the house and rampaging from room to room. The real screaming began as Megawatti's wounded, the household servants and anyone else they found were hacked to bits in an orgy of rising and falling blades. A few gunshots rang out, but mostly there was the fanatical howling of the *juramentado* and the sounds of a massacre. Prostitutes screamed as they were dragged from the bedrooms. Some fell screaming beneath the blood-drenched blades, while others were dragged off by men with a lust for more than just killing. Men in business suits who had obviously been Megawatti's guests were hauled out of their hiding places in closets and beneath beds. They pleaded for mercy in half a dozen languages as they were dragged into the living room and summarily dismembered.

Bolan's men stared down into the caldron of violence below. They had signed up to do the Mahdi's will. They'd had dreams of encountering the nonbelievers, of striking off their heads and making great slaughter among them. Instead they had been sent, some very unwillingly, to join Bolan's rifle corps and been made soldiers. As the chosen men gazed down onto the killing ground, they were like sober men at a party full of drunks.

The killers below were no longer human. They were like dogs, drunk on slaughterhouse blood.

The remains of the rifle corps looked down at the horror and then back at Bolan uncertainly. Ali looked sick. Suja's face was a blank, unreadable mask. Pedoy swallowed uncomfortably. "Makeen—"

Bolan ignored him as Jusuf entered the mansion surrounded by armed men. A Chinese man Bolan did not recognize walked with him. Jusuf took in the horror surrounding him and a thin smile crossed his face. Bolan's eyes went to slits.

Jusuf and his guards mounted the stairs. It was clear that they had not run *juramentado* but had watched the proceedings from a distance. The remains of Bolan's rifle corps stood at attention as Jusuf came to the landing. The Indonesian stared long and hard at Bolan's sword where it spiked Megawatti to the wall. "And where is the son? Isfan?"

The Chinese man looked Bolan up and down in hostile appraisal.

Bolan ignored him and glanced down the hallway to the suite adjoining Megawatti's. "Probably in there. With some guards."

"Fetch him."

The Executioner ripped his sword free of Megawatti, and the Pirate King fell facefirst into a puddle of his own gore. Bolan wiped his blade on the silk smoking jacket and sheathed it. He crouched next to one of the guards and drew a bayonet and clicked it onto the muzzle of his submachine gun.

"All right." Bolan raised the weapon. "Take cover."

The men pressed themselves against the wall or lurked in doorways as Bolan fired a burst through the door. A woman screamed and men shouted. Rifle bullets ripped back through the doorway in response.

"Yeah, I think he's in there," Bolan said.

"Fetch him," Jusuf repeated.

Bolan burned the rest of his magazine into the door. He kept his pattern in a circle the diameter of a saucer. He slid in a fresh magazine and took his last stick of dynamite out of his tunic. "Ali," he called out.

Jusuf watched with hawklike interest as Ali drew his lighter and lit the dangling fuse. Bolan looked at his remaining men. He was down to nineteen riflemen. They had taken more than fifty percent casualties. He wasn't going to forgive Jusuf for that.

"Be ready," he said.

Bolan walked up to the door and put his fist through the spot he'd weakened. He yanked it back and pressed himself against the marble frame. Bullets flew out in a hail. Bolan watched the flashing flame climb its sparking path up the fuse.

When there was half an inch left, he popped the stick through the hole.

The men behind the door shouted in horror. The women

screamed. Bolan raced down the hall and threw himself into an adjoining bathroom with two of his riflemen. The bathroom fixtures shook as the dynamite detonated. A flurry of wooden splinters and broken marble flew down the hall like shrapnel as the door disintegrated.

"Follow me!" Bolan charged through the black smoke filling the hall. The doorway was gone. He vaulted the section of missing floor into the suite of rooms. A white-suited guardsman bleeding out of both ears from the blast drunkenly aimed an immense revolver in Bolan's direction. The Sterling snarled in Bolan's hands and hammered the bodyguard backward and toppled him over a chair. Kalashnikovs erupted on Bolan's flanks. Another white suit staggered as the two automatic rifles chewed him up like a meat grinder. A pair of naked blond women screamed in hysteria behind the bed. Bolan burned down another guard, and his submachine gun locked open on empty. The last guard fell beneath Ali's and Pedoy's rifles.

"Die!" Isfan Megawatti burst out of the closet in his underwear screaming and spraying the bedroom with an FN assault rifle. "Die! Die! Die!

Fass cried out as she was struck and fell. Pedoy spun as he took a hit from the big battle rifle.

Bolan lunged. He hooked the barrel of Megawatti's rifle with his bayonet and slapped the muzzle skyward. Bullets shot into the ceiling. Bolan was wearing a black head wrap and greasepaint, but for a moment he and Megawatti locked gazes.

Isfan stared into Bolan's blue eyes and gaped in shock. "You—"

Bolan rammed his bayonet into Isfan's belly to the hilt. He ripped the eight-inch blade upward until it hit bone. The Pirate Prince let out a dying sigh and fell to the blackened carpet.

The two women would not stop screaming.

"Ali, take the women. Tell anyone who asks that I gave them to you as a reward for your bravery. When you have a chance, take them into the trees and hide them until we leave. Do you understand?"

"Yes, Makeen." Ali nodded. "I understand." The two women screamed uncomprehendingly as their savior dragged them away.

Bolan surveyed the carnage. The bullet had torn an ugly furrow through the flesh of Suja's shoulder. Pedoy had a similar wound, but the bullet had broken his collarbone. During Bolan's one week Warrior 101 intensive, he had taught his riflemen basic field dressing and two of his men were already tending to Suja's and Pedoy's wounds.

One of the surviving riflemen stepped up uncertainly. "Makeen?"

"What is it, Isah?"

"What would you have us do?"

"Locate all the men, dead, alive and wounded. I want a head count. Gather the weapons. We own the upstairs. Take what you want as spoils." The Executioner gazed at the body of Isfan Megawatti. "And take him to Jusuf with my compliments."

15

A great victory had been won. The Mahdi's enemy had been struck down. The Pirate King of the South China Sea was dead, and so was the heir to his throne. To the victor had gone the spoils. Rustam Megawatti's Cambodian mansion had been as richly appointed as the palace of any Saudi oil sheik. They had taken money, jewelry and valuables away from the estate in the millions. They had also sailed away with two of Megawatti's yachts. It had been a good haul.

Bolan lay beside Suja in their hut while the victory party raged outside on the beach. Her fingers drifted across his ribs. "You should be among them."

Bolan was in no mood to party. "Who's the Chinese man?"

Her nails trailed down Bolan's stomach. "His name is Chien Tien. Why?"

"He was giving me the evil eye on Kouprey."

"It is understandable. You killed his friend, Yaqoob."

Bolan had figured that, but now he had confirmation on the other PRC agent among the Mahdi's men. The question was how should he play it. He suspected Yaqoob and his partner had to have had a way to communicate with Beijing, but Yaqoob had died before Bolan could get any information. Unfortunately, both Yaqoob and his partner had orders to kill anyone who discovered their identity.

Bolan really needed to get a message out.

The music pounded on the beach. Men shouted and clapped, drunk on hashish and intoxicated with victory. "You should be among them," Suja repeated.

She was right. If only to maintain his cover and gather intelligence. Bolan heaved himself up to his feet. "I won't be gone long."

Bolan took a deep breath. He was exhausted. Half his riflemen were dead, and the survivors were men he might very well have to kill with his own hands. It was possible he might have to kill the woman he had just lain with. It wasn't a question of the lines blurring. The lines were crystal clear. They were just as ugly as hell, and getting uglier, and he saw them every time he looked in the mirror.

The Executioner looked at his reflection in the shaving mirror nailed to the wall.

His black hair was getting shaggy and falling across his brow. His beard and mustache had come in. His skin was ruddy bronze from exposure to the equatorial sun. Only his size and the blue eyes staring back in the mirror betrayed him. Bolan wound a red head wrap over his hair and slung his sword over his shoulder as he stepped out onto the tiny balcony overhanging the surf.

"Makeen!" Pedoy spotted him. His left arm was in a sling, but he waved his good one enthusiastically. "Makeen!"

A score of men looked around and happily took up the shout. "Makeen!"

Bolan scanned the torchlit crowd and saw that Jusuf and Chien were not chanting nor looking particularly pleased. The beach fell silent as Bolan drew his sword and held it high. "Abu."

The men on the beach bowed their heads in respect. Everyone knew the story of Abu's sacrifice. All of them had intended to run *juramentado* and martyr themselves to the cause, but Abu had martyred himself to save his fellows. They nodded, and the fallen young man's name murmured among them like the incoming tide.

Bolan broke the somber moment and pumped his sword into the air. *"Allah Akhbar!"*

The men on the beach roared. *"Allah Akhbar!"*

The hemp smoking and goat-gorging began again in earnest. Bolan sheathed his sword and descended the ladder down to the beach. Pedoy clapped him on the shoulder and shoved a smoking hot joint of goat into his hand. "Mak!"

Bolan circulated among the warriors congratulating his own men and the *juramentado* alike. He was a hero and the young men pressed around him, praising him and basking in his fame, hoping some would rub off on them. Every man carried one or more bladed weapons, but all the firearms had been collected and put back in the armory save for Jusuf and a squad of his personal guards.

The crowd parted like the Red Sea as Jusuf and Chien strode through them to Bolan.

"Come with me," Jusuf said.

Bolan stripped the remaining meat from his haunch of goat and tossed away the bone. He smiled at Jusuf as he wiped the grease from his chin with his fist. "Sure."

They walked along the beach until the lights of the bonfires grew dim, and several of Jusuf's personal entourage fell into step with them. All of them carried rifles. Bolan saw a lonely light in the distance ahead. Once again his main target was in sight, and again he was outnumbered and outgunned.

He was being granted another audience with the Mahdi.

The Expected One sat on a small rug contemplating the sea with a pair of tiki torches lighting his meditations. His huge sword bearer knelt behind him, and a half a dozen riflemen stood back discreetly.

Jusuf halted and held out his hand. Bolan unbuckled his sword and handed it over before kneeling in the sand.

"Imam."

"Makeen." The Mahdi turned his head and smiled. Bolan saw that he was not contemplating the sea, but the heads of Rustam and Isfan Megawatti. "You have exceeded all expectations. Even Jusuf has praised your ability and your bravery."

Bolan turned. "My thanks, Jusuf."

Jusuf nodded curtly. Bolan had no doubt that Jusuf had spoken well of him. The man was too smart to be the naysayer in the face of total victory. But he could feel the Indonesian's eyes on his back. He had no doubt Jusuf wished him dead, and by ordering him and his riflemen to take the lead in the attack he had been trying to engineer it. Instead, Bolan had walked out alive and a hero and the most popular man in camp. Jusuf also had to be intensely aware that there were twenty riflemen on the island who were unswervingly loyal to Bolan.

The Mahdi beamed. "How is Suja?"

It had turned out that Bolan was the most qualified battlefield surgeon on the island. He had stitched Suja's torn flesh with thread. The scar would be ugly, but the wound was clean and little more than a painful inconvenience. "She will be ready to fight within the week."

"Ah, good, good." The Mahdi's face shone like the sun, and again Bolan felt the power of the tiny man's personality. Again, Bolan wondered what was truly going on behind the facade of Jesus-like understanding in the huge brown eyes. "You bring so many blessings, Makeen. And Pedoy?"

Pedoy had not been so lucky. Isfan's bullet had broken the long, thin collarbone in a nasty fashion. They had hemped up Pedoy until he was feeling no pain, and then Bolan had probed and teased shards and bits of pulverized bone out of the wound before setting the shattered scapula. Bolan believed the bones would knit, but the scapula was shortened and some tendons in the shoulder had been cut by the bullet's passage.

"It will take some months before the wound is completely healed, and even then he will have to learn to wield a blade with his left hand."

The Mahdi nodded and gestured to Jusuf. The thin man brought Bolan's sword and laid it before the Mahdi. The little man drew the sword. It was clear the blade gave him great pleasure. He looked up and grinned impishly. "Have you seen my sword?" He nodded to the human mountain behind him. "Taiaishi."

The man rose with an ease surprising for his bulk and proffered the hilt of the Mahdi's sword.

Six rifles came just a little bit closer to pointing directly at Bolan.

Bolan drew the sword. The hilt was fashioned from the foot of a crocodile. Bolan felt the scaly hide of its ankle forming the grip against his palm. The clawed foot was sewn around a concealed pommel of steel. The blade was incredibly heavy. Well over three feet long with a simple diamond cross section. It was old, with some pitting and discoloration in the steel, but both edges were honed to razor sharpness. It was a blade designed to split shields and helmets and chop through armor of iron and steel. It was completely out of place among the short, sinuously curved slicing blades of Southeast Asia.

Despite its ridiculous length and weight it was incredibly well balanced.

"It is a *kaskara*."

Bolan had done some research when the word Mahdi had first been bandied around. The *kaskara* was the traditional sword of the Sudan. Some believed the design had been stolen from the invading Medieval Crusaders. Everyone who had historically fought the Sudanese commented on the size of their swords and spears, and the horrific wounds they inflicted.

The Mahdi sighed as he looked at the massive blade in Bolan's hands. "It was forged for the hand of first Mahdi."

The original Mahdi, who had fought the Egyptian and English armies in nineteenth-century Sudan, had been the son of a lowly, boat-building carpenter, though his father claimed to be descended from the Prophet Mohammed. Bolan handed the massive sword back to the tiny man before him. He was struck by how unnaturally large the little man's hands were. The

Mahdi's spatulate fingers closed around the hilt and lifted it as if it weighed little more than a willow wand.

"Always have we carried it. Throughout the generations." The man seemed almost in rapture. His eyes snapped down and locked with Bolan's. "You and I are much alike, Makeen."

Bolan allowed surprise to show on his face.

"Both of us carry the sword of our ancestor." The Mahdi's brown eyes were huge. They bored into Bolan with hypnotic force.

Bolan let his brow crease. "You are the descendant of the Mahdi?"

"I am the Mahdi."

Bolan stared.

The tiny man's eyes shone as if lit from within. "I am his reincarnation."

Traditional Islam was going right out the window, but the riflemen knelt at the Mahdi's words.

"I have returned."

"The Expected One," the men murmured.

"Once more I hold my blade in my hand. Once more I make war upon the infidel. Will you join us, Makeen?"

Bolan stared very steadily into the madman's eyes. "I will."

"Good, Makeen. Very good. You have brought so many blessings, and so many more shall you deliver." The Mahdi's religious fervor disappeared in an eye blink that caught even Bolan off guard.

"May I ask you a question?" His tone was blithely conversational.

Bolan nodded. "Of course, Mahdi."

The little man nodded toward the darkness. Two men came forward carrying a rolled Persian rug. It was lumped and swollen, and Bolan could see that something large was concealed within it. The two men knelt and laid the carpet in the sand. They grasped the fringed border of the carpet and heaved. The rug unrolled across the sand toward Bolan, and the fringe brushed his knees as it lay open and disgorged its contents.

The carpet lay like a bridge between Bolan and the Mahdi.

Marcie Mei's eyes rolled up at Bolan. Duct tape sealed her mouth. She lay before Bolan trussed like a chicken.

The Mahdi cocked his head inquisitively. "Do you know this woman?"

16

"She is my sister-in-law," Bolan said. "Her name is Mei."

The Mahdi nodded. "The sister of your wife, who was slain by soldiers in Mindanao?"

"Yes, Mahdi."

"She tells the same story as well." The little man looked at Bolan steadily. "She has been going from island to island, mosque to mosque, asking of Makeen Boulus. It came to our attention. She says she is alone. The rest of her family is dead. She has sold the land and received little for it and has used that to search. She says she has no one but you."

"I should have married her. It would have been the correct thing to do after what happened, but…" Bolan stared out onto the star-lit tide. "I was soul sick, and I took my boat and drifted instead."

"Indeed, it would have been charitable. Though your failure is understandable." The Mahdi raised an amused eyebrow. "And what are you prepared to do about it now?"

"What do you mean?"

"You are a lion, and yet, your status among us is…uncertain. Ties of marriage might, how may I put this delicately…cement you…among us."

Bolan let out a long breath. "A man who intends to run *juramentado* has no business marrying, Mahdi."

"Indeed, that is true." The Mahdi cocked his head once again in amusement. "But what if I told you that you have become too important to me to send you forth against the infidel with only the naked blade?"

"I would consider myself honored, but…" Bolan looked back meaningfully toward the camp and his hut above the surf.

"Ah, well." The Mahdi sighed innocently. "The Prophet Mohammed allows a man four wives.…"

Bolan marveled again at how the man could instantly change from father figure to friend to the voice of God in the blink of an eye. Bolan looked down at Marcie and allowed genuine discomfort to come into his voice. "I believe Suja would tear my testicles from my body."

The Mahdi laughed and his men joined in it. Mei's eyes narrowed over her gag in an unmistakably hostile expression. The tiny man shrugged. "It is possible I could speak with her about the matter."

"You do not seek to make life easy, Mahdi."

"Life is never easy." The Mahdi looked back toward the hut and then at Mei. "But some might call you doubly blessed. Wives to work and domestic tranquillity. What greater blessing could any man ask?"

The Mahdi's eyes were twinkling.

THE SOUNDS OF BATTLE were escalating. Streams of sizzling Indonesian were met by equally insulting Tagalog. Suja's voice kept dropping into an evermore guttural, snarling alto. Marcie Mei's rose into ever shriller shrieking. The reed walls shook.

Bolan sat in the sand beneath his hut basking in his domestic tranquillity.

The entire population of the island stood outside their huts and watched with great interest. A few of the men gave Bolan sympathetic looks. Most simply looked on in great amusement. A few appeared to be laying bets. All kept a prudent distance from Bolan and his double blessing.

The floor of the hut creaked with sudden footfalls, and Mei began screaming in earnest. The thud of blows could be heard all the way down the beach. Mei ran out onto the tiny balcony clutching her head. She flew down the ladder and ran shrieking and weeping into the trees.

Suja stepped out onto the lanai.

The onlookers all suddenly found something else to do.

The woman stood on the porch like a bloodstained valkyrie. Her hair was in wild disarray. She had ripped her stitches, and her shoulder was bleeding through her blouse. She shook as she pointed at Bolan accusingly. "You bring her into my hut? I will not be second wife!"

Bolan ducked as a two-foot length of rattan sailed past his head. Suja stormed back into the hut screaming. Bolan's bedroll flew out a moment later followed by his clothes and his sandals.

Bolan rose and walked through the camp after Mei. No one would meet his eye, though a number of men were grinning. Money exchanged hands.

Bolan followed Mei's trail into the jungle. He found her a few hundred yards in. She had slipped off her tunic and sat by a stream soaking her headcloth in the cool water and applying it to her shoulders. Magnificent welts were rising up across her back in purple stripes.

She looked at Bolan with anger. "Tell me you're not sleeping with her."

"Well…" Bolan shrugged. "Yeah."

"Jesus…" Mei grimaced and shook her head. "You know, I've never taken a beating from anybody outside of a sparring match. She's lucky I didn't kill her."

Bolan knelt beside the CIA field agent. "Don't underestimate her. She's a trained martial artist." Bolan continued, "You did a good job maintaining your cover."

"Cover, hell. I didn't sign up to be second wife to that psycho-whore."

"That's exactly what you're going to be."

Mei glared.

"Listen, no one knew if you'd be able to insert or not. Suja was an in, and she happened. We have to deal with it. You can go places I can't go and listen in on things I can't. If you're in my hut, you can cover for me when I need to go on a recon. For that matter if things go south, no one here knows you earned a marksman's medal or that you know which end of a kris is which. You're my ace in the hole, Marcie, and if that means you have to be second woman in the hut, deal with it. For the time being you are second wife and subject to her every whim. If you can't take it, I'll tell Jusuf to send you away."

Mei flinched. Bolan continued mercilessly. "You're a woman, and they think you're Muslim. There's a good chance they'll just dump you in some city rather than killing you. No shame. No blame. But in or out, Mouse." Bolan locked eyes with her. "I need to know right now."

"In." Mei spit out the word between clenched teeth. "You know I'm in."

"I know." Bolan nodded. "I just need you frosty."

"Frosty, hell." Marcie suddenly grinned. "I am ice cold."

Bolan took the cloth from her, and applied the cool compress to her bruises. She gave Bolan a long look over her shoulder. "She's in love with you, you know."

"I know." Bolan let out a long breath. "You called her a psycho-whore. Just so you know, she was sold into prostitution as a child. By her father."

Mei's smile dimmed.

"She has issues," Bolan said. "Tread lightly."

"All right." Mei paused in thought. "She doesn't hang out with the women, does she?"

"No." Bolan shook his head. "She doesn't."

"Then I'm a meek little second wife. Fresh from the farm, wide-eyed, terrified and obedient." Mei's eyes turned cunning. "And in a week I'll be her closest confidant."

"You're evil."

"I'm not the one sleeping with her." Mei's lips quirked. "And don't get any wild ideas."

"A man can dream." Bolan changed the subject. "What can you tell me?"

"Not much. I went asking for you from island to island, mosque to mosque. I got kidnapped one night in Tapul. I was at sea for about four days. No idea in which direction. Your buddy, The Bear, and I decided that it would be safer to go in without a tracking device and I'd try to make contact once I was settled in. What have you got on your end?"

Bolan kept the narrative short and to the point, culminating with the attack on Kouprey Island. "Then we hit the Megawatti residence."

"Oh, we heard about that." Mei shook her head. "That raised one hell of a shitstorm all over Southeast Asia. The Bear said that had to be you. What else you got?"

"The PRC is here. I had to kill one of their agents, but there's another named Chien Tien. You saw him last night. He shows up and disappears with Jusuf. He knows I killed his partner. Neither he nor Jusuf have that loving feeling for me."

Mei snorted. "I caught the vibe."

"The Chinese aren't in a cooperative mood. I tried to cut a deal, but their orders are to kill anyone who discovers them. My gut feeling is Chien has a communication device somewhere on the island. Other than that, we're waiting on the Mahdi's next move. You got anything else?"

"One thing. While I was on the boat, there were some men being transported in the compartment next to mine. I couldn't see them but I could hear them."

"What were they saying?"

"Don't know. It was in some Indonesian dialect. But they were sick. I could tell."

Bolan's eyebrow rose slightly. "What do you mean?"

"They were coughing. Deep rale, gurgling in the lungs, and they were moaning in pain."

"Anything else?"

"Yeah, last night, about a half hour before I was rug-rolled and delivered to you, they were disembarked. I heard them being carried out."

Bolan's instincts began running red flags left and right. "Half an hour?"

"Yeah, and then we motored away," Marcie said.

"You think they were dropped on a different island?"

"I'm positive, and then it took about ten minutes to come here."

"There must be another island close by." Bolan considered the situation. "The other Chinese agent said something about lepers before he died."

"Lepers? What did he say?"

"Nothing." Bolan frowned. "Just the word. Then he died."

"Well, the guys in the next compartment were coughing, gurgling and moaning." Mei pursed her lips. "From what I know, lepers don't feel much pain, but wet leprosy can go into the lungs. If you can't breathe, you'll wheeze and moan."

Bolan had only been to the other side of the island accompanied by an armed escort to see the Madhi. He had been told not to stray from the village without permission. "Why is the Mahdi transporting lepers?"

"Christian charity?" Mei suggested.

"Yaqoob was dying, but he thought it was important enough to mention. There has to be some kind of connection."

"Dunno." Mei shrugged. "You're the international man of mystery. What do you think?"

Bolan took a deep breath. "I think I'm going to have to go for a swim."

17

Bolan arose.

Mei sighed. "You're going?"

"It's time." He glanced down at his "bride." Mei's transformation had been incredible. She had gone from special operations dynamo to a meek and silent mouse of a second wife. She flinched at Suja's every gesture and obeyed her every command. In all ways both overt and subtle, she acknowledged Suja as the alpha female of the hut and of the island. Mei was an accomplished paramilitary soldier, but her primary training had been as a field agent. Blending into Southeast Asian cultures and being accepted by the locals was her stock-in-trade.

As predicted, within the week Bolan had come into the hut and found Mei grooming Suja's hair and found himself being shooed away as they indulged girl talk.

The Mahdi had spoken to Suja, telling her that Mei was Bolan's sister-in-law, alone and destitute. Grudgingly, Suja had accepted the woman into her hut. Marriage in the society the Mahdi had forged was a simple matter. The woman moved in and went to work cooking and cleaning and working in the gardens. Suja had magnanimously gone on an off-island errand and left Mei and Bolan alone for forty-eight hours.

It was past ten and time for Bolan to take a swim.

The first day of their honeymoon he had taken Mei to the other side of the island. They had been given permission, but Bolan knew they were being followed so they had spent the day frolicking in the surf. He had also taken a riflescope filched from the armory and surveyed the nearby island and taken a bearing on it with a stolen lensatic compass. The island was a green lump of vegetation in the reticule of the Chinese sniper scope.

Mei read Bolan's mind.

"Five miles, possibly more." She took an AK-47 bayonet from beneath her pillow and began darkening the chromed blade with lamp black. "Across open ocean and at night. You sure this is a good idea?"

"It's ten o'clock now." Bolan strapped on a watch. His own diving watch and everything else he owned save his sword had disappeared on his capture. He had convinced Jusuf to get him a watch for the purpose of timing attacks. The cheap plastic watch was marked a suspicious "water resistant," but it did have the benefit of a luminous dial. "I'm budgeting myself three hours there and three back."

"Three hours?" Mei sheathed the blackened knife and strung it on a leather cord. "But you have no idea what the currents are like."

"Nope." Bolan opened a clay jar of goat grease Mei had been collecting for him and began lubing up. Channel swimmers used a combination of lanolin and vaseline, but those were in short supply on the island.

The CIA agent wrinkled her nose at the rancid smell. "The sharks are going to love you."

"Grease my back."

Marcie greased Bolan's back. "Better hope there's no dogs on that island."

Bolan turned. "You have anything positive to say?"

"Yeah." Mei took in Bolan's shaggy hair and beard and his tanned body sheened with goat grease. "You look biblically sexy."

"Thanks." Bolan hung the sheathed bayonet and the compass around his neck. He stooped and kissed his second wife on the cheek. "Gotta go to work, hon."

He took his bundled clothes and cobbled together pistol and

crept onto the darkened porch. No one appeared to be watching. He slipped to the edge and lowered himself into the shadows beneath the hut. He crept along the water's edge until the lights of the village were a glow in the distance and then broke into a jog. The island was small, and it didn't take long to reach the other side. Bolan found the campfire he had made during his frolic with Mei on the beach and took a reading with the compass. He hid his bundle just inside the tree line and returned to the beach. The night was clear and brilliant with stars and a quarter moon to light the way.

Bolan stepped into the sea.

The water was lukewarm, but Bolan knew that would change as he got out into open sea. He pushed off, and his greased body slid into the water. It was a hot, still night, and the water was thankfully as smooth as a blanket. Bolan stretched out into a strong, distance-eating pace.

Bolan almost instantly went into the zone. His body went into autopilot and left his mind a detached observer. Bolan moved at a sixty strokes per minute pace you could set a watch by. Every thousand strokes Bolan would roll onto his back, breaking his pace to take a bearing with the compass. He had to allow for corrections if the current or tides pushed him off course, and he still had to show up on the other island in shape to run his reconnaissance and swim back.

Bolan rolled onto his back, kicking with his legs as he clicked open the compass. The glowing green needle hadn't deviated a hair. He was moving in a razor straight line. His body felt good. He checked his watch. He was making good time. Bolan gazed up at the silvery river of the Milky Way. It ribboned across the sky in a line directly toward his objective. He turned onto his stomach and his body instantly resumed the pace he had predetermined for it.

A lot of distance swimmers eschewed the night. With the darkness, awareness of the vastness and the primeval fear of the things that lurked between the swimmer and the bottom of the sea were heightened.

Bolan was not a professional distance swimmer. He was a soldier.

The night was his friend. The sea was his friend as well, though a treacherous one. Night insertions by sea were not new to him. He was naked and exuding the taste and smell of roasted goat into the water, but life was a gamble, the mission necessary and Bolan had rolled the dice. If something rose from the black depths he would never see it coming, but if that predator failed to take him with the first strike, then it would find it had run into another who dwelt at the top of the food chain. An Executioner armed with six inches of sharpened steel. Bolan had dismissed the issue the moment he had entered the water. He had no time to worry about the local ocean inhabitants. Until it happened it was a nonissue. Bolan had an objective and a pace to set.

Bolan rolled over with his ten-thousandth stroke. He checked his watch and his compass. The compass said he was still dead-on. His watch told him he had been in the water for two hours and twenty-five minutes. Bolan rolled over again and trod water. He scanned the horizon ahead. Under the starlit sky, his island objective was a vast black lump. Five hundred more strokes found Bolan with sand beneath his feet.

The Executioner came out of the surf, steel in hand, a half hour ahead of schedule.

Bolan broke into a slow jog around the island. It was much smaller than its sister across the strait, and it took him only twenty minutes to circle it. There was no pier, no boats and no signs of habitation on the coast. If people were living there, they weren't advertising it. As Bolan circled around the far side, he found a path and could see light through the trees.

Bolan crept into the interior.

He halted as he came to a village. It was encircled by a ten-foot bamboo stockade, the tips slashed at the top to make razor-sharp points. Bolan circled the village. There was only one gate in and out. He foraged around the perimeter and found no signs of gardening or agriculture, and on the coast there was no sign of any fishing going on. He concluded the village had to receive supplies from the outside, and for the majority of the inhabitants it seemed coming to the island was a one-way ticket. The freshly dug graves Bolan came upon behind the village were proof of their final destination. He came back full circle and crouched in the trees, peering at the gate.

It was a one-way ticket onto the island, save for the men with automatic rifles.

The Executioner had never heard of a leper colony that required armed guards. A very bored-looking Asian man in black pyjamas squatted against the gatepost. An assault rifle leaned next to him. The guard seemed to be devoting all of his concentration to the act of smoking a cigarette.

The state of alert on the island was not high.

Bolan moved back into the trees. He knelt by a pond he'd passed and smeared himself head to foot with mud. He returned and froze near the gate. The guard was still at his post, but he was gazing upward and talking to an Asian woman wearing a nun's habit.

The woman held her fists clasped before her and shook them pleadingly. The guard blew smoke and shook his head. Whatever the nun wanted, the answer was no. The guard offered her a consolation cigarette. The nun clasped her hands again and the guard reluctantly gave up his entire pack.

The nun disappeared inside the compound, and a moment later the guard followed her. It became very clear to Bolan that the function of the palisade was to keep people in, not out. He crept to the fence and peered through the cracks between the bamboo. There were three long houses made of bamboo and thatch and two ex-military wall tents. Two dilapidated prefabricated sheds stood off in a corner next to a plastic latrine that looked like it had been stolen from a construction site. Off in a corner, a generator sat beneath a thatch lean-to, sputtering and occasionally hiccupping. Two smaller, traditional circular huts had been erected behind the tents.

Bolan slipped through the undefended gate and entered the compound.

He stayed in the shadows, making his way toward the long huts. They had no windows, and he could see no light coming out from between the reeds forming the walls. Bolan could hear and smell, however, and he heard the moans and gurgles of dying men and could smell human waste and death. Bolan moved quickly to the other hut. Light shone from inside, but he could make out little through the tightly woven reeds. He listened to the sounds of suffering for long moments. He heard no conversation.

Bolan slipped through the hut's single door.

Nineteen Asian men lay shoulder to shoulder on reed mats. They were as skeletal and pale as concentration camp victims. Lesions covered their exposed skin, and the skin that wasn't open was mottled and discolored. Some of the men dribbled blood from the nose and mouth. Bolan knelt beside the closest man and looked at him beneath the light of the bare bulb above.

The man moaned, his eyes rolling in his tortured rest as Bolan looked in his mouth. His gums were inflamed and bleeding. Open sores dotted the corners of his mouth and eyes. Bolan pulled off the cotton cap the man wore and found only a few straggling patches of hair on the man's mottled scalp.

Bolan had seen the ravages of untreated wet leprosy before. It was horrible to behold.

This wasn't it.

These men were ghostly and skeletal from the advanced anemia that was plummeting their red blood cell count. The lesions on their skin were not the creeping necrosis of leprosy. They were slow-motion burns. Their mottled skin was due to the massive breakdown of the small blood vessels beneath the skin. An ugly chill ran down Bolan's spine.

Bolan rose and plastered himself beside the door as he heard footsteps outside.

The woman in the nun's habit came into the hut bearing a bucket of water and a basket of sponges. She knelt beside the first man and began to undress him. He moaned and opened his eyes but managed a smile for the nun. She put a cigarette between his ravaged lips and lit it. The dying man coughed and drew on the cigarette with an immense sigh as the nun began cleaning his sores and wiping his own waste from his body.

The dying man turned his head slightly and his red-rimmed eyes locked with Bolan's. The Executioner rolled his eyes as the man raised a palsied hand and pointed an accusing finger at him.

The nun turned. Her eyes went wide as she saw the naked, knife-armed mudman beside the door. Her mouth opened, and Bolan raised the lamp-blackened blade in his hand. The nun closed her mouth and continued to regard Bolan in horror.

"Sister." Bolan spoke low. "Do you speak English? Answer quietly."

"Yes. I was educated at Catholic school in Manila."

"Who are you?"

"Sister Hildegard."

"What are you doing here?"

"You're an American?"

"What are you doing here?" Bolan repeated.

Sister Hildegard looked around the hut. The men were asleep. The man she was tending to had sagged back into unconsciousness, and she took the cigarette from his mouth. "Sister Mary-Margaret and I were kidnapped from our mission in Mindanao."

"When?"

"About two weeks ago. We were put to work caring for the men in this camp."

"You realize these men aren't lepers."

"I don't know much about it. I had barely begun my medical training, but Sister Mary-Margaret said the same thing. She said these men are sick with something but—"

"Sister, these men are dying of acute radiation sickness."

Sister Hildegard's jaw fell open.

"Is there any work going on here on this island? Is there another camp where men are laboring?"

"No, the victims and supplies are dropped off by boat."

"How many guards are there?"

"Four."

"Where's the one who gave you cigarettes?"

"Felipe was getting off duty. He is kind, but the next on duty will be Yam. He, he is…" Sister Hildegard shuddered and cast her eyes down as she flushed with shame and despair.

It wasn't hard to imagine what a bored fanatic might do with a nun late in the night. Bolan grimaced. He was being forced to make a hard choice. "Listen, I can't rescue you right now."

Sister Hildegard gazed up at Bolan despairingly.

Bolan shook his head. "I'm undercover. I swam here from the island across the strait, and I can't carry you back with me. I don't have a radio, but I promise you, I will tell people you're here. For the moment, you never saw me. Don't even tell Sister Mary-Margaret. Do you understand?"

The nun looked heartbroken, but she nodded. "I understand."

"I will—"

Bolan moved against the wall again as a voice called from outside.

"Little Bird!" The man laughed unpleasantly. "Little Bird, are you there?"

A short, broad-shouldered man in khaki shorts and a black tunic came into the hospital hut. He held a dagger in his hand and leered down at the kneeling nun. "Forget the dying, little one. I want you to bathe me."

Sister Hildegard cast down her eyes in shame as she reached for the bucket and sponge. Yam grinned as he unbuckled his shorts. "You don't need those, Little Bird. Just use your—"

"Hey, Yam."

Yam started, half turning but lunging instinctively with his knife.

The Executioner shoved the blackened bayonet into Yam's gaping mouth.

Bolan let Yam fall facedown to the floor.

Sister Hildegard gasped, about to scream.

Bolan's hand clamped over her mouth. His blue eyes bored into hers and commanded her attention. "Wait one minute. Then start screaming. When Felipe and the other guard come, tell them Yam came in complaining about abdominal pain. Say he suddenly started throwing up blood. Do you understand, Sister? Nod if you do."

Sister Hildegard's eyes were still wide above Bolan's hand, but she nodded. Bolan released her. "One minute."

The Executioner moved toward the door. He glanced around the camp and then slipped back behind the hut. A few minutes later Sister Hildegard began screaming hysterically. The dying men in the hut began moaning and shouting weakly in response.

Felipe and two other men with automatic rifles burst from one of the tents. Felipe shouted at one of the men, who stopped, his rifle at the ready, scanning the compound. Felipe and the other man ran into the long hut. Rapid conversations in Tagalog followed.

The Executioner watched the tent intently. If there was a radio inside, this would be a golden opportunity. A portly woman in a nun's habit came out of one of the little huts. Felipe stepped out and shouted at her to come. The guard outside went back into the tent.

Bolan turned away. The exposure was too great. If he was going to go for the radio, he would have to kill all the guards. He didn't have the time to stalk them individually, and if Bolan were running the operation he would keep the hidden island incommunicado.

Bolan crept to the gate and disappeared into the night.

He had a long swim ahead of him.

18

Bolan dragged himself out of the surf. He'd taken too long. The tides had turned during the late hours of the night and churned the strait between the two islands into a caldron. Swells had risen up around Bolan, enfolding him like a matador's cape, and then fallen out from under him. He'd been forced to claw his way out of those sinkholes of the sea. The battle had sapped his energy, destroying his rhythm, and invariably his efforts took him off course. He'd spent one-third of the swim making corrections rather than forward progress. The mud he'd used for camouflage had sluiced off in the sea and had taken the insulating goat grease with it. Bolan was chilled to the bone and two hours behind schedule.

Dawn was rising behind him.

Bolan jogged around the island. The sun had not quite risen, so the village lay in a purple gloom. He reached the village as orange light began to spear across the tops of the trees. Bolan crept from fishing boat to fishing boat as he made for the hut.

The village was coming awake. The roosters were crowing and strutting between the inland huts. In moments, the timer on the village boom box would go off and the Call to Prayer would echo in haunting song against the backdrop of the morning surf. All would come from their huts, unroll their prayer rugs and face Mecca.

Jusuf, Raul, Chien and Pedoy came walking out of the trees. They were not looking his way, but it was a matter of split seconds and Bolan was naked and armed. The Executioner hurled his roll of clothing. The knife and pistol within gave the bundle weight, and it flew in a perfect spiral onto the porch of his hut.

Bolan threw himself into the sea with a splash.

He kicked outward underwater for a few moments. In his fatigue, he had forgotten to remove the compass tied around his neck. Bolan closed his hand around the brass compass and snapped the leather cord. He abandoned the piece to the sea and rose in the waist-high surf.

Jusuf and the others had walked down to the beach to investigate the noise. They stared as Bolan shook water from his hair and beard.

Bolan nodded at them wearily.

Jusuf observed him critically. "You look tired."

Bolan looked up toward the hut and grinned. "I'm exhausted."

Pedoy and Raul laughed. Even Jusuf smirked. "You should go up and dress. It is almost time for morning prayer."

"Yes, Jusuf," Bolan said and clambered up the ladder to his hut.

"Suja will be back tonight. There are bets about whether there shall be anything left of you tomorrow," Raul said, laughing.

Bolan shook his head as the locker room jokes began to fly. He kicked his bundle into the hut and flopped down on the sleeping mat.

"You're late." Mei rolled over and draped an arm across his chest. "How're the lepers?"

"They've got terminal radiation poisoning."

"Jesus…" Mei sat up. "Are you sure?"

"They have every symptom." Bolan shook his head as he thought about the dying wretches in the hut. "They've been exposed to radioactive material without proper shielding or decontamination procedures."

"How?"

"By the way they were gurgling and coughing, I'd say they'd breathed radioactive dust into their lungs," Bolan said.

"Radioactive dust? I still don't see how."

"My bet is they were handling reactor rods. I doubt they'd have the proper tools to open the rod casings, so they probably had to cut them open. Openly handling the rods would be lethal, but if the rods were spent they'd be shedding radioactive particles, as well, and shedding more as the casings were hacked open. Breathing in the dust sped up the process."

Mei grew very quiet. "You're saying they were manufacturing dirty bombs."

"They were doing the grunt work," Bolan said. "If you're packing nuclear material among explosives, you want the rods out of their casings so they blast apart completely and the radioactive material spreads and can contaminate as wide an area as possible. But I bet those men had no idea what they were working with, and no one bothered to tell them."

"Martyrs to the cause," Mei said.

"Jihadists these days don't seem to have many qualms about martyring people without their consent."

"But where? Where the hell did the Mahdi get nuclear reactor rods? I mean, his men are dangerous, but they're yahoos, hopped up on hash and swinging machetes. If they had assaulted a nuclear facility, the whole world would know about it, and for that matter, I doubt they would have the connections to buy the stuff."

"Five miles across the strait, there's twenty guys doing everything except glowing in the dark." Bolan's jaw set. "I have to get to a communication out."

"I've been over every inch of the camp in the last week doing women's work. If there's a radio, cell phone or computer in the village, I haven't seen it."

"Jusuf has one," Bolan said. "Either a radio or a cell phone he keeps on his person. I can't swear to it, but I believe Chien Tien has a transmitter of some kind hidden on the island. The PRC wouldn't send in infiltrators incommunicado. Not their style."

"So what are you going to do?"

"If the Mahdi is building dirty bombs, then we're running out of time."

"Yeah, and…?"

"And I'm going to have to take either Jusuf's or Chien's com gear and get a message out."

"That should be interesting."

"Hitting Jusuf would raise too many questions." Bolan unrolled his clothing and hid the Tokarev automatic pistol and the bayonet as he considered the task at hand. "Chien's our best bet."

"You pulled that win over Yaqoob right out of your ass. What are you going to do to get over on Chien?"

Bolan heard the sound of the call. "Pray."

BOLAN WATCHED CHIEN. The Executioner had finished his morning markmanship lesson. During the past week, he'd been training the Mahdi's chosen men in ones and twos. Bolan lay in the hammock he'd strung in the shade beneath his hut. A wide straw hat was pulled down low over his eyes.

From beneath the rim Bolan watched Chien's every move in camp.

Chien rose from where he was talking with Raul and began walking inland. Bolan rolled out of his hammock and took an oblique path through the village to follow. Chien walked between a pair of huts and disappeared. Bolan walked on unconcernedly to where Mei sat in a circle of women weaving and mending baskets. She smiled up at Bolan. Her eyes flicked toward the trees.

Bolan moved inland.

He followed the path that bisected the island. Bolan had spent some time in camp noting the pattern of Chien's sandals. In the soft ground and patchy sand of the path, his tracks weren't hard to discern. Bolan drew his pistol as he found the spot where Chien had diverged from the path and gone into the jungle.

The Executioner began stalking his prey, following the footprints, occasional crushed plant or broken stem. At the same time, he looked for trip wires or obviously set telltales. One hundred yards in, he stopped and crouched at the fringe of a tiny clearing.

Chien Tien squatted on his heels at the base of a palm tree. He had unearthed an aluminum case and appeared to be plugging it into the tree. Bolan looked closer and saw the squiggle of a line of dried sap running up the tree. The Executioner nodded. Someone would have to know exactly what they were looking for to recognize the line as the disguised antenna wire of a satellite link. Bolan suspected the dish was fixed facing the sky at the top of the tree among the fronds. He moved around behind Chien and silently emerged from the trees. Bolan didn't speak Mandarin, but he knew some phrases and he strung together a sentence with a decent accent.

"Good morning, Officer Tien."

Chien's shoulders hunched in surprise. Bolan spoke in English. "Stand up, slowly." Chien slowly stood and turned with his hands up.

"You?" He looked at Bolan in genuine surprise.

"Lose the blade." The Tokarev automatic pistol had no safety, and the hammer was already cocked. Chien looked down the muzzle a moment. He very slowly drew the heavy Chinese dagger from his sash with two fingers and tossed it into the bushes.

"And the gun."

Chien didn't bother to protest. Again with two fingers, he reached into his tunic and withdrew a small automatic pistol whose barrel was shrouded with a sound suppressor. He tossed the pistol in the sand by Bolan's toes, then kept his hands raised.

"I need your transmitter," Bolan said bluntly.

"You killed Yaqoob," Chien said.

"I offered to cooperate with him. He said he had orders to kill anyone who discovered him."

Bolan swiftly gave Chien the bare bones of the encounter, not omitting Yaqoob's offer of bamboo shoots being rammed in personal places. Chien nodded. "I do not doubt your story, and under normal circumstances my orders would be the same."

Bolan's pistol never wavered. "Normal circumstances?"

"Yaqoob is dead. We suspect something much bigger than piracy is going on. I have befriended Jusuf to a degree and like you have been put in positions of responsibility, but neither he nor the Mahdi have revealed their secret to me. I am working alone now. It will take time for my government to insert another agent, and I fear time is running out."

Bolan eyed Chien warily. "You'd be willing to cooperate?"

"Perhaps, conditionally." The Chinese agent looked grim. "Do you know what is going on?"

The Executioner decided to gamble. "The Mahdi is making dirty bombs."

He told Chien the story of his late-night swim and the radiation victims he found at the leper colony.

The Chinese agent's eyes slowly widened. "This is worse than we had feared."

"If we're going to trust each other—" Bolan made a small, meaningful gesture with his pistol "—you're going to have to give me something back. What do you know?"

"It is what I suspect."

"What's that?"

"A month ago, my country lost a freighter in the Malacca Strait. The ship was en route to Pakistan. The cargo manifest said that the freighter was carrying engine and airframe parts for fighter jets the Pakistanis buy from my country."

Bolan's own worst fears were being realized. "But it was loaded with reactor rods for the Pakistani nuclear reactor program."

"The rods were uranium 235," Chien confirmed. "Weapons grade."

Bolan frowned. "The Mahdi wouldn't have the technological wherewithal to make a thermonuclear weapon, but with a boatload of uranium rods and enough high explosive, he could reduce sections of major cities into irradiated ghost towns and leave ten of thousands of people to die the same way the hapless men across the strait are dying."

"As you can understand, this could quite possibly be a source of great embarrassment to my government," Chien responded. "The freighter was lost near the mouth of the Andaman Sea off of the Dreadnought Bank. Naturally, we sent a submarine to investigate, and it confirmed the hulk of the freighter was at the bottom of the sea. It was also highly radioactive and sunk nearly fourteen hundred feet below the surface. Salvage was deemed unfeasible, and letting it become public knowledge was politically unacceptable. The hulk was left to lay until a time it could be disposed of properly."

Bolan continued for him. "Only the ship didn't sink. It was taken by the Mahdi's pirates. They realized what they had and knew your government would come gunning for whoever had stolen it. So they unloaded most of the reactor rods, leaving a few broken containers for the Geiger counters to detect and scuttled the freighter. Your government keeps it quiet out of self interest, and the Mahdi gets his cleansing fire."

"Rustam Megawatti had ties to my government," Chien said. "He was getting unwelcome competition. My original mission was to infiltrate the Mahdi's organization, determine if it had ties to Islamic Jihad, and then vector in strikes to destroy them." Chien shook his head unhappily. "However, given what you have told me, my mission is now much more urgent."

"I need to use your transmitter," Bolan repeated.

"I am prepared to negotiate."

"No negotiation." Bolan put his front sight on the Chinese agent's chest. "I'm using it, right now. Get out of the way."

Chien tensed and then made a visible effort to relax. "Very well. I cannot stop you, but I beg of you. When you are done, let me contact my government."

Bolan considered the deal.

Chien spread his hands imploringly. "If you do this, then I will cooperate with you. Jusuf still does not trust you, but I have his ear. Neither of us knows where the Mahdi is or the location of the uranium. I believe it is most likely the Mahdi will load the uranium into boats filled with explosives and sail them into major Pacific ports. He has enough uranium to strike multiple targets and has undoubtedly kept many of the boats and ships his pirates have taken. It may take coordinated, multinational military action to locate and seize his weapons before he can sail them into their targets and detonate them."

Bolan kept his pistol on Chien. "You get one phone call after I make mine. Everything after that we play by ear."

"Agreed. You will need the codes to access the scrambler."

Bolan nodded. "Show me."

Chien bent toward the transmitter unit and suddenly snapped his wrist back at Bolan, who jerked his head aside. He felt the burn as glittering coins flew past his face, one of them slicing open his cheek. They were Razor Coins, one of the secret "sleeve weapons" of Chinese kung fu. They were a surprise weapon, not so much lethal but designed to take an opponent off balance.

They worked like a charm, and Chien was fast. Incredibly fast.

Chien's foot blurred into a kick. There was no cocking of the knee or setup. The kick just ripped straight-legged upward in one of Shaolin kung fu's "shadowless kicks." It was a technique that took years to master. Only Bolan's own battle-honed reflexes made him snap his head aside and prevented his jaw from being shattered. He still staggered and saw stars as Chien's foot clouted him on the side of the head. In the same heartbeat, Chien's hand chopped into Bolan's forearm before he could pull the trigger. The Executioner's hand spasmed open as his ulnar nerve was crushed and the force of the blow slapped the pistol from his grip. Chien's forearm uppercutted beneath Bolan's jaw in a forearm shiver that lifted the Executioner onto his toes.

Fingers sank into the pressure points of Bolan's already traumatized forearm like an iron claw. Chien's thumb thrust pulverizingly into the inside of the Executioner's elbow, and lightning shot along the nerves from his shoulder to his fingertips. Chien spun and knelt, and Bolan was inexorably drawn with him like the last man out in a game of crack-the-whip.

The Executioner's feet left the ground as he was thrown.

Chien did not release him to go flying into the trees. He retained Bolan's arm in his brutal hold. The big American made no move to resist. It would only serve to get his arm broken or dislocated when he hit. Instead he relaxed and went with the throw. He cartwheeled through the air over Chien's shoulder. The breath blasted out of Bolan's body as he slammed into the sand with bone-jarring force. Nevertheless, he'd managed to draw the AK-47 bayonet from behind his back before he hit.

Chien's free hand opened into a double-spearhand strike aimed at Bolan's eyes.

Bolan thrust the bayonet up defensively and the clip-point blade punched through Chien's palm and diverted the blow. Blood blossomed in a spray as the soldier ripped the knife free. Chien's iron grip on his other arm loosened, and Bolan attacked, slashing Chien's forearm open to the bone.

The enemy agent released his grip.

Bolan slashed at Chien's throat, but he was on his back and slashing backward. Chien jerked back and took a shallow cut across his chest. Bolan hooked his blade behind his adversary's knee to hamstring him.

Chien back-flipped clear of the blow.

Bolan heaved himself to his feet. He held his blade low before him in a knife-fighter's crouch.

Chien ignored Bolan and examined his injuries. He flexed his impaled left hand and grunted as it obeyed and made a fist. He wiggled the fingers of his right. The cut on his forearm was deep and bleeding, but no nerves had been cut. The Chinese agent's arms bent and his hands curled into claws as he dropped into a classic Praying Mantis fighting stance.

Bolan locked eyes with the agent over the point of his bayonet. "What the hell, Chien?"

"The Mahdi shall have his cleansing fire." Chien's eyes blazed. "The Infidel shall be struck down. As shall you be."

Bolan looked into Chien's eyes and saw the fervor of the *juramentado* shining. Bolan's stomach sank. There would be no negotiation. Chien had infiltrated the Mahdi's movement, and he had gone native.

Chien was a double agent for the Mahdi.

"You were feeding Yaqoob false information, keeping him alive to keep track of PRC movements." Bolan stalled for time to let Chien bleed. "You're sending false reports to Beijing."

"Yaqoob was a traitor to the faith and paid for it, struck down by an unbeliever. The old men in Beijing shall be made to pay for what they have done to the faithful in the western provinces." A horrible smile crossed Chien's face. "Hong Kong shall be their forfeit."

Bolan knew Hong Kong, one of the major financial and manufacturing centers of the planet, had nearly seven million people crammed into the city proper.

One couldn't ask for a better target for a dirty bomb.

"But first, Sydney, Honolulu, San Francisco…" The smile of the true believer shone on Chien's face. "And you, Makeen."

Bolan backed up as Chien advanced on him. His right arm hung useless at his side. It would take long precious seconds before Chien lost enough blood to affect his fighting ability, and in that time the Chinese agent could do serious damage. Bolan shifted his grip on his bayonet slightly. A knife throw was a fool's gambit. Worse still for Bolan was a left-handed throw.

But fighting one-handed against a martial-arts master of Chien Tien's caliber was simple suicide.

Bolan stepped forward. Chien guessed his intention, but Bolan whipped the bayonet around in a baseball pitcher's windup anyway. Chien instantly raised his arms to block his face and chest. His left leg lifted, his knee and calf protecting his abdomen and groin. Chien would accept a flesh wound to one of his limbs from the flying blade and then finish his opponent. Bolan closed and threw. At three feet, there was no time for the knife to revolve.

Bolan hurled the knife by the handle straight at the ground.

The six-inch blade sank like a lawn dart through the top of Chien's sandaled foot.

For an instant Chien wavered in his stance. He blinked in shock at the bayonet impaling his foot to the hilt. In that eye blink, Bolan's fist streaked between Chien's crossed hands and crashed into his throat.

Chien's trachea crunched beneath Bolan's knuckles.

Chien grabbed Bolan's arm before he could retract it. The agent's fingers dug into his opponent's arm, but he no longer had the strength to apply his paralyzing mantis-claw technique. Blood flecked his lips as he gagged and gobbled to breathe. Chien held Bolan's arm more like a lifeline to this world as his face purpled. Bolan ripped his arm free, cocking his hand back and stiffening his fingers to form a blunt ax for the killing blow.

There was no need. Chien fell forward. His face went blue as the broken bits of his voice box strangled him.

Bolan sagged against a palm tree.

His kidneys burned from the impact of the throw he had taken. His right arm hung at his side. He could barely feel it, but bruising rose up beneath his flesh where Chien's fingers had sunk in. Bolan pulled off Chien's head wrap and made himself a sling. Blood dripped from his cheek as he knelt in front of the satellite link. He didn't have much time.

He didn't have the access codes to the link's scrambler either. The keypad was arranged differently than most western com links, and Bolan did not recognize the tiny Chinese characters printed on them. There was no microphone that Bolan could see. Chien had already connected the link to the antenna.

Bolan flicked on the power, and a tiny screen glowed into life. He played with the keyboard a moment, and Chinese characters began appearing in vertical lines on the screen. He didn't know how to tell it what frequencies he wanted or how to put in the recognition codes for Stony Man Farm. Through experimentation, he found the dot and the dash button and the command that would transmit. Bolan began laboriously typing one-handed. He reread his message once and hit the button to transmit.

Bolan was sending a message in unscrambled Morse code across a nonsecure satellite link.

He began playing with the toggle, swinging it in tiny, growing circles as he kept resending the message. At the top of the palm tree Bolan could hear the motor of the tiny satellite dish as it rotated. A satellite link was like a flashlight beam. You had to shine it on the satellite you wanted to use to get your message out. Bolan had no way of knowing the coordinates of any U.S. or allied communications satellites, so all he could do was keep sending the message in wider and wider arcs.

Bolan spent ten minutes transmitting and then reburied the link in the sand. He looked over at Chien's body and considered burying it as well, but he was bruised and bloodied and Chien's disappearance would be suspicious. After a moment, Bolan unburied the transmitter once more and buried the two pistols for later retrieval instead. He groaned as he took Chien's weight across his shoulders and began walking back to the village.

19

Women screamed as Chien's body slumped from Bolan's shoulders. The dead man fell to the sand of the village square. Jusuf pushed his way through the murmuring throng. He took one look at the dead man and drew his pistol. He flicked off the safety as the muzzle came level with Bolan's chest.

Bolan's lip curled in disgust. "He was a spy."

The best lies were always interwoven with truth. Jusuf's finger stayed on the trigger, but the Indonesian would have known that Chien was a double agent and would want to know how Bolan knew. "What do you mean?"

Bolan laid out the facts, lying by omission rather than fabrication. "I killed Yaqoob, and I knew Chien neither liked nor trusted me. I saw Chien walk into the woods alone. I decided he and I needed to speak and settle our differences. I followed him, leaving my sword behind." Bolan spit in disgust. "I found him squatting before a transmitter. I confronted him. He attacked me." Bolan lifted his chin unrepentantly. "I slew him."

Jusuf ran his hawklike gaze over Bolan, taking in the grotesque bruising on his right arm and his flayed cheek. He judged them against Chien's wounded arm and hand. He eyed the long slash across Chien's chest, the bloody hole in his foot and the distorted, broken lump of his throat.

"You had a knife."

"So did he."

Jusuf jerked his head dismissively. "You did not have my permission to kill him."

"He was a spy."

"You did not know that."

"He attacked me." Bolan shrugged. "If I have committed a crime, let the Mahdi judge me."

Jusuf took a step forward. He lifted the muzzle of the Browning Hi-Power to point in Bolan's face. "I have the right to dispense the Mahdi's justice."

"Then let me fetch my sword." Bolan locked eyes with the Indonesian. "And let it be trial by combat."

Jusuf flicked the Browning's safety back on and holstered it. His hand went to the double-pointed saber sheathed at his hip. Bolan had no illusions. On his best day with both arms, Jusuf was the better swordsman. Bolan's luck, speed and some very dirty tricks had gotten him past several warriors he would have stood no chance against in a fair fight.

But there was no such thing as a fair fight.

Bolan looked to Mei where she squatted with the women. Her hand was beneath her sash. Ali stood to one side with his hand on his kris, tense but determined. Several of Bolan's riflemen shifted from one foot to the other, clearly conflicted about what was going on. No one in the throng looked happy.

The fact was Bolan was popular in the camp.

Jusuf looked Bolan up and down and jerked his head in dismissal. "Go to your hut. Rest. Suja returns tonight, and I think you will need it. We will speak of this again."

"Very well." Bolan did need a rest. The numbness in his arm had initially given way to tingling. Now a bone-deep ache was spreading through his arm.

Jusuf turned to Raul. "You and Tak watch his hut. I want him to stay in it while I investigate. Fetch him anything that he requires."

Bolan walked off followed by Raul and Tak. Mei walked past him carrying his sword. He gave her a wink as she passed, but she wasn't smiling. It took all of Bolan's remaining strength to climb the ladder and flop to the floor. He stared at the woven frond ceiling of his hut. He had managed to hurl a message out into space and had nearly been crippled doing it.

The ladder creaked as Mei eventually clambered up. She looked at Bolan's arm in horror and unstoppered a brown bottle. Bolan clenched his teeth as she began rubbing medicated wine into the grotesque bruising. He put his mind elsewhere and told her the story of what had happened.

"So what do we do now?"

"When you get the chance, go into the woods and retrieve the two pistols."

"Okay, and then?" she asked.

Bolan looked back up at the roof. God only knew who—if anyone—had received the message. "We wait and see who comes calling."

Stony Man Farm, Virginia

AARON KURTZMAN NEARLY choked on his coffee. If he'd had the use of his legs, he would have leaped out of his wheelchair. A number of computer screens sat on his desk. One of them was relaying a message. It was from the Australian Secret Intelligence Service. Australia was a staunch ally, and ASIS often worked closely with U.S. intelligence. One of their satellites had received a message. They had relayed the message to the U.S. National Security Agency. Certain codes in the message had sent up red flags that the message should be sent to the Justice Department where Hal Brognola recognized the significance.

The message had been sent over an unsecure channel. Kurtzman stared at the screen. Beneath a series of letters and numbers, terse sentences of translated code scrolled down his screen:

    pirates have stolen chinese reactor rods-break
    pirates manufacturing dirty bombs-break
    pirated ships probable delivery system-break
    probable primary targets ports honolulu sydney san
    francisco hong kong-break

Aaron Kurtzman's stomach sank. "You were right, Striker has been reacquired, Hal," he said.

Kurtzman shook his head as he read the rest of the message. The situation went from bad to really, really bad.

    location nuclear materials unknown-break
    status of weapons unknown-break
    enemy timetable unknown-break
    location mahdi unknown-break
    prc agents in mahdi organization-break
    prc agents dead-break
    this transmitter one shot deal-break
    my current location unknown-break

He clicked a key, and a six-foot flat screen on the wall brought up a geopolitical map of planet Earth. The ASIS satellite knew the exact location of the transmission. Kurtzman typed in the coordinates. The vast archipelago of the Indonesian islands came into brilliant prominence.

Kurtzman sipped coffee and smiled as the location of Bolan's transmitter appeared as a red dot in the Java Sea. "There he is," he said to Brognola.

Brognola's brow furrowed as he scanned Bolan's transmission site. There was no such thing as an unknown island anymore. Satellites had mapped the totality of the Earth's surface in minute detail, and Kurtzman's geopolitical software rivaled the Pentagon's. However, Indonesia consisted of more than seventeen thousand islands, and just because an island was known didn't mean anything was known about it.

Kurtzman scowled at the totality of information on the giant screen.

Geographically, the tiny island was simply a dot with a longitude, latitude and a landmass. Politically, it was simply a number and belonged to Indonesia.

There was no other information.

Brognola hit the intercom. "Barbara, get Calvin and Pol on a plane to Celebes. Have full warloads waiting for them. We need to make contact with Striker. Bear will give you a set of coordinates. I need the NSA to have satellites watching that island 24/7."

"I'm on it," Barbara Price replied.

Kurtzman turned to Brognola. "Hal, he transmitted from the Java Sea but across an unsecure channel. We have no idea who else might have picked up the message besides the Australians."

Brognola nodded. "I need to speak with the President. We have a situation."

Sanya, Hainan Island, China

CAPTAIN HSING-KUNG KAI stood in the colonel's office and stared at the printout in his hand. "You are sure, Colonel?"

Colonel Wan Lai Sin scowled at the captain. Sin was a grizzled pit bull of a man who had made his reputation as a special operations officer before the People's Liberation Army officially had special operations. That reputation had come from tiny, ugly battles that had never made the news or the pages of a history book and had taken place on both the Indian and Vietnamese borders.

Sin was old school, a lurker in the jungle, operating for weeks at a time subsisting on only what he could carry or kill until the time came to strike. Sin was the knife in the dark. The captain was the new school of special-operations commando. Captain Kai was powerfully built and high tech in his methods. He was a door kicker, armed and armored with the very latest technologies. His missions could be counted in hours and minutes. He would strike with overwhelming force and with the resources and technology of the entire PLA backing him up.

Sin sighed. "We know someone sent out a message on Tien's satellite link. The message implies that agents Chien Tien and Yaqoob Mu are dead."

"And the reactor rods?" Captain Kai was appalled. "Can this be confirmed?"

Colonel Sin shook his head wearily. "That is not confirmed. We did indeed lose a load of reactor rods destined for Pakistan, however, we believed they lay at the bottom of the sea. The navy has sent a submarine with combat divers aboard to make a thorough investigation, but it will take some days for them to reach the Andaman Sea."

Kai stood at attention. "What are your orders, Colonel?"

"The transmission was sent from a small island in the Java Sea. We do not believe it was sent by Tien or Mu. We must assume our agents are dead. By its nature, the message implies that there is at least one foreign intelligence agent on the island and he knows of our…dilemma. The reactor rods must be located and reclaimed. A strike team has been assembled, and it is converging on Jakarta as we speak. You, Captain Kai, will lead the strike force against the island. You will capture the leaders of the Muslims on the island. You will find the foreign agent and find out everything he knows. Find the location of this Mahdi and our nuclear materials so that other strike teams on standby can secure them. You and your men are authorized to use any and all methods of interrogation and coercion as well as lethal force against every inhabitant of the island to ensure the success of our mission."

Kai saluted smartly. "I hear and obey your orders, Colonel."

"You will then clean up the island. You will leave no loose ends." Colonel Sin raised an eyebrow. "You understand?"

"I understand your orders, Colonel, and I obey them without question."

20

"Hey sailor, want a date?"

Bolan stopped but didn't look around as the sound of Calvin James's voice came from a shrub at the edge of the forest. "How long have you been on the island?"

"About twenty-four hours," the shrubbery said. "It took about seventeen to acquire you. Once you finally came out of the hut this morning, I've been lurking for a contact opportunity."

"Sorry." Bolan sat down and took his arm out of its sling and began massaging it. To an outside observer, he appeared to be muttering to himself. "I was under house arrest there for a little while."

"House arrest?" James snorted in amusement. "Man, I saw Marcie come out twelve hours ago and then that lanky action tag in. I figured you were busy."

"I was."

"Really? What's Marcie's status?"

"We're married."

"Oh yeah?" James sounded amused. "What's the story on the tall one?"

"We're married, too."

"Damn."

"But Suja's part of the problem, not the solution."

"Suja…" Calvin savored the name. "Man, I wish I had your problems."

The former Navy SEAL medic's voice dropped concernedly. "Your arm looks like dog meat. Anything busted?"

"I don't think so, but one of the Chinese agents pulled some kind of iron claw action on it." Bolan shoved his mottled and swollen limb gingerly back into the sling. "I've been rubbing some home-brew bruise liniment on it, but it is messed up."

"Can't move it? Aches like tetanus?" James listed symptoms. "Feels like it belongs to someone else?"

"For starters."

"Here." The sound of Velcro tore. "I'm going to give you anti-inflammatories and some mild painkillers. Keep using the liniment. I'm also going to give you two syringes of localized hard stuff mixed with B-12 and cortisone. If you decide you have to use that arm, shoot up. It'll move, but you'll regret it later."

Bolan felt a package being shoved against his hip. He ripped it open and swallowed a handful of pills dry. "Thanks, Cal. Where's Pol?"

"About two hundred yards east."

"Where am I?"

"You're on the western edge of the Java Sea, big man."

"What's our status?"

"Find the Mahdi. Find the reactor rods. If we can't stop the floating dirty bombs, we vector in forces that can. As to how we do that, I was hoping you'd have some suggestions."

"Jusuf is the key. He's one of the Mahdi's top dogs."

"The skinny guy? Hawk-faced and walks around like he owns the place?"

"That's the one," said Bolan. "We get a line on him, we get a line on the whole deal."

"Just looking at him, I don't think snatching him is going to be easy."

"It won't," Bolan said, "and Pol isn't going to be able to snap him with the sweetness-and-light routine."

"So I'm going to have to break him." James was quiet a moment. Interrogation was one of his least favorite activities.

"Yeah, but fanatics love to talk. Chien Tien was a trained

PRC agent, and he couldn't help gloating and giving away their possible targets. I think you're clever enough to get something useful out of Jusuf before it comes down to jumper cables and pliers."

"He looks like a bona fide asshole, but I'll give it a try. We have one of the Cowboy's modified Tasers. If you can get Jusuf near the woods, I'll juice him and—" James suddenly started talking to someone else. "Roger that. Contact established."

"What've you got?"

"I got Pol on the line. Satellite recon says we have choppers heading straight toward the island, four of them moving fast and low. They ain't ours."

"I think someone else might've received my message."

Bolan took a syringe out of the medical package and stabbed it into the inside of his elbow. He pushed the plunger and felt the medical magic take place. The cocktail spread through his arm, masking the pain of crushed nerves, broken blood vessels and bruised bones.

The Executioner made a fist with his right hand. His arm felt like it was asleep except that he had complete control over it, like he'd hypnotized someone else's arm and had mental command over it.

"Nice work, Cal. We got an ETA on those choppers?"

James spoke low into his com link. "ETA fifteen minutes."

"I'd say they're Chinese. They're not waiting for dark. They're coming to kick ass and take back what's theirs before it becomes an embarrassment."

"That's the way I got it figured, too. How do you want to play it?"

"You and Pol stay back and stay low. You're our ace in the hole. Take action as you see fit, but try not to get spotted by any of our boys. See if you can take out their scouts."

"Roger that." The shrubbery rustled as James pulled a fade into the jungle.

Bolan broke into a run back across the beach. His voice rose like thunder. "Chosen men! To me!"

Heads jerked up all around the village. Ali and half a dozen of Bolan's riflemen instantly jumped up and ran to his side. Jusuf strode out a hut with his pistol in his hand. He didn't look amused. Bolan saw the saber drawn for the first time. It was a wickedly curved ribbon of blue steel with gleaming twin points. "What is it you think you are doing?" Jusuf demanded.

"I was on the other side of the island. I—"

Jusuf interrupted, "What were you doing on the other—"

"I heard helicopters."

Jusuf's face froze.

"They'll be here any moment. We have to arm, now."

"Raul!" Jusuf snapped his head, and Raul sprinted into the trees. The Indonesian turned back to Bolan. "If this is some kind of trick…"

"We're running out of time."

Jusuf holstered his pistol and raised his saber high. "Everyone! Arm yourselves!"

The Indonesian's hand clamped down on Bolan's injured arm as the rest of the warriors made a beeline for the armory. "Not you, Makeen."

Ali began handing out rifles and bandoliers of loaded magazines. Bolan noted with approval that his chosen men were the first to be armed. They swiftly checked their weapons, loaded them and were the first to come racing back.

"If this is a trick…" Jusuf repeated. He gave Bolan's arm a brutal squeeze. The mottled, swollen bruising turned white as Jusuf's fingers vised down into his flesh. "Your chosen men shall be your firing squad."

Bolan locked eyes with the Indonesian. "Move your hand, or I'll break it."

Jusuf's eyes flared in surprise.

Bolan kept the eye contact. Jusuf had made a mistake. He was too close, and he had holstered his pistol. Jusuf had put himself within grappling distance, and Bolan was pumped full of painkillers. If the twin tips of the saber moved even a hair, he would tackle Jusuf and snap his neck.

If he failed, Jusuf would cut him down.

But the choppers were coming, and Bolan was weary of the Indonesian and his pissing contest.

"I said move your hand."

Jusuf's eyes narrowed with rage. "You—"

"Jusuf!" Raul burst out the trees in full sprint. "Jusuf!"

Jusuf released Bolan's arm and took a prudent step back. His saber rose between them at groin level. "What did you see?"

"Helicopters!" Raul put his hands on his knees and fought for breath. "Four of them!"

"Civilian or military?"

"Civilian! But they are deploying men!"

"And who is coming out of them?"

"Armed men!" Raul gasped. "Dozens of them! In camou-flage! They're coming through the trees! They are moments behind me!"

"Do you have any idea who they are?"

Raul straightened. "Jusuf, I think they are Chinese!"

Jusuf's eyes flicked to Bolan, and a decision was made. "Get a rifle. Lead your men."

CAPTAIN KAI'S MEN moved like shadows through the trees. He had just over a platoon of men. He would have preferred a night attack with combat swimmers deploying from a submarine, but the urgency of the mission had dictated otherwise. They had to take the island as swiftly as possible without the Indonesian government becoming aware of it. Dragon Team consisted of a squad of special-purpose troops, Maritime Special Forces who had been off duty in Jakarta and every available intelligence field agent in the Indonesian islands.

They descended upon the village in a skirmishing line with a squad of men held back as a reserve. They were lightly equipped for speed and surprise. Intelligence reported the enemy was brave but poorly armed and not proficient with what firearms they had, preferring close combat with bladed weapons. Kai's men carried submachine guns, tear-gas and stun grenades.

The islanders would be dead or controlled before they knew what hit them.

"Chow, what do the scouts report?"

Lieutenant Chow put a hand to his earpiece. "Captain, scouts…" Chow's brow furrowed. "Captain, I…I cannot raise the scouts."

Captain Kai held up his fist and his line halted, crouching with their weapons ready.

"Try again."

Chow spoke quietly into his throat mike. "No response, Captain. From either Liu or Shin."

They had found no trace of sentries on the far side of the island. Even in the unlikely event someone had heard the helicopters on the other side, there should have been no time to mount an effective defense.

"Fatt." Kai looked to his sergeant. They had been through thick and thin together throughout Southeast Asia.

Sergeant Fatt crept ahead of the column, moving from cover to cover. He stopped and knelt as he came to some broken reeds. There were boot prints in the sand. He recognized one tread as PRC jungle issue. The other was a foreign pattern. Fatt read the terrain like a book. Shin had been deployed on the right front of the line. Someone had snuck up behind him. There had been a brief struggle. The heel ruts in the sand indicated that Shin had lost, and his body had been dragged away.

Fatt rose to a crouch and scanned the jungle. "Captain Kai—"

The thunder of a high-power rifle cut Fatt's communication short. An immense impact hit him in the chest, lifting him up onto his heels and dropping him back against a tree.

Kai knew the sound of a Dragunov sniper rifle from long experience. The enemy had a sniper in the forest. Initial surprise had been lost. The only course of action was to attack swiftly, overrunning the sentry and overwhelming the village. "Dragon Team!" Kai roared. "Attack! Attack! Attack!"

Attack whistles shrieked up and down the skirmish line, and Dragon Team stormed forward. Their sound-suppressed submachine guns whispered in their hands and shivered the jungle foliage.

The rifle thundered again above the sound of the charge, and Chow staggered and fell, his face going fish-white as the bullet imbedded in his heart and dropped his blood pressure to zero. Kai caught the flash of the rifle in the trees and hurled a stun grenade. "There!" he roared. "The sniper! The sniper!"

Dragon Team loped forward like wolves for the kill.

"Chosen men!" a voice boomed in English. "Fire!"

The stun grenade detonated, but its sound was eclipsed as a line of automatic rifles roared into life point-blank into Dragon Team. Men twisted and fell in the surprise onslaught.

"Fall back!" Kai screamed through his com link. "Fall back and reform!"

"Attack!" the enemy commander roared. "Go! Go! Go!"

The enemy assaulted through the trees. Their rifles fired on full-auto, their fixed bayonets gleamed. The sniper rifle boomed and boomed on rapid semi-automatic above the sound of the smaller caliber automatic rifles. Dragon Team was being slaughtered. "Fall back!" Kai repeated. "Reserve forward and—"

"*Allah Akhbar!*" The war cry thundered in the forest. Men came out of the trees on Kai's left flank. They sprayed pistols and automatic rifles one-handed while they waved shining steel blades in the other.

Kai slammed a fresh magazine into his submachine gun. He hammered down a charging rifleman in front of him and then put a burst through the belly of a man screaming in on his left.

Dragon Team had been sucked in by the sniper's draw, then

counter attacked and flanked. The battle was going hand-to-hand. Captain Kai fired his Type 64 dry and dropped the spent weapon, clawing for his pistol as another rifleman closed on him.

A voice shouted a few yards away. "Ali!"

Kai whirled. His machine pistol cleared the holster on his thigh.

In that split second, Kai caught sight of the figure exploding from cover. He was larger than the men around him by a head. His blue eyes blazed as he lunged holding a Dragunov rifle in a low guard. The Dragunov was the only sniper rifle in the world with a bayonet fitting, and sharpened steel hung from the muzzle. Kai swung his pistol up. He was fast, but his opponent moved with liquid speed.

The bayonet slapped Kai's machine pistol aside and plunged into his throat. Kai dropped his pistol as the blade cut through arteries and severed his ties to this world.

BOLAN CHARGED ACROSS the island followed by his riflemen and a mob of crazed fighters. They ran hot on the heels of a few of the Chinese who had managed to retreat. The Chinese were shot in the sand as they burst out of the trees.

"Helicopters!" Bolan shouted.

Bolan's men opened fire on the aircraft. Two were rising up, and the engines of the other two roared into liftoff power. The islanders boiled out of the trees firing their weapons. The helicopters were civilian aircraft, three Bell-Augustas and a French Dauphin. The massed rifles ripped into their cockpits, spiderwebbing the glass with bullet holes and cracks, and painting the interiors with bloody spray. The mob ran forward, leaping into the open cabins with naked blades and slaughtering anyone still alive.

The Dauphin rose and spun on its axis as bullets poured into it. Smoke bled out of one of its exhausts, but it was a twin-engine aircraft. It dipped its nose over the surf and fled out over the waves chased by the streaming lines of tracers.

Bolan watched the helicopter fade out of range. "Chosen men! Head count!" he called out.

Bolan's riflemen ran to him and assembled. They were twelve. Bolan had started out with over a platoon. Now he barely had a squad. "Spread out," he ordered. "Search for survivors. I want prisoners if there are any left alive."

Jusuf came out of the trees. His pistol was holstered, and he was wiping blood from his saber with a rag of torn Chinese camouflage uniform. Back in the trees, high-pitched screams began issuing from the battlefield. The sound of the women's screaming was matched by the sound of men howling in agony. The women of the village had come for the fallen with their knives.

There weren't going to be any prisoners.

"You have done well," Jusuf conceded. The Indonesian was all too aware that without Bolan and the training he'd given his men the entire island would have been wiped out.

Bolan ignored the compliment. "We have to leave the island and disperse. These are Chinese soldiers. I do not know what the Mahdi has done to anger them, but we have destroyed them. The Chinese will want vengeance. More will come, in overwhelming force."

"You are correct. I have contacted the Mahdi. He agrees. Boats are coming. Meanwhile, we run a sweep of the island, gather everything of value and burn the village."

"Very well. I will give the order to my men."

"Give me your rifle. You are coming with me, now." Jusuf's smile reappeared briefly. "The Mahdi wishes to speak with you."

21

Bolan blinked as Jusuf removed his blindfold. He sensed the speedboat ride had taken about an hour. If the island had been on the western edge of the Java Sea, that told him he was probably on the island of Sumatra. He looked around and found himself in a tiny courtyard. The Madhi sat cross-legged on a blanket by a tinkling fountain. His giant sword bearer stood behind him holding the mighty, cruciform blade. A pair of men Bolan did not recognize stood in the corners of the courtyard armed with submachine guns.

"Ah, Makeen." The Mahdi rose and embraced Bolan warmly. He stood back and looked sympathetically at Bolan's arm, but for a moment the Executioner caught the look of pleasure in the madman's eyes as he gazed at the grotesquely lumped and discolored limb. "Once again, you have exceeded all expectations. You saved many of my followers from death at the hands of infidels."

"I did my duty, Holy One."

"Indeed, and more." He gestured toward a blue-painted wooden gate in the courtyard. "Come, walk with me."

Bolan followed the little man out, and Jusuf and the sword bearer were right behind them. The house was a small, crumbling Spanish-style villa. They followed an overgrown stone path through the trees to a cove. There were no other houses in the cove, and Bolan assumed it was a private estate. Moored at the stone pier was the speedboat they had arrived in. Next to it was one of Rustam Megawatti's pleasure boats taken from Kouprey Island. A shrimper was moored next to the yacht.

Bolan kept the smile off his face.

Beside the fishing boat was his yacht.

Concealed in her hull, he had weapons and communications gear. The tracking device meant that the Farm knew where the boat was. He would only need a few moments alone.

"Your boat is beautiful." The Mahdi turned his gaze lovingly upon Megawatti's giant yacht. "But can you handle a boat such as that?"

Bolan ran his eyes over the Pirate King's floating palace. The gleaming white ship looked to be about forty-five meters and powered by twin diesels. The yacht's clean, aerodynamic racing lines and tinted windows made it look more like a fighter plane than a ship.

Bolan's stomach tightened.

There was nothing clean about the startling number of fish, crabs and seabirds bobbing belly-up against the hull. The shrimper had a similar ring of death around it.

They were deathships.

The cargo they carried hidden in their bellies was lethally radioactive, and piloting any of the craft to a destination of more than a few miles would be a death sentence. So would going aboard his yacht and accessing the gear hidden in the hold. Bolan knew just walking up the pier past them had exposed him to radiation.

There was also another unpleasant possibility to consider. If there were opened reactor rods on board, the ionizing radiation they were giving off was most likely to have fried the electronics of his communications gear and the tracking signal.

It was very likely that he was off the map again.

"Yes," the Executioner answered. "I can pilot such a boat."

"Good, very good."

"Where are my wives, Holy One?"

"Do not worry." The Mahdi's shining smile returned. "They shall meet you soon."

Bolan wondered if the Mahdi meant they would meet him soon in the afterlife.

"Come with me, Makeen." Jusuf started to lift his hand toward Bolan's arm and thought better of it. He smiled, and there was nothing shining or beatific in it. "There is someone I want you to meet."

The Mahdi and his men stayed gazing down at the death fleet while Jusuf led Bolan back up the path. The fields had gone wild, but the land had clearly been part of a small plantation of some kind in the past. They walked to a low clapboard building that had probably once been quarters for servants or workers. Two men with submachine guns stood outside the door. Bolan lifted his nose slightly as he smelled smoke that was harsher than the hand-rolled cigarettes the Mahdi's men usually smoked.

Bolan's battle instincts began ringing the alarms.

They walked into the ramshackle building. A man sat in front of a coffee table in a rattan rocking chair. He was a powerfully built Caucasian, unshaved with shaggy brown hair, dressed in a cheap rayon Hawaiian shirt, khaki shorts and sandals. His nose was broken and there was an obvious knife scar on his chin. A Zastava .357 Magnum revolver was tucked casually into the front of his shorts.

Bolan had been to Bosnia on a number of occasions. He recognized the smell of the cheap, unfiltered Drina cigarette hanging from the man's lip. Jusuf and the two men with submachine guns stood behind Bolan. The man stubbed out his cigarette and rose, smiling.

Jusuf's voice dripped venom. "Makeen, I would like you to meet one of your fellow Bosnians. Dragicevic, this is one of our best men, Makeen Boulus."

The jaws of the trap slammed shut.

Bolan stuck out his hand.

Dragicevic grinned and said something in Bosnian.

Bolan struck instantly.

The Bosnian flew backward. The force of the blow sat him

down violently, and both he and the rocking chair rolled into a backward somersault.

Bolan waited for several long seconds. With each heartbeat, he expected the bullets from the guardsman's guns to come ripping through his back. He slowly turned and glared at Jusuf. "That was foolish."

Jusuf's pistol was aimed at Bolan's face.

Bolan scowled. "I understand you wished to test me, but when you told him to see if I spoke the language, you should not have told him to insult me."

Jusuf's eyes slid to Dragicevic, who was spitting teeth and making a feeble attempt to extricate himself from the broken chair.

Bolan did not speak more than a few phrases of Bosnian he'd picked up on missions, but every soldier knew the choicer insults of any country he visited. Dragicevic had opened up with a modern favorite.

"His words involved a horse, my pregnant sister and my mother's grave." Bolan looked back at the Bosnian as he managed to push himself to a sitting position. "And had I let him finish, my retarded father watching from his wheelchair."

Jusuf looked to Dragicevic again. The Bosnian wiped blood from his chin and nodded ruefully. "It is true."

Bolan knew he had only seconds before the man said something that he wouldn't be able to answer with his fist. He ignored the gun at his head and stepped over to the fallen man. Bolan stuck out his hand to help him up. "Come."

Dragicevic nodded and took Bolan's hand. The pointed guns lowered.

The Executioner heaved the Bosnian up to his feet and then pivoted violently. He hurled the man over his shoulder at Jusuf in a textbook flying mare judo throw.

Jusuf's pistol barked once before Dragicevic and Jusuf violently collided. They fell in a tangle of limbs, taking one of the guardsmen with them. Bolan scooped up the wreckage of the rocking chair and flung it at the standing guard. He instinctively knocked it aside with his weapon, but in that moment the muzzle of his submachine gun was off target.

Bolan grabbed the coffee table and charged with it held before him like a shield. Wood splintered next to Bolan's face as a burst tore through the table. Bolan charged as if he had every intention of going straight through the wall.

The Executioner hit the guardsman like a battering ram.

The guard was crushed between the table and the wall. For a moment his weapon was pinned against him and pointing off to one side. Bolan took a step back and swung the table like giant flyswatter. Between the wall and the slab of teak it was the guardsman's skull that failed.

Bolan flung the cracked table aside and ripped the submachine gun from the dead guardsman's hand.

Jusuf's pistol fired on semiauto from the floor. Dragicevic's Magnum revolver erupted deafeningly. Bolan hurled himself out the window as the other guardsman's submachine gun joined the fray.

The Executioner rolled to his feet, ignoring the glass shards sticking out of his arms and shoulders. He couldn't afford a firefight. His number-one priority was to get out a communication and have the radioactive death fleet seized.

Bolan ran for the trees.

Stony Man Farm, Virginia

"WE'VE LOST HIM." Hal Brognola's jaws worked as he savaged his cold cigar and leaned over Aaron Kurtzman's shoulder.

"We've misplaced him." Kurtzman stared woefully at his screens. He punched a key, and eleven red dots blinked into life in the six-foot close-up geographic image of the Java Sea. Eight of the dots were spread along the coast of Sumatra. Two of the dots were heading northeast toward Borneo. Another was heading south for Java. "As of forty-five minutes ago, we suspected he was on one of those eleven boats that vacated the island."

"What are Calvin and Pol's status?" Brognola asked.

"They have confirmed the island was attacked by PRC forces. Striker led the attack, and it was a complete wipeout except for one helicopter that managed to escape and fly back to Sumatra. Calvin and Pol did an intelligence recon, but there wasn't much. The Mahdi's people burned the village. I have them extracting by submarine within the hour and we'll land them in Sumatra. The CIA station in Jakarta already has a helicopter en route to their location. They'll be hot on the pad waiting for the go signal."

"So we have nothing." Brognola scowled.

"Right now, he's a needle in a haystack. We just don't have a lot of assets in Indonesia except for intelligence gathering operatives. The Australians have SAS units, but they're operating up in the New Guinea highlands along the Indonesian border. Like I said, we have an attack submarine picking up Cal and Pol. Once they've extracted, I want to deploy the sub roughly in the middle of the Java Sea. If we can identify the dirty ships, I believe she has the speed for us to vector her in and intercept. The Navy is deploying the Pacific fleet in a screen between Indonesia and Hawaii. The Australian navy is doing the same along their northern coast." Kurtzman raised an eyebrow at the man from Justice. "I believe we should inform the Chinese that Hong Kong is on the target list."

Brognola nodded. "I'll tell the President."

"Meantime…" Kurtzman leaned back with a sigh. "Striker really needs to make contact."

THE DAILY TROPICAL DELUGE hammered the earth. The rain was as hot as sweat and fell in vertical, bulletlike lines. Bolan eyed the villa.

His hunters were stone-cold killers, and there were more than a dozen of them, but they were not jungle fighters. If he'd had a decent rifle, he could probably have eliminated all of them in the course of a day. Instead, he had a sixty-year-old submachine gun with a single, partially spent stick of ammo. The gun was reliable but only accurate to fifty yards under ideal conditions. To use it to any effect, Bolan would have to get close, too close, and the second the gun spit fire he would announce his location and his pursuers would swarm him in a rush.

Still, Bolan owned the jungle, and he had easily managed to lead his pursuers deep into the jungle and then double back on them.

Bolan slipped back into the bunkhouse and found the guardsman he'd killed still lying on the floor. He stripped him of his four spare magazines and the parang thrust through his sash. Bolan stalked through the rain and fallow rubber trees toward the villa.

"Makeen!"

Bolan froze as Jusuf's voice called out.

"Makeen! I knew you would double back. You must send out a signal. Did you know we are on an island?"

A flare shot into the rain and detonated in a burst of red light. Jusuf was calling back his dogs.

Bolan's blood ran cold as Jusuf stepped out onto the back patio with Ali held before him like a shield. Ali's arms were bound behind his back, and Jusuf held him by the hair. Rain flicked from the points of Jusuf's blade as he tapped the flat of it rhythmically against his calf. "Come, Makeen! Come out, or the traitor dies!"

Bolan gazed at Jusuf's head through his gun's open, fixed iron sights and considered his options. The weapon only fired on full-auto, but a skillful operator who was light on the trigger could snatch off a single shot. There was really only one choice. He would have to get closer. Bolan became one with the mud. He belly-crawled, moving an inch at a time through the foliage.

"Come, Makeen!" Jusuf shouted. "The game is over! Come out!"

Bolan suspected Jusuf's idea of fun and games had only begun.

"Makeen!" Ali shouted. "Do not—"

Jusuf drove a brutal knee into Ali's kidney. Ali grimaced and nearly buckled.

"Makeen?" Jusuf raised his saber and placed it against Ali's back. Rain dripped from the Indonesian's jaw as he grinned like a wolf. "Then let his blood be on your hands."

Ali screamed as Jusuf shoved the blade into his back. The young man fell to his knees, and Jusuf pulled him back up by his hair. Jusuf pushed the blade upward and then twisted his wrist. Ali screamed and screamed as Jusuf shoved the blade through him with surgical precision. The twin tips erupted from the front of Ali's shirt beneath his breastbone.

Bolan kept creeping forward.

Jusuf had expertly twisted the blade through Ali's body, giving him a wound that would take hours, possibly even days to kill him. Ali howled in torment.

"Come, Makeen." The blade turned ever so slightly, eliciting more sounds of agony out of Ali. "How can you let the young man suffer so?

It was the sniper's draw, done only with a saber. Jusuf was waiting for Bolan to expose himself by charging to save Ali or shooting to put him out of his misery.

With every twist of the blade, Ali screamed like the damned in hell.

Jusuf shook his head in mock sadness and let go of Ali's hair. "You lack mercy, Makeen," he called out.

The young man shrieked like an animal as he slid off the blade and collapsed on the tiles. His screams were reduced to horrible groans.

Jusuf held up his saber and watched as the rain washed the blood from his blade. "Were you afraid of hitting your young friend?" The Indonesian stood, arms spread and waiting for Bolan's bullets. "Here I am."

Ali screamed anew as Jusuf kicked him in the wound in his back. Bolan's face was a battle mask. For all his sadism, Jusuf was a true believer. He was willing to die so that Bolan would be exposed and prevented from getting out word.

"You disappoint me, Makeen." Jusuf lowered the saber. "Let us appeal to your romantic side."

Sujatmi Fass stepped out into the rain. She led Marcie Mei onto the patio like a dog, but rather than a leash, one of Suja's iron combat tongs held Mei by the throat. The barbed pincers pricked her flesh and blood ran down her collarbones. Mei stumbled after Fass, choking and weeping with her arms bound. Raul and Dragicevic came after her. The Bosnian grinned through his mashed lips as he pointed his massive revolver at her back.

Half a dozen gunmen stepped out of the villa, not bothering to hide anymore. Three of them were Bolan's own riflemen, including Isah and Pedoy. They were grim-faced as they scanned the jungle. "Makeen!" Pedoy stepped forward with his AK-47 in his good hand and screamed in his broken English. "You lie! You betray us! Makeen!"

Fass released Mei and Jusuf took her by the hair. "Let us end this, Makeen. Come out, and she and Ali die easy. If not…" He placed the tips of the saber against Mei's back.

"Remember the mission!" Mei screamed. "Don't you—"

Her body locked in a rigid arch as Jusuf pushed the tips of his saber an inch into her flesh. She suppressed her scream through sheer will.

Raul laughed unpleasantly. Bolan could hear the hunting party coming in the distance behind him.

"Come out, Makeen!" Pedoy's voice cracked as he shouted.

Bolan looked very hard at the young man. Pedoy was screaming, but his face did not match his voice. His eyes searched, but they did so with a strange desperation. He was waiting, hoping for something to happen. Pedoy looked back a moment and met the eyes of Isah and the other two riflemen. They quietly drew and fixed their bayonets without the order of their commanding officer.

Jusuf drew back his saber for the thrust. "She dies, Makeen!"

The Executioner roared over the sound of the falling rain. "Chosen men!"

Bolan charged.

Pedoy whipped around and shoved his AK-47 at Jusuf's head like a giant pistol. The rifle was awkward, and Pedoy was too slow with his injured collarbone. Jusuf leaped back a step, and his saber moved upward in a vicious slash. Pedoy's rifle fell to the tiles in a spray of blood.

Mei fell to the ground, and Dragicevic pointed his weapon at her head. Fass lunged. The sharpened iron teeth of the tongs dug into the Bosnian's wrist. She yanked, pulling the gun off-line. She twisted her wrist and tore out the arteries and nerves going to Dragicevic's gun hand. The weapon fell as Fass's second pair of tongs closed on his throat. She snarled and yanked the tongs back. Her adversary's esophagus came away with it.

Raul raised his rifle to kill Fass.

Bolan skidded to a halt and raised his gun. The range was still long, so he lowered his aim as he squeezed the trigger. The steel snarled with recoil in the Executioner's hands. The burst shattered Raul from his pelvis to his breastbone, his rifle falling unfired to the ground as he collapsed.

The patio was a point-blank firefight. Bolan's riflemen had the initial surprise, and they shot down the Mahdi's men without mercy. Steel rang as Fass and Jusuf exchanged a blinding flurry of Indonesian *silat* techniques. Bolan took aim at Jusuf. "Suja!" Bolan yelled. "Back off!"

She lunged into Bolan's line of fire.

Her tongs shot for Jusuf's throat in a double thrust. Jusuf parried them aside and thrust his saber into the woman's stomach. It was no careful, surgical probe as he had done to Ali. The twin points sank into Suja up to the hilt. The six-inch razor-sharp notch they formed gathered her guts and severed them in one motion. Her body folded around the blade.

"Suja!"

Jusuf grinned at Bolan over the woman's shoulder as he brutally yanked his sword from her belly and shoved her aside.

Bolan squeezed his trigger and held it down.

Jusuf swayed like a snake. Bolan's bullets ripped stucco

from the wall of the villa. Jusuf dived behind the fountain. The Executioner tracked him, his weapon sending up geysers of water. Jusuf rolled out of sight back into the villa.

Bolan charged forward. The firefight was over. All of the Mahdi's men were dead. Only Isah and a rifleman named Toy were still standing.

"Jusuf!" Bolan roared. "Get—"

A gray metal cylinder the size of a beer can bounced onto the patio. Bolan recognized it. The cylinder was a white-phosphorus grenade.

"Run!" Bolan flung his feet forward into a baseball slide across the wet tile. He caught the grenade and threw it into the fountain. The grenade detonated.

Isah and Toy grabbed Fass and Ali and dragged them toward the jungle. Mei and Pedoy supported each other as they staggered after them.

Water would not stop burning phosphorus, but it was ninety times denser than air, and it would seriously dampen the spread of the molten metal streamers. The stone sides of the fountain would contain a great deal of the blast and funnel it straight up.

Bolan scrambled to his hands and knees as the fountain erupted. Burning white phosphorus and superheated steam shot into the air in a gray column. Bolan sprinted for the jungle as boiling water and burning metal fell to earth.

He knelt beside Fass.

Mei sat beside her desperately trying to plug her wounds with her head scarf. Fass lay in the mud hemorrhaging front and back.

"Jesus…" Mei fought a losing battle. "Her stomach, her intestines, liver, spleen, she's been shredded inside, she's—"

"I know," Bolan answered.

Fass was dying in agony.

Her teeth clenched as she looked up at Bolan. "Jusuf…never trusted you. He contacted Dragicevic days ago, and he had never heard of you. When we left the island, Jusuf had his men take Marcie. Ali tried to protect her, and he was taken, too."

Blood spilled over Fass's lips, and her body locked in a ripple of pain. "I guarded her. She told me what the Mahdi planned. I believe the West must be punished, but to strike their cities…" She grimaced horribly. "I will not be a part of killing children. I went to your riflemen. They said they would follow you if you asked it."

"You did well, Suja." Bolan held her face. "Where will Jusuf go?"

"There is an island, a few miles south of here. That is where the Mahdi is. That is where he will take the boats."

"The boats?"

"Hoja was here on the island with crewmen. You will find the boats…gone."

"Jesus…" Mei wept uncontrollably as they watched Sujatmi die.

"Get a gun." Bolan's voice was as cold as the grave. "They're coming."

Shouts came from the edge of the plantation as the hunting party charged through the trees. Mei ran back to the patio, picking her way past bits of phosphorus and picked up a rifle.

Bolan slammed a fresh magazine into his gun. "Reload, make ready. Set for semiautomatic," he said to his men.

Isah and Toy reloaded their rifles.

"Isah, use the tree to the left. Toy, go right."

The men flanked Bolan to either side and knelt behind cover. Mei took a position a few feet from Bolan by a stump.

The Mahdi's men burst from the trees, spraying weapons and waving blades as they came.

"Fire!" Bolan commanded.

Isah's, Toy's and Marcie's rifles cracked on rapid semiauto, rapidly moving from target to target. Bolan's submachine gun hammered off burst after burst. The range was short and the enemy coming straight in. In seconds, the twelve fanatics were dead or dying.

Bolan reloaded and rose. The rain fell hissing onto bits of

the still burning phosphorus, popping yellow sparks as the burning metal and the rainwater violently reacted. Bolan methodically began searching the bodies.

In Dragicevic's pocket he turned up a cell phone. Bolan flicked the phone open and frowned. The little digital screen showed zero bars of signal strength. He pocketed the phone and kept searching.

Raul had a handheld radio.

Bolan flipped up the antenna. It was probably used for communicating with the boats and the other island. However, if NSA had the area under surveillance, there was a good chance they might pick it up. Bolan tuned to the Farm frequency. "This is Striker. Repeat, this is Striker, over."

Nothing but static came back.

Bolan switched to a different frequency he had memorized. "This is Striker calling *Flawless Victory*. Repeat, Striker calling *Flawless Victory*, come back."

Static popped across the line.

Mei came to the patio. Her arms were covered with blood up to the elbows. "Ali's in a bad way. In this wet and heat, he's going to go septic in a matter of hours."

Ming Jinrong's mellifluous voice spoke loud and clear through the radio receiver. "This is *Flawless Victory*. Tell me, my friend, where are you?"

22

Flawless Victory

"My thanks, Sifu." Bolan covered his right fist with his open left hand and bowed his head slightly in the Shaolin kung fu salute.

Ming beamed. He was clothed head to foot in bloodred velvet trimmed with white lace. "The pleasure is mine, Mr. Cooper."

"My personal doctor is seeing to your young friend, Ali. He has been stabilized and shall live. Your friend Pedoy's hand was badly injured, but he will regain full use of his arm. Marcie's wounds were unpleasant yet superficial and have been tended. How else may I be of assistance?"

"I need your help."

Ming sighed. "You know you have but to ask."

Bolan had made his decision. "Here's the situation. A Muslim extremist group has stolen nuclear reactor rods. They've packed them into stolen ships with high explosive and turned them into floating dirty bombs. I know they have at least three ready." Bolan looked steadily into Ming's eyes. "Hong Kong is one of their targets."

"The Pearl of the Orient." A light came into Ming's eyes. "I shall not allow it."

"I was hoping you'd say that." Bolan pointed off the bow. "There's an island south of here. That's where the Mahdi and the bomb-boats should be. I want to launch an immediate assault."

"Then you will pleased with certain modifications that have been made."

Bolan eyed the big man warily. "Modifications?"

"Fung!" Ming clapped his hands. Fung and three crewmen pulled the bolts from the collapsible container box on the prow, and the sides clanged down. Bolan gazed at the Ontos tank destroyer.

Modifications had been made.

It was freshly painted a bright red, including the six 106-mm recoilless rifles. A .30-caliber Browning medium machine gun had been reinstalled in the commander's cupola. Squares of re-active armor blocks had been bolted across the frontal armor. The most intriguing change was that the Ontos was no longer chalked in place by its road wheels.

The little tank was sitting on treads.

Bolan was grinned. "Tell me we have an engine."

"Oh, indeed." Ming sighed happily at his monstrosity. "She has been brought back to full operating specifications. Except for the color. That was my idea. Do you like it?"

"Very dashing," Bolan said. "How'd you manage it?"

"You couldn't even begin to imagine." Ming leered slightly. "And you might not want to."

Bolan left that one where it lay. "I need a phone."

"Do use mine." Ming handed Bolan a satellite telephone. Bolan punched in the number and codes. He waited a moment as the Farm's computers digested his codes and where the signal was being bounced from. Kurtzman picked up on the first ring.

"Striker!"

Bolan quickly gave Kurtzman his coordinates. "Bear, what assets do we have on hand? All I've got are Ming's crew and two chosen men."

"Chosen men?"

"It's a long story, but we need backup."

"The Australians have a flight of F-111 strike bombers hot

on the tarmac in Darwin. They can be there in an hour and fifteen minutes."

"Not good enough, and we can't afford a bomb hitting any of those boats. If they go up, the prevailing winds will take the radiation cloud to the coast of Sumatra. Have them launch and then track anyone who gets past us. What else have you got?"

"How about Calvin and Pol? Will they do?"

"Where are they?"

"In a helicopter on the coast of Sumatra and not far from your position. "I'll vector them in."

"Good. Ming and I are assaulting in thirty minutes."

The island

MEGAWATTI'S YACHT WAS missing.

Bolan sat in the cupola of the Ontos and scanned the objective with his binoculars. He could see the enemy on the shore. There were dozens of them, and the way they were scurrying around it was plain the enemy had seen *Flawless Victory*, as well. The island was much like the one Bolan had just left, a cove, a beach and a pier. Except rather than a crumbling Spanish-style villa, the manor on this island was built like a medieval fortress with stone walls and a crenellated roof.

The dock was lined with speedboats and fishing trawlers. Bolan's yacht and the shrimper were there, but an open berth gaped where Rustam Megawatti's motor yacht should have been.

Bolan spoke into his radio. "One got away, Ming."

"One is missing. It shall be found," Ming said from the bridge. "In the meantime, let us give them a volley."

Bolan trained his recoilless rifles on the manor. Given its apparent age, the walls actually had been designed to stop the iron cannonballs of eighteenth-century pirates.

The long dead architect had not envisioned 106 mm high-explosive shells.

Bolan fired his spotting rifles, and the two .50-caliber tracers streaked across the water and hit the wall in a spray of dust and stone chips. "Ming! Tell your men to clear the decks."

Ming's men slid down the ladders below deck or ran behind the bridge.

"Clear!" Ming called.

Bolan pumped the electrical trigger. "Firing One! Firing Two! Firing Three! Firing Four!" The four recoilless rifles belched fire from both ends in rapid succession. A ten-foot section of the wall erupted in shattered rock and flashing orange fire.

"Firing Five! Firing Six!" Bolan hit his trigger, and two rounds streaked through the gap in the wall and impacted the manor. "Hsuan! Chang! Reload!"

Fung's loading team leapt out of the back hatch bearing fresh rounds for the rifles. A pair of ragged black holes oozed smoke from the second floor of the manor, and fires flickered and burned within. Armed men were spilling out of the building like ants from a broken nest. Fung's team slid fresh shells into the breaches of the rifles and slammed them shut. Hsuan and Chang slapped the sides of the Ontos to signal the rifles were loaded and leapt back through the hatch.

Bolan flipped his selector switch and fired all six guns at once.

The six high-explosive shells hit the manor in a single, simultaneous explosion. The entire front of the manor vanished in black smoke and fire.

"Magnificent," Ming said.

Fire rose into the sky. The front third of the manor collapsed in a landslide of rock and rubble.

Bolan shouted down into the hull. "Fung, tell them to reload One, Two and Three with beehive, Four through Six HE!"

Fung shouted in Mandarin, and Hsuan and Chang leaped out again to swing open the red-hot rifle breeches and reload. The Mahdi's men swarmed toward the pier.

Bolan fired his spotting rifles and the tracers ripped wood from the dock. "Firing One! Firing Two! Firing Three!"

The pier collapsed in ruptured pilings and shattered planks. Smoldering speedboats drifted away from the carnage of the decimated dock. A blackened fishing trawler began burning in earnest and joined the drifting fleet. The other end of the pier remained standing. Bolan's yacht and the shrimper lay at dock untouched. He couldn't afford to lob explosive shells in their direction. The Madhi's men swarmed toward the death ships armed with rifles and RPG-7 antitank rockets. Bolan traversed his guns and pumped the trigger. "Firing Four! Firing Five! Firing Six!"

Three hundred steel needles expanded out of the muzzles at over twice the speed of sound. The mob rippled like wheat as the invisible clouds of fléchettes passed through them like a deadly wind.

"Fung! All six HE!"

Fung gave the order, and his men responded quickly. The pier was littered with bodies. The mob was falling back on the manor.

"Ming! We need to secure those boats, storm the manor and find out where the other ship went!"

"My men are ready."

"The pier isn't big enough for *Flawless Victory.*"

"Then we shall make an amphibious landing."

Ming was going to run them aground.

Bolan could feel the throb of *Flawless Victory*'s engines as Ming took her to full steam. "Fung! Get Chang and Hsuan inside and button up!"

The little engineer snarled at his men. The burning fishing trawler snapped in two beneath *Flawless Victory*'s prow as the freighter surged forward like a juggernaut.

Ming spoke happily across the radio, "Brace for impact."

The Ontos lurched on its steel pallet as *Flawless Victory* rammed sand. The hull groaned and steel screeched as the freighter ran aground. The freighter creaked and with a horrible moan began to tilt to starboard. Bolan's stomach dropped, and Hsuan and Chang screamed as the Ontos and its pallet slid six feet across the deck.

Rifle and machine-gun fire began slamming into *Flawless Victory* from the manor.

Ming's men ran onto the deck. Some hurled cargo nets over the side, while others returned fire. The freighter's crane swung around, and a squad of men ran to attach the Ontos's pallet cables to the massive hook. One of the men pounded his fist on the hull and gave Bolan the thumbs-up before jumping away and grabbing a rifle.

"Winching," Ming announced. The cables went tight. Bolan's stomach lurched again as the tank lifted up off the deck and swung out over the surf. "Lowering."

"Brace yourself!" Bolan shouted to his crew.

Fung grabbed his steering wheel. Hsuan and Chang grabbed each other. The Ontos rocked on its tracks as the pallet hit the soft sand. Water splashed up into the open cupola. The Ontos was in four feet of surf.

"Hit it!" Bolan commanded.

The engine roared like a beast as Fung hit the ignition button. The Ontos slid as her tracks tried to grip the wet steel of the pallet. The tank slewed about sideways, and the chassis rocked as her treads suddenly bit into sand. Fung turned the wheel, and the tank crawled toward shore. Ming's men swarmed down the cargo netting and jumped into the surf. They held their rifles over their heads as they waded forward and followed the tank onto the beach.

It was D-day on Mahdi Island.

Bolan shouted into his radio over the sound of gunfire. "Ming! Tell your men to clear the back of the tank!"

Ming stood on the prow of his grounded ship with Mei and Du by his side and shouted through a megaphone. His men naturally clustered behind the tank to put its metal hull between themselves and the incoming fire, but all of them had seen the back blast of the recoilless rifles firing, and they didn't have to be told to clear the area twice. They fanned out to either side at Ming's order.

The Ontos clanked up onto the beach, and Bolan swiveled his guns onto the manor. "Firing One! Firing Two!"

The rest of the manor's front wall crumbled under the onslaught. Bolan raised his aim slightly. He flipped his selector switch and hit the burning manor with all four barrels at once.

Ming strode out of the surf with Mei and Du beside him. He raised his sword high as he shouted through the megaphone. "Fix bayonets!"

The hard end of forty M-16 rifles rattled as cold steel was fixed. "Charge!"

Ming's men answered with shouts of their own. They followed their master's sword and charged the burning manor with their rifles blazing. Bolan fired long bursts from the commander's machine gun to cover the attack. "Fung! One through Four beehive! Five and Six HE!"

Hsuan and Chang jumped out. The Ontos's Achilles' heel was that the guns had to be reloaded from outside the vehicle. Sporadic gunfire answered back from the manor and the surrounding grounds. The single tank on the beach attracted their attention like a magnet.

Hsuan screamed as a bullet struck him. He spun from the half-loaded guns and fell as he was hit again. Chang slammed his last breech shut and slapped the side of the hull before running to finish Hsuan's loading. Bolan spied Isah and Pedoy on the left flank of the tank. They knelt and fired their rifles to cover Ming's advance. "Chosen men! To me!"

Bolan's remaining two riflemen jumped up and ran to the tank. "Isah! Pedoy! Watch what Chang does! Do it!"

Chang didn't speak English, but loading the recoilless rifles was mechanically very simple. Doing it with incoming fire sparking off the hull was what took a steady hand. Isah and Pedoy slung their rifles and watched Chang reload with utmost concentration. The last rifle breech slammed shut on a loaded round. "Get in!"

The three-man loading team jammed themselves into the

cramped hull as the Ontos began crawling forward. The hull of tank rattled and pinged with bullet strikes. Bolan traversed his rifles, giving any enemy strong point a barrel. "Reload! All beehive!"

Chang, Isah and Pedoy leaped out.

The Mahdi's remaining men rose from their positions in the rubble. The Mahdi had summoned the faithful to the island, and whoever was in command had kept a reserve in the bowels of the manor. Even with all the casualties, well over a hundred men rose with guns and blades to take the fight hand-to-hand.

"Fung!" Bolan shouted. "Forward!"

The Ontos's rifle was empty, but Bolan held down the trigger of the Browning .30 and fired into the advancing horde. Fung ground the gears, and the Ontos pushed on. Bullets screamed off the hull of the tank. Ming's men stood their ground and shot as the mob roared forward. It wasn't going to be enough.

They were going to be overrun.

"Sarge," Jack Grimaldi said suddenly in Bolan's earpiece. "Be advised, button up. Ming, have your men fall back."

A green Huey helicopter swept around the far side of the cove. It swooped over the grounded *Flawless Victory* and then higher over the battlefield. Calvin James and Rosario Blancanales hung out of the open cabin doors on chicken straps with M-60 E 4 light machine guns in their hands.

Bolan fired the Browning dry, dropped inside the tank and slammed the hatch. James and Blancanales opened for business. Their machine guns ripped vertical smoking lines of tracers down into the rubble, sweeping the risen enemy like scythes. The Ontos guns were empty, but Fung kept the tank rumbling forward. Men screamed as they went down under the treads. Bullet strikes, rifle butts and stone struck the Ontos as the fanatics physically assaulted it. The tiny tank lurched as men leaped on top of the vehicle and tried to tear their way inside.

"Jesus, Sarge," Grimaldi's voice spoke across the radio in mock disapproval. "You're infested."

The top of the tank rattled as the Stony Man gunners swept the attackers off Bolan's hull with their machine guns. The armor of the Ontos was thin to begin with, and the armor on top was the thinnest. Bolan cocked an eyebrow at the roof of the tank. The steel dimpled and bubbled under the machine-gun fire as if it had been heated to a boil. Chips of paint flew off violently. Bolan thumbed his throat mike. "If you guys don't ease up we're going to be Spam in a can."

The hammering suddenly stopped. "You're clear, Striker," Grimaldi came back. "Consider yourself deloused."

Bolan popped the hatch with his Beretta 93-R drawn. The rubble around the manor was strewed with the dead and wounded. He gazed up at the orbiting Huey. James hung out of the helicopter behind his gun and gave Bolan the thumbs-up.

Bolan saluted and scanned the grounds. "JG, what kind of movement do you have?"

"Looks all clear," Grimaldi came back. "I have no enemy movement around the manor or the surrounding grounds. Will continue to orbit."

Bolan surveyed his vehicle. The top of the turret was cratered like the surface of the moon. The new red paint was stripped and scored and covered in blood and gore. Rifles One and Five had been yanked out of alignment.

"Fung! Reload! Forget One and Five! Half HE! Half beehive!"

Fung shouted at the crew, and Chang led Isah and Pedoy out of the tank and began reloading. The Browning .30 needed reloading, as well.

"Fung, pass me up a fresh belt."

Fung handed up a 100-round belt of ammo. Bolan opened the Browning while Chang slapped the side of the Ontos that rifle three was ready.

"Ming, how are we doing?"

"I have seven men down, thirty-three effectives."

"All right." Bolan laid the belt in the feed. "Advance your men. I want to search the grounds for—"

"Sarge!" Grimaldi shouted.

A man appeared in the last doorway standing in the manor. The man had an RPG-7 antitank rocket across his shoulder. The rocket tube blew fire back into the manor as the weapon launched. There was no time to rack the action on the Browning and bring it to bear.

Bolan hit the trigger for rifle Three. "Down!" he shouted.

Chang, Isah and Pedoy hit the deck as Bolan and the rocketeer exchanged fire. The distance was twenty yards. The beehive munition had no time to expand. The one hundred darts passed through the rocket operator as if he were tissue and left him in collapsed scarlet rags.

The rocket hissed as it accelerated out of its tube. Bolan dropped into the tank as the 82 mm warhead hit. The shaped-charge warhead detonated, and the reactive armor Ming had fitted on the frontal arc of the Ontos's armor exploded in response. The little tank bucked like a bronco under the double detonations. Fung jerked back as the steel in front of his face blackened and threw off heat, but the reactive armor had done its job by exploding into the path of the RPG's shaped charge. The lethal jet of molten metal and superheated gas that would have cooked everyone inside the Ontos had been dispersed and diverted.

"Sarge!" Grimaldi called out.

Bolan drew his Beretta. "We're all right."

"Sarge, I saw two men. You still have another hostile in there."

Calvin James spoke. "Yeah, I saw him too, through a hole in the roof. He's a white boy. We've got him pinned down."

Bolan considered that bit of information as he popped the hatch. The entire front of the Ontos was black, and radiated heat in waves. Isah, Pedoy and Chang dusted themselves off and got back to loading. Ming's men arrayed themselves in an arc facing the front of the manor.

"Hey!" The Executioner used his limited Bosnian. "Come out!"

The fire rose higher in the remaining corner of the manor. Rubble shifted as supporting beams cracked.

"I killed Dragicevic!" Bolan called. "Come out! Or I kill you!"

Nothing moved except fire and smoke and the helicopter orbiting overhead. Bolan switched to English.

"You've got five seconds to come out or I'm going to drop that burning hellhole down on your head! Fung! High Explosive! All six barrels!"

Chang began reloading the barrels to HE.

"One!" Bolan counted. "Two!"

A white cloth waved around the corner of the blackened door.

"Three! Move it!"

The man stepped out and stared down the six 106 mm muzzles facing him. He was short and thickly built. His shaved head and his face were covered with several days' worth of stubble.

"You speak English?" Bolan called out.

The man nodded. "Yeah."

"What's your name?"

"Vaclav."

"Isah, Pedoy." Bolan jerked his head. "Bring him!"

Bolan's remaining riflemen grabbed the Bosnian and dragged him to the tank. They shoved him to his knees beneath Bolan's unforgiving gaze.

"Where's the Madhi?"

"He..." The man swallowed with difficulty and looked away.

"He took the boat," Bolan stated. "Where?"

Vaclav chewed his lip and started sweating. The Bosnian was a Muslim, and a terrorist, but Bolan suspected he was technical assistance like Dragicevic, not part of the martyr brigade.

"I'm going to ask you one last time."

"I...I am not afraid to die," Vaclav announced without much conviction. He began shaking like a leaf.

"Good." Bolan nodded to Isah and Pedoy. "Put him under the treads! Fung! Hit it!"

Vaclav screamed as the chosen men knocked him to the

ground and held him down by his arms and legs. Fung glee-
fully gunned the engine, and the Ontos clanked forward several tread-lengths toward the Bosnian's feet.

"North!" Vaclav screamed. "He went north!"

"What's his objective!" Bolan thundered.

"Hong Kong!" Vaclav shrieked. The Bosnian shuddered at
the enormity of his betrayal. "Hong Kong!"

Bolan slapped the side of the turret. "Fung!"

Fung made a disappointed noise and cut the engine. Vaclav
collapsed and wept in the shadow of the tank.

"Who's with him?" Bolan demanded. "Jusuf? Hoja?"

"Yes," Vaclav said.

"How many men?"

"A dozen, perhaps…more."

Ming walked up and sheathed his sword. He surveyed the
damage to his tank. His eyes gleamed as he took in the blackened and dented steel. Like his dragon-carved broadswords, the
Ontos was part of his weapons collection. He had seen it bloodied in battle, and he was well pleased.

Bolan kept his attention on Vaclav. "Where are the rest of
your men?"

"I was commanded to get the other two boats launched
within the hour and repel any attack. Some of the men may have
run for the trees, but…" He looked around at the sea of bodies
that stretched from the pier to the manor.

Bolan nodded. "Where are the rest of my men?"

"Your…men?" Vaclav flinched and couldn't meet Bolan's
eyes.

"Yes. My men. Chosen men. They're not here. Where are
they?"

Vaclav began shaking so badly his teeth rattled.

"Where!"

"I had no part!" Vaclav screamed.

Bolan leaped down from the tank and heaved Vaclav to his
feet. "I'm going to ask you one last time."

Vaclav pointed toward the back of the manor. Bolan marched him through the rubble. Behind the manor the trees had been strewed with camouflage netting. Beneath the canopy pieces of timber had been driven into the ground to form crude crosses.

"Jusuf...Jusuf considered them..." Vaclav was blubbering. "Unreliable...after some helped you on the other island."

Bolan's face was stone cold. Tears rolled down Isah's and Pedoy's faces. The chosen men had been crucified.

Several were still alive.

"Cut them down." Isah and Pedoy went to their comrades.

Bolan thumbed his mike. "JG, set her down. Cal, I've got men who need immediate medical attention."

Ming surveyed the scene and dispatched a dozen of his men to help. Mei had approached and stared at the atrocity in horror. Bolan gazed long and hard at the men who had died in agony because of their loyalty to him. He put his bitterness aside and turned his attention to the matter at hand.

"Ming, the Madhi's on his way to Hong Kong."

"So I understand." Ming glanced back to where *Flawless Victory* lay beached. "I fear I shall not be able to overtake him."

23

"Bear, I have situation."

"What kind of situation?"

"The Mahdi got away with one of the boats. Best intel is that he and over a dozen of his men are on a one-way ticket to Hong Kong."

Kurtzman stared at his screens. "This…is not good."

"What's our current relationship with the PRC on this one?"

"Hal just got out of a meeting with the President. The Chinese are still denying that they're missing any nuclear material."

"It's not missing, Bear. It's coming home to roost."

"Yeah, well…" Kurtzman punched up a six-foot map of the China Sea. "How far out do you figure the Mahdi is?"

"He couldn't have left more than an hour ago."

"Well, that's the good news." Kurtzman hit keys, and his map exploded into a view of the Java Sea and Sumatra. "Even with his diesels at full throttle, he can't have gotten far. The *Corpus Christi* is on her way to you at full speed. She'll reach you in an hour, and I'm betting under emergency war power she can overtake the motor yacht in two or three."

"And do what?"

The question lay between them.

Bolan's voice was cold reality. "All she can do is torpedo her or hit her with a missile."

"That's better than irradiating half of Hong Kong," Kurtzman said.

"You explain that to the people on the coast of Sumatra."

"I read you." Kurtzman leaned back in his chair. "Well, I can tell Hal to advise the President to bring in the Chinese."

"No, not yet. It's the same situation. They'll send in a sub or fighter planes and blow up the yacht. They'll consider the political fallout preferable to letting Hong Kong get slagged."

"We could advise them to let the yacht reach open ocean before hitting it," Kurtzman said.

"You trust them to do that?"

"No. No, I don't. God only knows what they'll do or find politically expedient. You're right. We have to take control of this one." Kurtzman had a sudden thought. "We deployed radiation detection gear to Sumatra for Calvin. Has he examined your yacht or the shrimp boat?"

"He just got done. The shrimp boat is at LD 50 plus. The yacht is radiating at LD 100."

Kurtzman's short hairs rose. LD 50 was shorthand for Lethal Dose 50, where one-half of the population exposed would be expected to die of radiation poisoning. It was the equivalent of taking five hundred rads. LD 100 was Lethal Dose 100%. No one exposed got out alive.

"Calvin said the differences are due to boat design. The yacht is a sailboat with very little room on board. If she's pumping a thousand rads, she must be packed to the gills. The shrimper is a lot bigger and has two holds belowdecks. If they've surrounded the nuclear material with plastic explosive and bags of fertilizer, the crew could be partially shielded." Bolan paused. "You have an idea?"

"Maybe." Kurtzman hit keys and he brought up a file on radiation levels on a monitor on his desk. "I'm thinking if Megawatti's yacht is anywhere near as poisonous as the other two maybe we should just—"

"Let them go," Bolan said.

"Not just let them go, Striker. I mean we track them close, real close, like we have the *Corpus Christi* wear them like underwear with her torpedo tubes flooded and ready. But it's over fifteen hundred miles to Hong Kong. Maybe we just let the Mahdi and his boys sicken on their own radiation and die somewhere in the middle of the South China Sea. Then the sub can tow the yacht someplace where we can secure the nuclear material for disposal or we could even tell the Chinese where it is as a goodwill gesture."

"I don't know." Bolan considered the Mahdi. "I think the Mahdi would have packed this stuff pretty carefully. The yacht and the shrimp boat are lethal, but maybe he intended to tow them close to their destinations and then crew them at the last moment. He's nuts, but I don't think he's stupid. And being the man he is, I'm betting if he starts to sicken on that yacht, he's going to detonate it close to something as a last act of defiance."

Kurtzman ran every possible permutation in his head and every outcome came up ugly. "Striker, as of my last conversation with Hal, this is your call. I've got the *Corpus Christi* on its way to you and Australian strike fighters hot on the tarmac in Darwin. How do you want to play it?"

"I've got a helicopter that can hold eight men. I can cobble together a team with the assets I have here."

"Not to throw it back in your face, Striker—" Kurtzman liked where this was going less and less. "But you put together a team...and do what?"

"I don't know."

Kurtzman was appalled. "For God's sake, Mack! You said yourself he has over a dozen men. He'll see you coming. Even if you don't lose half the team fast-roping onto the yacht, you still have to secure the detonator. If it even looks like things are going that way, he'll blow it anyway."

"Probably."

"Probably!" Kurtzman took a deep breath. "You're making this up as you go along."

Several long seconds of silence passed. "Bear, I'm on a chopper."

"Mack—"

The line went dead.

"I NEED A TEAM." Bolan looked at Calvin James. "You got a blade?"

James slapped the Gerber Mark II combat knife sheathed at his hip. "'Course I do."

"Get a bigger one." Bolan turned to Blancanales. "You got your staff?"

"It's in the back of the chopper." He looked at Bolan suspiciously. "Why?"

Bolan ignored the question. "Ming, I have room for eight on that chopper. You want a seat?"

"Indeed." Ming sighed. "I shall see this through with you, unto the end."

Bolan bowed slightly. "Thank you, *Sifu*."

Marcie Mei glared at Bolan defiantly. "Don't even think about telling me I'm not going."

"Actually," Bolan said wearily, "I'm counting on it."

"Oh, well…good." Mei blinked as she was taken aback. "Because I am."

Du sighed and rested his shotgun over his shoulder. "You know if Marcie is going, I'm going."

"I was counting on that, too." Bolan called out to the men helping the crucifixion victims. "Isah! Pedoy!"

The last of the chosen men rose and came forward. Bolan gazed back toward their fallen comrades. "You two want some payback?"

Pedoy was so choked with rage and sorrow he couldn't speak. Isah had gone cold. "If you follow the Mahdi, then we will follow you to hell, Makeen."

"Good. Because that's where we're going."

A radioactive hell was their destination. Being blown sky high was the likelihood. He thumbed his mike. "JG, get ready to take off."

Sumatra

"There she is." Jack Grimaldi pointed out across the water. Rustam Megawatti's motor yacht was moving up the coast. The helicopter threw up rooster tails of spume as it thundered barely six feet above the water in pursuit.

"You know this Mahdi screwhead is going to blow the ship," Calvin James stated cheerily.

"I am afraid I concur," Ming agreed. "I am hoping you have some kind of plan."

Blancanales stared hard at Bolan. "We're not just dealing with a fanatic, Striker, but the head of the whole cult. These guys traditionally like to go out in a blaze of glory and take a lot of people with them, you know."

"Yeah, I know." Everyone on the chopper was aware of it.

"I know you have some kind of plan." James flashed a rueful smile. "But I don't think we're going to like it."

"No, brother, you won't like it." Bolan considered his plan. It was pretty much suicide. "But I'm open to suggestions."

"Well, I don't see how we can stop him from detonating if he wants to." James tilted his head toward a five-foot-long molded case in the back of the cabin. "But we've got a Barrett .50 with armor-piercing ammo. I say you get behind that bad boy. We hold off two hundred yards behind the Mahdi, pop his diesels and leave him dead in the water. If he wants to blow himself up, let him. If he doesn't, we have the *Corpus Christi* sink him from a distance. There aren't any major cities for miles."

Bolan pointed toward land as the helicopter swept past a fishing village.

The west coast of Sumatra was relatively unpopulated, but terraced paddies hugged the hillsides, and out on the water the sinking sun silhouetted the platforms of oil derricks. If the bomb went off, no thriving metropolis would be reduced to a radioactive ghost town. The casualties would be in the hundreds rather than hundreds of thousands, but the villagers and oil workers who made their living along the stretch of coast would suffer for decades to come.

"Yeah...all right. I read you." James let out a long breath. "But how are you going to keep that from happening anyway?"

"This guy's a maniac. He's fused the Sudanese Mahdist movement with the Filipino *juramentado* cult."

Blancanales raised a wary eyebrow. "And?"

Bolan loosened his sword in its sheath. "We're just going to have to appeal to his psychosis."

James looked heavenward. "Jee-zus Christ..."

Bolan nodded. "We bring them up on deck and we take the ship, hand to hand."

"You're nuts," Mei said.

The Executioner knew the plan was insane, but he could see no alternative. "The yacht will be packed with reactor rods, explosives and the propane tanks. That means it will take only one stray bullet to set the whole thing off. I think there's about a two percent chance we can take that yacht without blowing it up." Bolan looked toward the coast as they passed another village. "But I want to give these people that chance. I understand if anyone here doesn't want in, but I need everyone on this chopper. Either we're all in, or we abort and go with Calvin's plan. I need to know now."

The crazy light was back in Ming's eyes. "I am in."

"Man..." James shook his head at Bolan. He drew a long-bladed kris with one hand and filled the other with his own fighting knife. "Why are you even asking?"

Blancanales picked up his bo staff from behind his seat without comment.

"Marcie?"

Mei's grin was in place, but her eyes were hard. "I owe that Jusuf scumbag."

Everyone looked at Du.

Bolan shrugged. "This isn't your fight, but short of Ming you're the best man with blades we've got."

"I'm a Macao boy, but my sister lives in Hong Kong. I owe Marcie my life. And besides…" Du scowled out the cabin door at the coast. "My father was a fisherman. These people deserve a chance."

Pedoy and Isah didn't need asking. It was clear they wanted payback.

Ming removed his scarlet jacket and loosened his waist-coat. "Then we are agreed."

Bolan leaned into the cockpit and tapped Grimaldi on the shoulder. "Bring us alongside at about fifty yards. Go slow. Let them get a good long look at us and then get in front of them. I want to deploy on their bow."

For once, not even a hint of a grin was detectable on the pilot's face. "This *Pirates of the Caribbean* bullshit is bullshit. You read me?"

"I read you." Bolan's voice was quiet, but implacable. "Just do it. Then get the hell out of range."

Grimaldi pulled the Huey up off the yacht's starboard side. They paced the boat for long moments. No one was visible on deck, and no motion was visible through the tinted windows. Everyone on the helicopter waited for the yacht to blow. At their proximity, the explosion would swat the chopper out of the air.

Rotor wash hit Bolan as he stepped out onto the skid. He held on to the cabin door with one hand and hung out in plain sight.

The door to the yacht's bridge opened, and Jusuf stepped onto the deck. Bolan and Jusuf's eyes met across the distance. Bolan slowly drew his Beretta 93-R. He took the machine pis-tol by the barrel and dropped it into the sea.

Jusuf smiled as Bolan drew his sword. The Indonesian drew his saber and the cleaver from his sash and stood waiting.

"JG, take us in. If we fail, vector in the *Corpus Christi* for the kill."

"Goddamn it—" The Huey pulled ahead and cut across the yacht's bow. Grimaldi brought the chopper to a three-foot hover. Bolan jumped off the skid, and hit the deck. His boarding party deployed behind him.

Isah and Pedoy dropped the magazines from their rifles and fixed bayonets.

Bolan waved Grimaldi off, and the Huey rose away from the yacht. Grimaldi dipped her nose, and the chopper thundered away out of range. All was suddenly very quiet except for the hum of the yacht's engines.

Hoja walked out onto the deck. The boat captain's nose was bleeding, and he had sores around his mouth. The Mahdi's six personal guards followed him. Ten more men came out of the main cabin. Most of them showed signs of radiation burns or sickness. All of them stank of the hashish they were using to counter the symptoms. Bolan's skin prickled. Every second they stood on the deck, he and his team were taking rads. They needed to take the yacht in ten minutes, or their exposure level would start climbing toward the black magic number Lethal Dose 50.

Their opponents had already passed that marker, if not LD 100, but it would take hours if not days for the radiation poisoning to kill them. At the moment they were feeling no pain and the odds were three to one.

The Mahdi and his giant Sudanese sword bearer were nowhere in sight.

Bolan spoke quietly. "Ming. I'd say it's fifty-fifty that Jusuf has a detonator, and you're the only one who can take him in a fair fight."

"I understand." Ming's broadswords rasped horribly against the sharpening steels embedded in the sheaths as the giant swordsman drew. He pointed his blades at Jusuf in challenge. Jusuf's ugly smile slid across his face.

Kris daggers, parangs and curving Southeast Asian steel of every description filled the hands of the Mahdists.

Calvin James whispered to Bolan. "Find the Madhi and the master switch. We'll keep these punks busy."

"Right, when I say—"

"*Allah Akhbar!*" Hoja screamed. The fat little captain moved quickly. The rest of the Mahdists rushed forward in a mob.

"*Allah Akhbar!*"

Mei moved to intercept Hoja. He took his parang in both hands and swung it like an ax. Mei crossed her long and short kris daggers and staggered as she blocked the blow. Hoja swung his parang again and again in frenzied chopping blows to break her guard.

Jusuf did not join the charge.

"You!" Ming roared. Jusuf only smiled as one of his men lunged screaming at Ming, thrusting with a knife in each hand. The giant gangster swept the double attack aside like Moses parting the Red Sea. His broadswords clanged together in a vicious scissoring motion that left both blades imbedded in his opponent's temples. Bone splintered as Ming put his foot in the cultist's chest and ripped his weapons free from the dead man's head.

"Now, Jusuf, you and I—"

Jusuf's cleaver flashed through the air. Ming staggered as the square, chopping blade sank into his right shoulder. Blood turned Ming's scarlet waistcoat a wet maroon and his right-hand sword fell to the deck.

Blancanales whirled his staff as he was attacked. Steel rang as Du's double butterfly knives wove a web of steel around him. Calvin James cut the throat of the Mahdist before him, and two more charged in to take the fallen man's place. Isah and Pedoy fought shoulder to shoulder, thrusting and parrying with their bayonets. The team's only advantage was that in the close quarters the Mahdists couldn't all swarm in at once to surround them.

Bolan skirted the melee and ran for the main cabin. Jusuf grinned and watched him go. The Indonesian made no move to stop him.

Bolan kicked in the door to the main cabin. The salon was huge and richly appointed with teak panels and brass furnishings. The stench of hashish and fertilizer was overpowering. All of the furniture had been removed except the wet bar on which sat several burning water pipes. The salon was stacked to the ceiling with propane tanks and bags of fertilizer. Nestled in the middle was a small fortress made of bricks of C-4 plastique. Nestled at the center of the bomb were ten six-foot-long metal cylinders. They had been crudely hacked open with power saws.

Bolan's stomach sank as he looked at the exposed yellow-green rods of uranium 235 nuclear fuel that formed the heart of the bomb.

He turned as the Mahdi's sword bearer came up from below-decks. The huge man had to stoop to enter. In his hands he carried an ax that looked more suitable for killing water buffalo than men. The giant's eyes were a web of hashish-inflamed veins. He hefted the ax. "Infidel."

Bolan lunged.

Their blades rang. For all his rolling bulk, the huge Sudanese moved with the speed of a wrestler. Bolan's sword clanged as he blocked a wild swing that sent a shivering ache down his arms. There was no room to maneuver. Bolan blocked a second, sledgehammer blow and his injured arm nearly buckled. Their weapons crossed and locked together momentarily. The Mahdi's man hurled his shoulder into Bolan, crushing his bad arm and bouncing him off the bar.

Bolan rose shakily. His arm spasmed as he tried to bring his hand to his sword. He let it fall limp as his opponent went for the kill. The giant swung, and Bolan put up his blade to block. Steel rang and the force of the blow staggered Bolan. He was thrown over the bar. His sword left his hand as he fell in a cascade of breaking bottles and glasses.

The Sudanese behemoth raised his ax and chopped the bar in two. He grabbed the shattered wood in one hand and ripped it away to expose Bolan. The soldier threw a whiskey decanter into the giant's face. The Sudanese snarled and swung his ax like a baseball bat. Bolan ducked, and the bar mirror shattered as the ax head smashed through it and sank into the wall.

Bolan's fingers found the hilt of his sword.

As his opponent tugged on the haft of his ax, Bolan swung and lopped off his right arm at the elbow. The Sudanese screamed and staggered backward, leaving his ax in the wall and clutching his spraying stump. He screamed again and fell back into the nest of high explosive in the middle of the room. Bolan took a ragged breath and followed him.

The scream rose as the bleeding man regrouped. He came at Bolan wielding a five-foot rod of uranium in his remaining hand. The metal rod whooshed through the air in a wild swing at Bolan's head. The soldier ducked, and the soft metal bent around a propane tank with a clang.

Bolan's sword blade sank into the Sudanese giant's skull with grim finality.

The Executioner pulled his sword free and staggered over to the bomb to look for the receiver. He figured it had to be buried somewhere within the mass of material. Bolan noticed the sound of the melee outside had stopped.

"Makeen!" Jusuf shouted from out on the deck. "Come out!"

Bolan looked at the bomb wearily. He didn't have the strength to pull apart the mountain of fertilizer bags, propane tanks and piled plastique. Every second he spent in this room ramped up his exposure level.

"If you do not come out in five seconds, I will detonate the bomb!"

Bolan knew Jusuf was going to detonate it no matter what happened.

Mei screamed in pain.

Bolan staggered toward the door. He noticed that the shattered mirror behind the bar had concealed a hidden compartment. There were two shelves. One was filled with stacks of money. A cell phone, a bag of white powder and a gold plated N-Frame Smith & Wesson .357 Magnum revolver sat on the other.

Bolan grabbed the pistol and opened the cylinder. It was loaded with Winchester Silvertip 125 grain hollowpoint bullets.

He snapped the revolver shut and thrust it in the back of his sash. "Coming!" he shouted.

The Executioner took up his sword.

He walked slowly back onto the deck. The Mahdi stood with his massive sword across his shoulder. Jusuf stood beside him. Both the Mahdi's and Jusuf's swords were caked with blood to their hilts. The cultists were all dead.

Bolan's entire team was down.

Ming lay on the deck. The handle of Jusuf's cleaver still stuck up out of his right shoulder, and his waistcoast was ripped open where he'd been run through. Mei lay curled in a ball clutching an ugly wound in her side. Du groaned and held the right side of his face. Blood streamed between his fingers where his eye had been cut out. Blancanales was propped against a deck locker. His bo lay a few feet away. He'd been pierced through both shoulders. Isah lay on his side and clasped his hamstrung right leg. Pedoy had jammed the stumps of his wrists into his armpits to staunch the bleeding.

Calvin James leaned against the rail. He looked up at Bolan and shook his head helplessly as he pressed his hands against the bloody wounds in each of his thighs.

Jusuf surveyed Bolan's hanging arm critically. "I left your people alive. I want them to watch this." The Indonesian held up a black plastic box. "I want them to watch you try."

Bolan looked at Ming. Blood bubbled over the gangster's lips. "I tried."

Bolan nodded. "Seven Triple Bursting technique."

Ming blinked. The Executioner's eyes met the Mahdi's and then Jusuf's.

Jusuf beckoned Bolan with his blade. "Come, Makeen. I have waited for this for some time."

"Take me." Bolan stepped forward and let his sword slip from his hands. The dadao clanked to the deck. "But let Marcie go."

"Jesus, Matt!" Marcie said.

Jusuf spit in disgust as he raised his saber. "You disappoint—"

Bolan slapped leather.

The gold-plated pistol flashed from behind the Executioner's back. He squeezed the trigger, and the .357 Magnum revolver thundered like dynamite in his hand. Jusuf staggered as the hollowpoint round hit him in the chest and mushroomed to three times its normal diameter. The gun rolled in Bolan's hand as he fired and fired again. The gun hammered Jusuf. His sword fell from his hand with the fourth shot. He raised the detonator before him like a charm, his thumb spasming for the button, but Bolan's fifth and sixth shots toppled him over the rail.

Smoke oozed from the muzzle of the empty revolver.

Bolan waited for Armageddon.

All that came was the splash of Jusuf's corpse hitting the water.

The Mahdi screamed, the sound rising from a howl of inconsolable loss to a shriek of hatred. His massive sword rose to slice Bolan in two.

Ming's left hand clamped around the Mahdi's ankle.

Bolan stooped and picked up his sword.

The Mahdi shrieked and drove his sword down into Ming, pinning him to the deck. Ming grinned up at the Mahdi through bloody teeth as he held him in a death grip.

The Mahdi's head whipped up as the Executioner's shadow fell across him.

He screamed in naked fear as Bolan swung his sword with all of his might.

The curved blade sheared diagonally through the Mahdi's collarbones, shattering his ribs and finally coming to a stop against his spine. Bolan ripped the sword free, and the little man fell.

Bolan thumbed his com link. "JG we need immediate extraction. Radio the *Corpus Christi* and have them tow the yacht away from shore. Advise CIA Sumatra station we have seven badly wounded and need medical teams ready." Bolan watched the chopper come thundering in even as Jack Grimaldi spoke.

"Inbound, Striker. Will advise *Corpus Christi*. Sumatra station will have medical teams ready on arrival."

Bolan knelt beside Ming. *"Sifu."*

Ming lay motionless. His huge hand was still clamped around the fallen madman's ankle. Even in death, a ghost of the old light seemed to haunt his eyes. His death mask was a bloody smile.

"You said no guns." Calvin James shook his head and smiled.

"I had to improvise."

"How's the arm?"

Bolan tried to move his hand and found that his limb would obey him. The painkillers had long worn off. The feeling came as a searing ache that emanated out of the bones. The ache turned to fire as Bolan made a fist.

The Mahdi hissed at Bolan from the deck. His huge eyes bored into Bolan's sustained by some terrible vitality. "Infidel...I shall rise again."

Bolan picked up the Mahdi's sword.

The ancient blade was an invaluable antique. The Mahdi claimed it had been forged for the first Mahdi. It was the symbol he had carried in his unholy jihad to bring radioactive fire to the world.

Bolan took the ancient sword in both hands and snapped it across his knee.

The madman's mouth went slack with shock as Bolan tossed the broken pieces into the sea. The Mahdi's eyes glazed over. His chest sank with a bubbling sigh and did not rise again.

"Nice," James said approvingly. "Now can we get out of here? We're getting microwaved every second we sit around on this tub."

"Yeah." Bolan picked up his sword and slid it back into its sheath. "Let's get out of here."

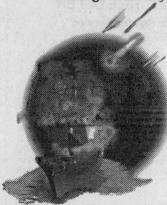

TAKE 'EM FREE

2 action-packed novels plus a mystery bonus

NO RISK

NO OBLIGATION TO BUY

James Axler
Outlanders®

The war for control of Earth enters a new dimension...

REFUGE

UNANSWERABLE POWER

The war to free postapocalyptic Earth from the grasp of its oppressors slips into uncharted territory as the fully restored race of the former ruling barons are reborn to fearsome power. Facing a virulent phase of a dangerous conflict and galvanized by forces they have yet to fully understand, the Cerberus rebels prepare to battle an unfathomable enemy as the shifting sands of world domination continue to chart their uncertain destiny...

DEADLY SANCTUARY

As their stronghold becomes vulnerable to attack, an exploratory expedition to an alternate Earth puts Kane and his companions in a strange place of charming Victoriana and dark violence. Here the laws of physics have been transmuted and a global alliance against otherwordly invaders has collapsed. Kane, Brigid, Grant and Domi are separated and tossed into the alienated factions of a deceptively deadly world; one from which there may be no return.

Available at your favorite retailer.

GOLD EAGLE®

GOUT36

DEATH LANDS®

Labyrinth

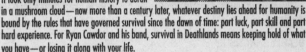

In a ruined world, the past and the future
clash with frightening force…

NO TIME TO LOSE

It took only minutes for human history to derail
in a mushroom cloud—now more than a century later, whatever destiny lies ahead for humanity is
bound by the rules that have governed survival since the dawn of time: part luck, part skill and part
hard experience. For Ryan Cawdor and his band, survival in Deathlands means keeping hold of what
you have—or losing it along with your life.

BORN TO DIE

In the ancient canyons of New Mexico, the citizens of Little Pueblo prepare to sacrifice Ryan and his
companions to ancient demons locked inside a twentieth-century dam project. But in a world where
nuke-spawned predators feed upon weak and strong alike, Ryan knows avenging eternal spirits
aren't part of the game. Especially when these freaks spit yellow acid—and their creators are the
whitecoat masterminds of genetic recombination, destroyed by their mutant offspring born of sin and
science gone horribly wrong….

In the Deathlands, some await a better tomorrow, but others hope it never comes….

GOLD
EAGLE®

GDL73